# NOT CATCHING LOVE

Accidental Love

Book 5

SAXON JAMES

*To Kate*
*Thank you for being the best (and only) feral romance sensitivity reader*
*and cracking me up with your highly professional live reacts.*
*I only wish I could have hurt your feelings more.*

# Content Warning

*This book contains mentions of past traumas, including abandonment, neglect, and childhood abuse. There is trauma dumping and severe anxiety attacks.*

*Xander's opinions on mental health and psychologists are his own and don't reflect reality or the author's own opinions.*

## Thank You

It's such a huge moment to finish a series and I want to say thank you, so much, to everyone who fell in love with our Bertha boys. The outpouring of love for Xander has been incredible to see and whether this book turns out the way you were hoping or not, just know that little shit directed his own story.

It's a huge relief for me to know he's finally living his best life.

In all honesty: not everyone will like Xander in the first part of this book. Mental illness isn't a pretty thing to live with and I didn't shy away from writing all of his highs and lows. If your mental health has taken a hit, or you relate to Xander more than you'd like to, as always, it's okay to tap out if needed.

So grab some snacks and your drink of choice, and get ready for our last visit to Big Boned Bertha.

(While every effort has been made during the editing process, if you're someone who likes to spot and report ninja typos, you can send them to: admin@saxonjamesauthor.com)

# PART ONE

# Chapter One

Xander

The blankets wrapped around me are getting suffocatingly tight. No matter how much I beg my brain to switch off, to relax and let sleep come, I only get more wired.

Like this itch in my brain. Just irritating enough that I can't ignore the way it's infesting me. There's something about the house getting dark, and still that's a perfect recipe for the terror that lives in my head. The pathetically frequent loop of my friends and all the things that could go wrong during their day tomorrow presses on my chest so heavy and real it makes my eyes prick.

Madden tripping and falling on a big pair of garden scissors.

Rush being hit by a bus he's waiting for.

Molly … well, he works from home, so the risk is lower but not nonexistent. He could electrocute himself on a toaster. Fall down the stairs. Befriend some wild animal that bites him and transmits a fatal disease.

Then I'd never have my Molly again.

It's getting harder to breathe now.

My skin feels like it's rattling, and it takes all my feeble willpower to stay put in bed.

I've reached the point in my anxiety spiral where I usually scramble from my room and hunt down one of my roommates. Seven and Molly are first on my list because they'll squish me between them and help scare some of the scaries from my brain. I know they *want* to help me too, but more and more lately, it feels like I'm overstepping. Like, they've got them, and I'm … someone to deal with.

That clawing in my chest gets clawier, and I throw off my blankets and get up. It's as far as I'll let myself go though. I pace toward my door on socked feet and then back again, trying to talk myself back from the edge. Trying to remember that everything is fine, and my roommates are okay, and everyone is breathing and alive and *o-fucking-kay*.

I suck in a breath that feels like glass shards and move over to my window. The chia pet sitting there is a cute clay unicorn pot with rapidly growing plant hair and was gifted to me by one of my roommates. Madden always spoils me with presents, but as the most recent Bertha boy—what we call all of us who live in Big-Boned Bertha house—to find his forever love, I can feel him pulling away too.

They all are.

Every single one of my roommates has a partner, and all I have is stupid anxiety.

My own personal ball and chain that's less of a ball and chain and more of a cage that looms over me. And maybe it's less of a husband and more of a boogieman. I'm constantly waiting for that shit to jump out and drag me into its grasp.

Like tonight. Like most days.

Will this fear that we're all going to die morph into more? I'm usually only one bad thought away from a debilitating panic attack, so why not tonight?

I run my fingertips over the chia pet's grass hair and try to ground myself against the weight clogging my chest. There's a small part of me that hopes that it does kick in because then I'll get Seven and Molly's attention without having to pathetically climb into their bed.

And I'll see Derek.

It's both a terrifying and exciting thought.

Derek is my angel. The nurse who's always there to deal with my stupidity. I hate him seeing me during a meltdown while simultaneously craving his presence. When things get too loud and overwhelming, he's there. He's my calm, my anchor, and I'm confident I'm head over heels in love with him.

Too bad he doesn't see me as more than that sick guy he has to look after sometimes.

With a surge of panic that he might suddenly walk into my room, I dig at my hair, trying to get it into place. Trying to make it look perfect.

A car passes quietly out on the street, headlights cutting through the shadows of the leafy front yard. It's that little burst of humanity that has some of the chest-heavy anxiety shifting.

I guess that means no Derek tonight.

The disappointment at not getting to embarrass myself in front of him is ridiculous.

I'm sure if I got back into bed, the death stress would come again because I'm not exhausted enough to pass out. This whole having to sleep every night thing is bullshit, and maybe if people needed less of it, I'd have fewer episodes.

Or maybe not.

My friends have their own lives now, and even though they don't mean to, they have less and less time for me.

The thing is, I knew better than to get attached. I tried so hard to be guarded. I tried so hard not to let anyone into my life except for Seven, but then we moved here, and the guys gave me no option but to love every single one of them. For the first time, I had a family.

Now, I'm losing them again.

Because everyone gets sick of me eventually, and when Seven finally, eventually, walks away, it will kill me.

Not metaphorically.

People die of heartache all the time, and he'll be the one I can't survive without. When we were foster brothers, he was that first glimpse I ever had of someone wanting to love me. I soaked up his attention like a sponge, and when he aged out and had to leave, I thought that was it for me. I didn't think I'd ever recover, and while my anxiety and panic attacks were one thing before that, it was the first time I ever thought I really might die.

Now, Seven has his Molly.

Objectively, I know it's a good thing that Seven has someone to rely on like I rely on him, but the petty side of me wishes nothing ever changed. Because it's changing, and I already know it's for the worst.

Seven's started therapy, and ever since, there's distance growing between us.

Therapy is toxic. All therapists want to do is point out what a horrible human you are. They don't help; they just break you down until you're an empty shell who can function because you're not you anymore.

I don't need those mind games. Seven doesn't either.

I was doing perfectly fine until my family all decided they needed more.

There's talk of Madden moving out. It won't be long until Christian and Émile have their own place too. Gabe already left us, and soon enough, I'll be the only one left in this big, empty house, and little by little, they'll forget about me.

*Urg, these voices.*

My eyes screw up against the relentlessly intrusive thoughts, and I viciously shake my head for a brain restart.

I'm not letting the negativity win. No matter where my friends go, I'll still love them, and they'll still make time for me. They'll have to. Anything else would be unbearable.

Before that train can shoot from the station, I grab the little plastic container from under my bed and leave the room. I need to confirm that everyone is okay. That they're sleeping peacefully, and in a few hours, they'll wake up, and everything will be normal.

The container in my hands rattles softly, plastic on plastic, as I approach Christian's door. Slowly, silently, I turn the handle and slide the door open.

He and Émile are tucked up in bed. The covers are thrown off and bunched around Christian's legs, and Émile's arm is slung over his chest.

I ache for that kind of love. For being so close to the other person that I need to find them, even in my sleep.

The important thing is that they're both alive, so that's two down, five or six to go.

I close the door, snap open the container, and pull out two stick-on googly eyes. A shadow of a smile tugs at my lips as I stick them to the round door handle, and then I turn it all the way until the tension stops me and release it.

The knob flings back into place, and the eyes go all loopy until one black dot sticks to the top and the other is out to the side.

My new friend looks like a deranged *Alice in Wonderland* character.

I chuckle and flick between the eyes so the black dots settle back into place.

"I a-dore you," I whisper to my new friend before giving him a soft pat and moving on.

Madden is sleeping, splayed out and buck naked, muscular chest rising and falling softly. I linger, taking in his body, his cock, wondering *why* it does nothing for me. I like to pretend that it does, but I think more than one thing broke inside me when I was younger, and I never learned how to fix it.

It's a struggle to not linger on those thoughts as I pull the door closed and make another little friend.

Hunter and Rush are in the next room, sleeping soundly, and I leave a friend there too.

Then, the final door makes me pause.

The second I open it, I'm going to be tempted. Seeing Seven and Molly asleep will tug at my willpower because I know the comfort I'll get by climbing into that bed. I wish I could give them boundaries, but I struggle with separation from them more than anyone, and whenever one of them tells me no, it's not like hearing it from other people.

Their no means I hate you. I'm sick of you. I never want to see you again.

I grit my teeth and stick the eyes to the doorknob first this time, and then I lean in for a heart-to-heart.

"You need to help me," I tell it. "You have to make sure that once I've confirmed they're alive that I leave again, okay? You're like … like their guardian. Or their guard. Something to stop me from being able to enter. Got it?"

I'm assuming the door says yes because it's not like doors can think for themselves.

I grip the handle, remind myself that I *will* leave, and slowly open the door. My breath is a ball in my chest as all the worst-case scenarios flash through my mind—them both, eyes open and unresponsive, or victims of a break and enter, or buried under a collapsed ceiling.

The room inches into view. It's dark, clothes strewn on the floor with a crack of light from outside peeking through the heavy curtains.

My favorite mop of hair is splayed out on a pillow, and beside him … nothing.

A slice of panic hits, and I remind my brain it's being stupid. Getting ahead of itself. There is no way in hell that Seven got up for a glass of water and had a heart attack on the way downstairs. There's no way he's gasping for breath somewhere.

No way, no way, no way.

I cross the hall to the stairs as fast as I can and don't even try to keep quiet as I throw myself down them. Seven has to be here somewhere. He has to. He's like me in that he struggles to sleep, and the perfectly logical explanation is that his thoughts are getting too loud for the night. It's not the first time, won't be the last, but I need to *find him* and be sure.

I need to be certain.

I need to see him.

Need to—

"Z?"

Relief explodes through me, and I do a one-eighty to find Seven's followed me down the stairs. All six foot three of his redheaded, tattooed form steps off the bottom stair and onto the polished wooden floor. He's okay. He's alive. I can breathe again.

"Ah, hey," I say.

He studies me. "Hey. Everything okay?"

"Sure, of course, why wouldn't it be?"

"I thought an elephant had gotten inside and fallen down our stairs."

I slide my foot in a circle over the floorboards. "Sorry."

"Don't be sorry. Tell me what's wrong."

I glance up, and all of my insecurities, all of my worry and anxiety and every little thing that's ever popped into my head and spun me off course, tries to get loud. "Nothing. Everything is okay now."

He doesn't believe me, which isn't a surprise because we know each other inside and out.

"Why are you awake?" I ask.

"Stupid, flop damn nightmares."

"Need a hug?" I suggest, desperately hoping he says yes because I can't leave this hall without one.

His lips twitch. "Badly."

I cross the hall to throw myself into his arms, and I'm reminded why this is my favorite place in the world. Seven is like a shield for my spiraling thoughts. He can't stop them, but he gives me an extra layer of protection, and sometimes that's enough.

# Chapter Two

Derek

I close the lid on my formicarium, grinning at my newest addition to the group.

A queen ant.

Finally.

I've had a few ant farms over the years, but they all saw the familiar pattern of demise without a queen to keep the population replenished. It was one of those things where I wasn't sure if I wanted to completely commit or if it was a fun thing to keep my mind active.

Keeping ants started as a hobby. A way for me to have a pet when my life was too busy for one that needed constant care, and now … well, now it's turned into a custom-built, six-foot by six-foot formicarium in what I call my "bug room."

Look, I'm a normal guy—I have a job as a nurse, I volunteer for dance classes at the nursing home up the street, and I have friends I catch up with a few times a week.

But I also really like bugs. They're fascinating and under-rated—ants most of all.

And while I'll defend my love of bugs to the death, I'm also incredibly grateful this was a post-high school passion. I got to be the cool football player there, and the best part is that my teammates who never moved out of town? Yeah, they're stuck with me. Bugs and all.

Speaking of. My phone lights up with an incoming call from the guy who's been my best friend since middle school. "Derek, tell me you got her," Manny says.

"I did. Now I have to make sure she stays alive."

"Fucking A. And ehh, I'm not worried about that part. You have a way with those creepy things."

I tilt my head as I watch a line of ants follow each other along the dirt. "Creepy? I think they're cute."

"Yeah, well, you would. You don't exist in the same world as the rest of us."

He can give me shit about this all he wants, but I know for a fact that on Saturday, he and his daughter have tea party dates, and he tries a different tea flavor each week.

If he likes tea, I can like—my gaze casts around the room at all the little bug cages I have in here—*all this*.

"How was the hot cross bun flavor?" I ask.

"Nowhere near as nice as I thought it would be." He audibly shudders. "So … given any thought to moving yet?"

Not this again. I grew up north of the city where there's lots of land and wildflowers and freedom. The plan was to stay there for the rest of my life, basically, but then I got this job at the immediate care office of the pharmacy, and it made sense to move closer to work. For … reasons. Recently, Manny's been talking about subdividing the land he inherited from his parents to boost his daughter's college fund, and I was offered first dibs.

It's tempting. I could make my dream of keeping bees a reality.

When I say I'm a bug guy, I mean it. I don't know that I want to go full-blown apiarist, especially with all the travel I want to do as a nurse, but bees are so vital and important that managing a hive feels like the ultimate privilege.

Leaving this tiny two-bedroom isn't an option yet, though, because I *need* to be here. It's why I moved in the first place. Sure, having to commute wouldn't have been ideal, but it's not uncommon in Seattle, and I would have dealt with that if circumstances were different. Most of my colleagues do.

None of them have to get here at a moment's notice though.

The blue-haired, anxious ball of snark and sweet passes through my mind, but I push him right out again. I might stay to make sure I'm available for him, but I make it my mission to not think about him unless he's right in front of me.

It's why I keep so busy.

"I've told you," I say to Manny, voice bordering on patience and frustration, "I have a lot going on here."

"But imagine being neighbors," he pushes. "We could turn the land between our houses into a football field. Teach the kids how to play."

"The kids. All those kids that I currently have. *Those* kids."

He snorts. "You know I'm talking in the future."

We'll see. I'm thirty-five this weekend, and it's starting to feel like a lot of things that were "future" goals should be now goals, and I've barely scratched the surface. I thought at this age I'd be traveling, maybe doing some kind of Nurses International thing, but those plans have been put on hold the last few years because of one person.

I'm at a loss for what to do about it because cutting him off when he needs me feels cruel, but continuing the way I have been is wearing on me.

I lean in to inspect my ant colony, hoping the queen will take and not go on a homicidal spree with all her worker friends. These little rays of happiness I give myself are what I need to focus on.

"You talk about future plans like you're not mid-thirties," I point out to him.

"Whoa now. That isn't ageism I hear in your tone, is it?"

"No, it's reality."

"Fuck, reality. My thirties have been the best years of my life."

Well, that makes me feel like shit for mine being on hold. The good part about doing nothing big with your life and having no dependents to rely on you is that you end up saving a good chunk of money. When I finally pull my head out of my ass and accept Manny's offer, I'll be doing it with financial confidence. I only wish I could accept it now.

"Still meeting Saturday?" I ask.

"You really think any of us will miss a birthday game? No way, man."

There's eight of us left from our high school days, and we meet up on each person's birthday to play a friendly game of four-on-four football.

So, that's something at least.

And for right now, it has to be enough.

---

I'M ABOUT to clock off from my shift when Constantine rounds the corner into the break room. He pins me with his "guess what" look.

"Xander?"

"On his way."

Right, well, I guess I'm staying a bit longer, then. I clock out and head for the front room, where I normally see people who stop in with health questions or give vaccinations. It's also where I see Xander for his health anxiety.

He's such a tricky one to deal with because where I thought I was doing the right thing by stepping in to help when he had a panic attack in the pharmacy, it slowly evolved into ... more. Every attack, every spiral, every episode where he's sure he's dying and can't pull himself back, he ends up here. At first, it was months apart. Then weeks. Now, well, this is the second time I've seen him since last Monday.

I ignore the unprofessional nerves that hit and head out the front to wait for him.

It doesn't take long for Xander's friend Seven to walk in, carrying Xander in his arms.

They're a real pair, and Seven is the main reason they caught my attention in the first place. He's well over six feet, tattooed just about everywhere, and is speaking so softly to the tiny, blue-haired man he's currently carrying.

The man I've become way too invested in.

Xander is shivering all over, struggling to breathe, and he hasn't grasped where he is yet.

Seven lays him on the bed, and I approach.

What I do for Xander is mostly triage because there's nothing physically wrong with him; it's all his anxiety preying on his senses. He needs a psychologist but flat out refuses to see one, and for some reason, that same anxiety has decided that I'm someone who can be trusted. He refuses to calm down until I've seen him.

"What's wrong?" I ask, letting my professional demeanor slip into place.

Seven crosses his broad arms, face tense like it always is when I see him. "Appendix."

This is the tricky part. That fine line between making sure I don't completely blow off Xander's claims on the off chance something is wrong while not giving them more weight than I should, which would play into his anxiety more.

I'm so not the person cut out for this.

Not least of all because it's starting to really fucking hurt to see him in this state.

"I need you to lie back," I tell him, and once he does, I reach for his hand. "I have to lift your shirt and inspect the area. Squeeze my hand twice if you're okay with that."

His small, clammy hand tightens firmly around mine twice, giving consent for me to inspect him. Xander's a small guy, more noticeably with his shirt up, and I commit to focusing solely on feeling the site of the pain.

"Does this hurt?" I ask, pressing gently.

He shakes his head.

"This?"

He shakes again. I go over his front, then get him to sit up so I can check the back. I'm not a doctor, so I can't give a definitive diagnosis, but I do know that step one is getting him to calm down, and then if he's still in pain, we can take step two.

So far, thankfully, we've never needed step two.

Once his back is cleared, I shift until I'm standing in front of him and lean forward so he's forced to meet my eyes.

"There's no pain to indicate a burst appendix," I tell him. "The first thing I need from you is to take your breathing and heart rate down so I can check your vitals. Does that sound okay?"

Tear tracks streak through the makeup on both his cheeks, and I have to swallow to clear out the lump building in my throat. I don't know how his friends can stand seeing him this way. I've had training for handling distraught patients, but this gets to me more every time I see him.

"This panic attack isn't you," I remind him. "It will pass.

I'm here to help. I'm going to count my breaths, and I want you to copy me."

We go through the usual breathing exercises, and it takes a few minutes, but eventually, Xander's panic evens out. He's still shaking, still crying, and seeing him like this? It's a real effort to keep up my professional front when all I want is to pull Xander into my arms.

Lines blurred for me a few months ago, and while I've always cared and wanted to help him, I can feel those protective urges building into something more.

Something I can't let take over.

"D-Derek …" he whispers between inconsistent breaths.

"Hey, I'm here." I pull up a chair to sit next to him. The need to reassure him and make sure he's okay is consuming.

"S-sorry."

"Don't be. Just take your time."

He nods, blue hair falling over his forehead as he looks down at his lap. With the way his head is angled, I can't make out his freckles or those unusual-colored eyes, but that's for the best. I'm already too familiar with everything about Xander Moore.

It takes longer than usual until I can't hear his breathing anymore, and his slim shoulders fill with tension.

"Thanks," he grits out.

And now that he's not panicking anymore, this is where I come in with the tough love. Judging by the way he tensed up, he's ready for it. "How's therapy going?"

He scowls, eyes immediately meeting mine. "I'm *fine*."

"No, you're not."

"I don't think you're supposed to tell people how they feel."

"But isn't that why you come to me?"

He scrubs at the tears on his cheeks. "I never ask to come here."

"You don't need to ask. You know I'm here if you need

me." I lower my voice to give myself the impression that Seven can't hear our conversation in the tiny room. "This is the second time this week."

"Sorry I haven't miraculously learned how to fix myself."

"Your snark doesn't work on me. Your mental health isn't your fault, but that doesn't mean you can't do something about it."

His lips turn down.

"Have you at least looked up some of the resources I gave you yet? I can't help you if you don't make the effort."

Xander glances over at Seven. "I'm bored. Can we go now?"

Seven's gaze pings between us before dropping to the floor. "Sure, Z. Whatever you want."

They both leave before I can get another word out—or shake them; I'm pretty fucking ready to do that too—and I lean back in the chair and cover my face with my hands.

A long groan slips between them.

"Good visit?"

I startle at Constantine's voice. "Don't ask."

"You look like you could use a drink."

"Or twelve." But we both know I won't do that. There's every possibility Xander could be back here again tonight. "Are we still on for dinner tomorrow?"

"Of course. It's your birthday."

At least someone cares about that. "I should never have mentioned it. And Constantine, no cake. Seriously."

"I heard you the first ten times."

We'll see about that.

## Chapter Three

Xander

"You're such an old person," I complain as I hold the wool Auntie Aggy is using. The knitting needles clack together as she works on what I can only assume is a sweater that belongs to a blob creature.

"Shush and help me."

I eye the blue, lumpy ... whatever that is. "I don't think you're very good at this."

"You're ruining my concentration," she snaps.

"And you're ruining a perfectly good ball of wool."

Aggy huffs and sets the monstrosity aside. She's in her late seventies and sharp as a tack. Ever since our ragtag group moved in next door, she's called us her lost boys and unofficially adopted us as her honorary grandchildren. Or *great*-grandchildren. She is *very* old. "I've never knitted before."

"Then why are you knitting *now?*" I wrinkle my nose.

"Because there's a man at the nursing home who likes unflattering knitted sweaters."

"You have the unflattering part right."

"This is not my wheelhouse." She runs a delicate, veiny hand over her forehead. "I could swing dance that mother fucker to death, but a sweater? Still, when you're my age, you work with the options you've got."

I sigh and grab my phone, opening a video on how to knit. "This really is Rush's expertise," I tell her. "Why don't you ask him to knit one and pass it off as your own?"

"You really think so little of me?"

I give a flat look to her fake-offended tone. "Have you forgotten that I was here when those religious missionaries showed up, and you told them that you already signed the contracts for your soul with Satan and that God should have come knocking ten years earlier? Then offered to put them on a waitlist?"

"Okay, so maybe I'm going to hell for that one, but that doesn't mean I need to get the big man any more offside by lying. Ah, *more*." She leans toward my phone. "What's it saying?"

"That you're a terrible knitter."

She waves a hand. "What else is it saying?"

I watch the video tutorial for a few more seconds and glance from the screen to her mess and back again. "Yeah … we're going to have to start over."

"Of course we are."

I spend the morning with Aggy, helping her learn how to knit a hideous sweater while she tells me about Gerald. The man's name is *Gerald*. I will definitely have to die before I turn eighty because the dating pool sounds bleak.

"You had another episode yesterday?" she asks casually.

"What of it?"

"I told you, boy, you're not allowed to die before me. I have dibs."

I scowl. "You really think I want to see you die?"

"Well, I flat out refuse to see you die, so you better take your vitamins because if you try to leave first, I'll dig you up myself and recreate *Weekend at Bernie's*."

"That's a fucked-up movie."

"It is, and I'd prefer not to spend my last years in jail, so cool your jets and stop wishing for the end."

"I don't wish for it."

"Oh, yeah? Let me see your search history on the Google for today."

There's no way that'll happen. "How do you even know that's a thing?"

"I'm still incredibly hip."

"And then you said that."

She scowls, tugging at the wool. "Tell me you haven't looked up anything medically related today and I'll drop it."

Would *are consistent hiccups something to worry about* and *the veins in my hand are super bright blue* be considered medically related? Thankfully, I have no issues lying to an old lady.

"Nothing."

Unfortunately, she has no issues calling me out on it either. "Bullshit."

"Aren't old ladies supposed to be sweet and bake cookies?"

"Molly and I are baking cookies later. I happen to be multifaceted."

"Choc chip?"

"Since I'm such an old lady, I'll throw in some raisin ones too. Just for you."

The devil's cookies. "Come on, you're not *that* old. Barely look a day over seventy-five."

She stares at me with all the disappointment she's capable

of. "Have I taught you nothing? Can't even suck up right. What is the world coming to with the youth these days?"

"And now you sound ninety."

When I first met Agatha, I was more careful about what I said. I used to be desperate for her to love me and always craved her attention, but then one day, she asked if I'd taken up people-pleasing as a sport. I wouldn't normally suggest to an old lady that maybe we could swap, and *she* could be the one with a backpack full of trauma while I'm the one with a backpack full of judgment, but it made her laugh. So now I'm convinced Aggy is as fucked-up as the rest of us, and I'm not sure where the stereotype of easily offended old people came from, but it missed her.

I'm grateful. My roommates might be my brothers, but she's like the matriarch I never had. She gives me the attention I crave, never makes me feel like I'm an imposition, and she genuinely loves us all. She's adopted us as much as we've adopted her, and it's yet another reason why I'm so scared of change.

What happens to Aggy if some of us move out of Big-Boned Bertha? Does she replace us with the next lot of shit-heads who move into the house?

Feathers of panic brush my heart.

"Aggy … what would you do if Seven and Molly moved into their own place?"

She's focused back on her knitting. "Buy them a toaster and pray they don't burn it to the ground?"

"But they'd be gone."

She glances up. "From Seattle? Where are they moving to?"

"Well, nowhere. But they might. They probably will— Molly's dad lives in Massachusetts—and then where does that leave the rest of us?"

She fixes me with one of her stern looks. "Happy for them. That's where it leaves us."

"I don't know if I will be."

"You will."

"Why are you so sure?"

"Because you'd never do anything to hurt either of those men."

She's got me there. Seven deserves the world, and I'd been —and still am—so happy that he found Molly. Molly is the pure sweetness neither of us ever had in our lives, and I love him to death, but they scare me. There'll eventually be a day where it's not Seven and Molly and Xander, just Seven and Molly, and I'll never survive it.

"And they wouldn't hurt *you*," Aggy says, pulling me out of my funk. "No one is moving to Massachusetts."

She gazes at me with murky brown eyes, and I gaze back.

"You have a lot of cataracts," I whisper.

"And you have a lot of nerve," she whispers right back.

"Can you promise to live for another … fifty years so that I never have to be alone?"

"Nope. Come and teach some art lessons at the nursing home, then you'll never be short on old people to dote on you."

"I hate everything about that idea. Take one for the team, won't you?"

She squeezes my knee. "No. Dear god, no. That sounds horrendous. But I will promise not to leave until I know you're looked after. So, if you could get moving on that, it would be much appreciated."

My thoughts drift to Derek and his gorgeous face and the way he both gives my heart little wings and makes me want to poke out his eyes, all at the same time. Emotions are complex, do not recommend.

It'd be so much easier not to have any.

I never learned that skill. My emotions are either happy or

sulky or *kill them all*, and there's no in-between. There's also very little pre-warning, which will come out from one minute to the next. I can be having a great day, and then suddenly, everything will be shit, I'm shit, everyone is shit, and I take a very deep dive into a very shallow pool. I try to be cute and happy like Molly, but that sunshine doesn't reach the swampy marshlands my brain bobs along in.

"Bit hard to do that when the man I want doesn't want me back."

"Your nurse friend?"

"Uh-huh."

"I should think not."

That surprises me. "What do you mean?"

"There are rules about patients and the people treating them for good reason."

"*Really*?" I eye her skeptically. "You're all about breaking rules."

"Only when it makes sense. I don't believe in breaking rules just to break them. People who make stupid rules are stupid to believe they won't be broken, and that's on them as far as I'm concerned."

"Well, I think the rule about patients is stupid."

She watches me for an uncomfortably long time. "I love you, but you're being shortsighted. Your own damn community has been accused of being predatory for too long and fought too hard against that image for you to play with that man's job. He's a gay man in the medical field, and you're the person he's treating. What do you think people would say and assume if something happened between you when there's such a clear imbalance of power?"

No one could ever say something horrible about Derek Knight. "There isn't though. Derek doesn't have any power over me. I know what I want, and I go for it."

"And while that's one of my favorite things about you, not

24

this time you don't. I mean it. You've had your brain addled by far too many people who should have done right by you, and until you put some effort into fixing the damage they did, you can't claim to be in your right mind about anything."

"Oh, fuck you."

She laughs. "What's wrong? Are you going to throw a tantrum, sweet pea?"

"Don't you know that you can't talk to people like that these days?"

"Yes, I do find people these days struggle to tell the truth." She studies me. "Help me out here. Which part of what I said don't you agree with?"

"I'm not an idiot. I know what I want."

"What you think you want."

I scoff. "You're an expert on me now?"

"My baby boy, I'm team Xander. I'm team you do whatever you need to. I'm not pushing you either way when it comes to therapy, but I will when it comes to your nurse. I forbid it."

"You *forbid* it?" I tug at the sweater. "Does Grandaddy Gerald forbid it as well?"

"He will if I ask him to. I know you've never been given a boundary in your life, but this is me giving you one."

The funny thing about never having boundaries? I don't know *how* to have them. So I hear Aggy speak, but an angry little gremlin catches the words and filters out any meaning.

Derek's the one I want, and if he'd stop talking about goddamn therapy every time I saw him, he'd be the perfect guy.

Aggy either wants me happy, or she doesn't.

Boundaries or no boundaries.

## Chapter Four

Derek

"Happy birthday!"

I internally die inside as Constantine leads a singing line of restaurant staff from the kitchen and into the dining area. He's holding a cake way too big for the two of us, and I want to crawl under the table and pretend like I'm not here.

That jerk.

I'm already physically sore from the football game with Manny and my other friends today; now, he's going to make me emotionally sore from the betrayal.

The whole time they're singing "Happy Birthday," the smoke rising steadily from the candles, I glare at him. He smiles at me.

Who needs enemies, huh?

"Thirty-five, you old bastard!" Constantine shouts as the servers resume the not-a-spectacle side of their jobs.

"Say it louder. I think there's an old lady in the corner who didn't hear you."

"Thirty-fucking-five!"

I drop my forehead into my hand. "Can I fire you yet?"

"Thankfully, you're not my boss. Blow out the candles and make a wish, grandpa."

"Original." But I do it because I might be a whole decade older than Constantine, but I still know how to be a good sport. As for the wish? I don't know where to start. But even as I think that, Xander flits through my mind.

Fuck.

*I wish he'd fight for himself.*

Maybe it's a waste of a birthday wish, but it is what it is.

Even if it means never seeing him again, I'd be happy to know he's not at the mercy of his anxiety, and while no one ever asked me to be, I'd kind of like to not be at the mercy of it as well.

"What did you wish for?" Constantine asks, helping himself to a large chunk of the rich mud cake.

"Nothing specific."

He gives me a pointed look. "Lemme guess, it has some-thing to do with an X."

"Fuck off."

"That's confirmation." He shoves a big bite into his mouth and keeps talking. "You've put your whole life on hold to be around if he needs you. Don't think none of us have noticed."

"Don't know what you mean."

"You moved a block from the pharmacy. We're not idiots."

"You sure about that?" I point my fork at him. "You're spraying food everywhere."

"I'm enthusiastic."

"You're an animal." I'm also exaggerating, as gross as it is to watch him talk with his mouth full. Anything to get people off the topic of Xander, who already takes up too much space in my life as it is. I'm pathetic, and I'm wasting the best years of my life, but I can't *not* do it. He needs me, and I'm full of stupid conflicty feelings over being happy whenever I get to see him and knowing that I'm only getting to see him because he's sick. Which makes me a selfish bastard.

Reason number one for why a nurse shouldn't fall for his patient.

And reason number one for why I'm not supposed to think of him unless he's right in front of me.

"Still going out?" Thankfully, Constantine has remembered to swallow this time.

"Sure. Why not?"

"Not drinking though, are you?"

I hum noncommittally. "We'll see."

He snickers into his next bite. "Uh-huh. Sure."

As the only two openly gay men at the pharmacy, we hit it off fast. It's a large chain store that's open round the clock, and statistically, there have to be more queer people working there, but *he's* the one I'm stuck with.

As much as I might give him hell, and he teases me about being ancient, I'm glad to have him. Fuck knows without Constantine in my life, I'd be even more engrossed in my bugs than I already am. He reminds me to leave the house.

"It's been about three months since I got laid," he continues, like we're not in the middle of a busy dining room. "This work schedule is bullshit."

"That's where saving for a house will get you."

"My point is, don't you dare stand me up. I need this, big D."

"That's a no on that nickname, but I will definitely be there."

"Good. Wear something slutty for me."

I flip him off and grab some cake for myself.

Given that I've gotten through the whole day with no phone calls from the pharmacy, I'm taking that as a good sign. Would I like to see Xander for my birthday? I'd like to see him every day, but it's selfish of me. The longer it goes between visits, the better; I just wish I wasn't always waiting around for them. At one point, my life used to be fun.

In college, I was constantly at frat parties and hooking up. I took road trips at a moment's notice, stole mascots from our rival school, was always up for a dare or a stupid decision … when did I get so *old*?

"I'm stuffed more than a star stripper's thong," Constantine announces. The couple beside us glances over, and I give them a tense *don't listen to him* wave.

And there I go being an old man again.

It's almost instinctual at this point, and I wonder if I can get that fun guy back or if he's well and truly dead.

"Question," I start cautiously, half-convinced I'm going to fuck myself over with this. "Want to check out a different club tonight?"

"New dick pool? Sure."

"Do you know of any with … cage dancing? Or stages? Platforms? That anyone can use?" It's been a long time since I made a spectacle of myself, so why not now?

The smile that stretches across his face is wicked. He's trying to grow a mustache that hasn't completely caught on, and instead of making him look older, it makes him look maniacal.

"I bet I could find one. Are you going to give me a show?"

"Not sure yet." I rub at the stubble on my jaw. "I want to try something different, maybe get back some of the fun I used to have."

"Before a certain blue-haired man turned you into a prisoner in your own house?"

"Shut the fuck up. This was way before Xander. Before I

started working in a pharmacy and realized how messed up things are for people. Maybe I grew a heart. Or got jaded."

"Well, I'm going to find your jaded ass a club where you can get up and shake your chaps to your ass's content."

"I won't be wearing chaps, but thanks for assuming I own some."

"A harness?"

That gets a laugh from me. "What part of my vanilla, boring-as-hell existence do you think took a break to buy a harness?"

"I'll bring one for you. Show off that chest—you'll have all the gays drooling."

Well, if I don't get in a cage, that's a mild way to draw attention amongst all the other men who'll be wearing one. "Fine. It's my birthday, fuck it."

Constantine fist pumps. "Wait until Susan finds out about this."

"Susan will *not* find out about this."

"I'm going to take pictures, just for her."

My hand slides over my face as I remind myself he's teasing. Susan is a constant thorn in my side and the only customer assistant rep who refuses to call me when Xander comes in. She's made it clear she thinks there's something *untoward* going on between us, and I hate that she's not completely wrong. I also hate that of the two of us, she's the one in the right.

So tonight, I'm giving myself a *fuck it* moment. I'm going to pretend I'm back in college again. No responsibilities. No constant worry about the future and what's next. No yearning to travel and not being able to leave a ten-minute radius from my house.

Mid-life crisis, here I come.

I might even turn my phone off.

There's no way I *will*, but I can pretend.

Constantine and I part ways after he pays for dinner, and I head home to get ready.

A harness and cage dancing. Hopefully, a hookup.

What else are birthdays for?

## Chapter Five

Xander

"This is going to be great," I say for the umpteenth time, sandwiched in between Seven, Molly, and Madden. I'm holding on to Seven while he holds on to the bus handle overhead, and while I'm glad he's taking one for the team, I'm going to have to monitor him for E. coli or a staph infection. This man never takes his damn health seriously.

Molly pokes me in the cheek. "What's going to be so great about it?"

"Well, Madden's excited, so I'm excited. Hey, maybe tonight, I'll even find someone to hook up with. Finally. I can't wait." I think I'm convincing? No one questions me on it, at least. The last time I forced myself to go home with someone, I had to fake a panic attack to get out of there. All I know is the thought of *doing* things with him made my skin crawl. That's not supposed to happen. I'm supposed to want sex. I'm supposed to be sexually active and a total deviant and be all nom nom for the cock.

I don't think I'm doing the right kind of gagging over it.

When I think of sex, I think of cuddles and neediness and being close to the other person. Snuggling with some random I've met on the dance floor sends my brain into overdrive, questioning when he showered last, if he brushes his teeth properly, and if he's had sex in his bed since he last washed the sheets.

I run my eyes over my friends. I've seen Madden naked enough to know that I'm not attracted to him, but letting him touch me? I think that would be okay. Seven? I shudder. We might not be blood related, but he's my actual brother, as far as I'm concerned. Molly? He's sweet and sunshiny, and I love him with my whole heart. I could maybe have sex with Molly.

I wouldn't because I understand *some* boundaries, but thinking in an objective, could I actually go through with it way, I maybe could.

Possibly.

But a nameless, faceless stranger?

It's like a dark, sludgy feeling creeping over my skin.

The bus pulls up to our stop, and I climb off with my friends. The club is loud with a short line out the front, and thankfully, it isn't cold enough yet to deter all the mesh shirts and booty shorts.

Booty shorts like I'm wearing now.

While I follow the others toward the queue, I sneakily make sure that my outfit is perfect. The vest is snug, my shorts are high, and my over-the-knee socks are perfectly aligned. My chest tightens at not being able to check my hair and makeup in this lighting, and I'm trying to ignore the chipped nail polish on my thumb. If I think about it too deeply, I'll never walk into the club. I did everything I could to look perfect, and I'm not perfect and—

"Z?"

I hurry to catch up to Seven and give him my best "I'm fine and happy" smile. He doesn't need to know that every day, I regret not making him tattoo on my eyeliner. I also want more freckles, but I'm too scared of him getting annoyed with me to bring it up. Last time we talked cosmetic tattoos, he got angry —something he never would have done before. It's all therapy's fault, I'm sure of it. So now, I have no choice but to keep these self-conscious thoughts to myself in order to keep Seven and Molly to myself too.

We get inside the club, where it's immediately a good ten degrees warmer, and follow the hall down to the main area. It's late, so it's already jammed full of people, and I look around in awe.

I've never been here before, but Madden suddenly decided an hour ago that we needed to get our butts down here imme- diately. It didn't give me anywhere near enough time to get ready, but here I am, dressed sweetly, in a sea of horny men.

There aren't only men here, of course, but that's what it feels like. Like I've stepped into a sea of expectations I'm not ready for, and the sharks are circling. Judging. Inspecting. Trying to determine if I'm worth their time. As much as I'm not interested in any of them, being rejected guts me, so to distract myself, I turn to Molly. "Look at all the hot guys here tonight. I'm totally going to find my Daddy."

Molly laughs. "Anyone standing out to you?"

"Not really—"

"What about him?" Madden shouts into my ear, long arm appearing over my shoulder as he points across the room. On the back wall are all these raised platforms at different heights, topped with shiny gold cages that have people dancing inside.

I inspect the one he's pointing at, but it's not until the man turns around that I realize why we're here.

"D ... d ... d ..."

"Derek?" Seven finishes for me.

"Here," I choke out.

"Dancing," Molly teases, nudging me with his bony elbow. I'm too transfixed to bat him away.

My nerves are exploding so hard I'm worried for a second I'm being hit with a stomach flu. But it passes. And Derek is still up there in a harness and pants too tight for words.

I have no idea if he's a good dancer or a bad dancer, but he sure as hell is a sexy dancer, and my tongue swipes over my lips as I watch him.

Derek? Derek is someone I could have sex with. I'm not sure where the lines are with my comfort levels and why him and not Seven when they're both huge protectors in my life, but thinking about Derek's hands on me makes me shivery. And it has nothing to do with the fact that every time I see him, he's disinfecting them.

Probably.

Maybe.

Who fucking knows, but sex or no sex, I know how he makes my heart ache.

All I have to do is picture his big arms and how intoxicating it would feel to be buried in them.

My lust snaps when a man with overinflated muscles climbs up onto the platform beside the cage and runs his hand over Derek's calf before continuing up his leg.

"What. The fuck. Is he doing?"

Now, normally, I do my best to be sweet Xander. Like a puppy. Or a kitten. If I'm cute, people will want to keep me.

But I never learned how to share as a child, and now, a filthy little gremlin lives inside me.

And seeing that man's hands on Derek?

The gremlin is activated.

I'll sooner pull off my Derek's head than let someone else play with him.

"We're in a club. Guys touch," Seven says, like I haven't caught the scent of blood.

"Over my dead body."

I push forward into the crowd of people around me, my friends calling after me as I disappear. It's easy enough to give them the slip when I'm shorter than almost everyone here, even with my platform sneakers on. The same sneakers I use to stomp the feet of anyone who gets in my way.

The swelling heat is making me sweaty, and I need to get off this dance floor before my makeup runs or my hair gets sticky. Especially if Derek is going to see me like this.

I reach the platform and climb up to where the guy is now rubbing both of Derek's legs as Derek rolls his hips toward him. If there weren't bars around my man, I'd bite his fucking dick off. Before either of them see me, I grab Mr. Handsy from behind and yank him away. I might be small, but I'm stronger than I look—and I'm a sneaky motherfucker with no issues catching someone by surprise.

Whatever it takes.

The guy, caught off guard, loses his footing and hits the platform with a *thud* that can almost be heard over the music.

"The fuck?" he shouts, springing back to his feet, but before he can take a step, Derek steps out of the cage and puts himself between us. The man goes for me, but Derek's hands catch his chest, and I almost swoon at how Derek holds him back. "Walk away."

"That little fuckwit pushed me over."

I give the asshole my devil smile and blow him a kiss from behind Derek's back.

"You're fucking dead!" He lunges for me, and Derek catches him as Seven and Madden show up. The raised platform isn't big enough for all of us, but that doesn't stop Seven from joining us and hauling the guy from Derek's grip.

"Touch my brother, and I end your life. Got it?"

Seven is a scary motherfucker. Head and neck tattoos. Angry red hair. Absolutely enormous size. Sweetest heart in the world, which this guy has no way of knowing about.

It's very obvious who's coming away the winner in this scenario. The man, flushed in the face, jerks himself away and jumps from the platform, flipping me the bird as he disappears into the crowd.

As soon as he's gone, I ignore Seven's *you're in big trouble* glare and redirect to Derek as he turns to face me.

"Xander? What the hell are you doing here?"

Those wide, kind eyes search mine, and I swear I can smell the heady scent of his sweat.

I forget how to form a sentence. Every other time I see Derek, I'm too far gone to appreciate it, and once he calms me down, I'm too embarrassed and angry with myself to stick around for long. Here, now, where I'm having a good night and he's not reminding me that my brain is a shithead liar who lies, I have no idea what to say to him.

I barely remember to close my mouth.

"Umm … hi."

The corner of his lips twitches. He has the sweetest eyes of anyone I've ever seen. "Hey."

"You're here."

"And so are you."

"I am." I've never seen Derek out of his uniform that he wears at the pharmacy, but I'm seeing a lot of him now. He's got a chunky belly and a solid chest sprinkled with dark hair. And big arms. He's not overly big like Seven, but he's a nice big. A cuddly big. I'm dying to know what his hugs are like. "Hi."

Derek cracks up. "We've covered that." He glances at Seven and Madden. "You here with, umm, anyone else?"

"Just Molly." No date. Not me.

"Ah …" The eye contact is heart-stopping. "Well, I might go—"

"Want to grab a drink?" The words spill from me before I can stop them.

Derek's mouth opens. Closes. "With you?"

I nod. And nod. And nod. Like I've forgotten how to stop.

"Okay, but if we grab a drink together, I'm going to need you to say actual words." His breathtaking smile comes. "You know that's how a conversation works, right?"

"Give him a second and you won't shut him up," Seven butts in.

Derek turns to him. "I'd prefer that over him being mute. If it's okay with you?"

I throw Seven a look, begging him to help me out here.

"Fine …" But Seven doesn't look happy about it. No doubt he thinks I'll get into more trouble, but with Derek's attention on me and him not bringing up the nasty "T" word—therapy —my happy, little kitten is back.

"Let's go."

I follow Derek, more careful of the people dancing than before as we make our way to the bar. Now that I've calmed down, I genuinely feel bad about all the pushing and almost hurting that guy, and I hate that I can't control myself sometimes. I hate that something in me snaps. I hate that the little gremlin always, always wins, but it's the thing that defended me when no one else would, and slipping back into that is easier than fighting all the time.

I'm struggling to believe Derek's here. Like, I could reach out and touch him. Smell him. Listen to him talk and drown in his steady gaze.

"What are you drinking?" he asks.

"Whatever you are."

"Sorry to say that I'm on water tonight."

"Oh." Does that mean he's here with someone? "Are you designated driver?"

"Nah, I …" He shakes off whatever he was going to say. "Don't always need to drink, you know?"

"I'll have water too, then."

"If that's what you want."

I can handle my alcohol, but there's no way I'm going to risk getting drunk in front of him. Not Derek. He's a real adult. Put together, stable, handsome, with a grown-up career and no demons in his closet.

But he's also seen me at my worst, and here he is, choosing to spend time with me anyway.

Because Derek is my real-life Prince Charming.

Now, if only he'd do that part where he sweeps me off my feet.

# Chapter Six

Derek

Well, this is the stupidest thing I've done in a while, but I was not expecting Xander to show up while I was dancing half-naked in a cage. It's the first time I've seen him outside of the pharmacy, and apparently, I wasn't prepared, and my mouth got carried away.

But we're celebrating. We can have one drink. For ... my birthday? That we're seeing each other during a time when he doesn't think he's dying?

Whatever feeble excuse there is, I'll find it. I have one chance to enjoy being in his presence, so I'm going to shamelessly take it.

I grab our drinks and turn to hand Xander his, keeping my eyes firmly on his face. Not that it helps. Xander is an inhumanly pretty guy.

He's got some kind of white, glittery powder over his cheeks, his dark blue hair is messily styled, and his pink lips give an illusion of innocence, but I've heard some biting remarks fly from them.

Those same lips curl into a smile, head tilted back slightly to look up at me. "See? You don't see me like this much, but I'm normal most of the time."

"I'm not a therapist, but I'm confident you're not supposed to talk about yourself that way."

Irritation flits across his face. "I can talk about myself however I want. I can't hurt my own feelings."

"I don't think that's true."

His purple eyes take on that slightly deadened look they get when the conversation isn't something he wants to be talking about, and I remind myself that it isn't my place. Xander isn't my responsibility, no matter how I might have rearranged my life for him, and if he wants to get help, he will. Constantly pushing it when I'm practically nobody to him isn't going to do a thing.

"But enough about that," I say before he can get annoyed. I tap my glass against the one he's holding and force myself to meet him on a level he's comfortable with. "To *normal.*"

He lights up from the inside out. "To normal."

I take a long sip of my water, realizing that I'm not sure what to say. We've never had a conversation outside of work, and there's so much about him that I don't know and so much I *want* to know. Honestly, it's probably for the best that nothing changes.

I've never been good at doing what's best for me though, so here I go, walking into a brick wall.

"You're an artist, aren't you? You do paintings?"

"Primarily." He turns the glass in his hands. "But I play with a lot of different mediums. I'm not good at any of them though. I've been lucky."

"What do you mean, lucky?"

"I sell enough to get by. Have some savings. Nothing special."

Savings? I chuckle. "In this economy, that does sound special."

He scowls, and it's a skill how quickly he yo-yos between annoyed or frustrated and sweetly happy. "There are people way more talented than I am, but for some reason, the algorithm pushed my stuff, and it turns out people like horrible art. Who knew?"

"Considering I haven't seen any of it, I'll have to take you at your word that it's horrible."

"Smart."

"How did you get started with this horrible art?"

He shrugs, and it draws my attention to his shoulders—which is a whole neck lower than my gaze is supposed to go. "I always had that itch. When I'm creating, I'm not thinking about anything else. It helps when … it just helps. I'm self-taught, which is why my work isn't great."

I'm sure that's not correct at all, but I let it go. Talking to him is like a minefield. "How do you self-learn something like that?"

"Practice. Sketching. Art books from the library. YouTube."

"I could do all of those things and still barely draw a stick figure."

A glimpse of a real smile crosses his face. "Everyone can draw a stick figure. You seem like the kind of guy who can do anything."

Heat creeps up my neck and into my cheeks. "I wish that was even close to being true."

"Aww, are you getting all shy on me now?"

"Not shy. Just making sure you manage your expectations." It would be awesome to tell him that I can do anything, but there's something very cool about being human too. I'm not perfect, and that's okay. Fuck, this conversation is enough to drive home that point. "What do you do other than paint?"

Xander hesitates, then changes the subject. "I'm boring. Let's talk about you."

If there's one word I could use to describe Xander, last on that list would be boring. I want to know more about him, but here in a crowded and loud club, while his roommates linger on the periphery, probably isn't the place to get into anything personal.

I shouldn't be getting into anything personal *at all*. No matter how much I talk around the issue, my attraction to Xander is inappropriate.

"You know, it's *really* hard to hear in here," I reply. Plus, talking about me is a dangerous fork in the road where I can either confess to my life suddenly centering around him, or I can direct the conversation to bugs.

I love my bugs. Not many other people do though, and I'm not sure I want Xander knowing about that side of me. I'm better off calling it quits, finding Constantine, and getting the hell out of here. I never should have agreed to this drink.

"I'm okay," Xander says quickly, stepping in closer. His big purple eyes hit mine, and a wave of lust sweeps through me.

There's no doubt in my mind that if Xander and I had met any other way, I would have asked him out already. My body responds to him on a primal level, but knowing the little that I do about his past has a softness building behind my ribs.

I might not have all the details, but I know enough that the urge to protect Xander never shifts. He deserves someone who will look after him, support him, hopefully get him the help he needs instead of being a prisoner in his own head.

I can't be that guy. I can't be the one who gives Xander what he needs, and I really have to remember my place.

Which is nearly impossible when he's looking at me like this.

It's my job to make sure lines aren't crossed and expectations are clear, especially when the next time I see him, I'll be clinically checking him over while I talk him back from a panic attack.

I'm unlucky that the first guy I've ever wanted is my patient, but if he wasn't my patient, I never would have met him in the first place. It's a vicious loop. I'm constantly at war with myself through every interaction.

"I think I'm getting tired," I say reluctantly. Every cell is reaching toward him, begging to stay here and talk to him, get to know him better, but it's a slippery slope, and I've already given him mixed signals by agreeing to be alone like this.

There's fun and spontaneous, and then there's reckless. Reckless isn't something I want to be, especially not with someone like Xander.

He's a strong man who's been through a lot, but I can imagine that he lets himself get hurt way too easily.

"We can go and sit down somewhere," he says, moving even closer again. "Or maybe go and get something to eat."

"I had a big birthday dinner."

"What did you have?"

I know I shouldn't answer, but I can't think of another way around it. "Burgers."

"I love burgers."

We sort of stare at each other a moment before I work out what I'm doing. "That's because they're delicious." I fake a yawn. "I'm going to find my friend and head out though. It was nice seeing you."

"Can we dance?" Xander blurts. "Just once. First. Before you go."

No. We absolutely cannot dance. If we dance, I'll touch him, and I'm not strong enough for that. He doesn't make it easy to turn him down either, not with how hopeful his expression is, but I have to, so I do. Something fundamental in me dies with every word out of my mouth.

"Sorry. Really beat. That's what happens when you turn thirty-five. You get old."

"I didn't know you were thirty-five."

Hint, hint. Xander, I'm too old for you. I know he's twenty-eight, but if I hadn't been given that information, I would have assumed early twenties. Seven years is still too much of a gap. For us, anyway.

Xander links a delicate finger around one of the straps of my harness, and the feel of his skin against my midsection sends ripples over my body. It's not like I've never touched him before, but *he's* never touched *me*.

"One *quick* dance," he pleads.

I deserve a fucking award for staying strong. "I *really* have to go."

Xander snatches his hand away like he's burned, and I hate that I've put that deadened look back in his eyes. "Fine. Go. There are plenty of other men who'll want to dance with me."

Looking like that? I have no doubt.

The thought of other guys dancing with him doesn't sit right, but there's literally nothing I can do about it. If this is Xander hitting on me, he's going to have to deal with that rejection and find someone else to have fun with. There's no way I'll be able to look him in the eyes or not get overinvolved next time he's having a panic attack if we hook up, and that's if I forget the whole code of ethics I have as a nurse. Which I can't.

So as much as I want to believe this is us hanging out and chatting, that the suggestion to dance is a friendly one, I'm getting the distinct impression that's not what's on his mind.

And when it comes right down to it, I can't go there with someone I view as breakable. Vulnerable. I want to make everything right for him and protect him from his demons, but the real world doesn't work that way.

Which is exactly why there are rules about medical professionals getting involved with patients.

No matter how many times I try to tell myself that it's only triage and breathing exercises, that excuse doesn't hold water. When he's having an episode, I'm the one he seeks out.

And I always make sure I'm available for him.

In some ways, I'm enabling him more than his brothers do, but it was never supposed to be this way. It started and then … never stopped. So here we are, locked into an endless loop that's getting worse instead of better.

I know what I need to do. The constant availability is giving him a crutch, and cutting off the supply—or at least stepping back gradually—needs to happen. The feeling has been sneaking up for a while now, but even after years of being at his beck and call, I can't do it.

I'm a hypocrite.

I lecture his roommates about them not wanting to help him, and here's me, also too weak to actually do what he needs. I keep telling myself I'm that last line. They have the power to help make sure Xander doesn't get to the stage where he thinks he's dying, but none of them will do it.

I don't have a choice.

Which is bullshit because we all have choices.

I need to start making the right ones.

# Chapter Seven

Xander

The whole way home, my mood is infecting my friends. There's that little voice telling me I need to cut it out before they get sick of me, but I can't. The sourness in my limbs is biting. I wish we'd never gone there and that Derek had been free to hook up with that asshole who was pawing him. At least the two of them look like a pair that makes sense. A pair who can have a fast and dirty encounter in a public bathroom before going their separate ways, whereas me and Derek? There isn't a world in any multiverse where I make sense being with him.

"Sorry, Xander," Madden mutters. "I saw the club post that video of him and …"

And what? Thought it would be a good idea to rub my face in what I can't have?

I'm not going to snap at Madden though, no matter how infected I am. Seven is the one who gets that side of me, and I won't share it with anyone else. No one else can handle me like that.

Though I'm getting the impression lately that Seven doesn't want to deal with that side of me either. The irrational side that I know is wrong, but whenever that side comes out, I don't want to control it. I want to feed the gross, slimy feelings until I feel exactly as pathetic as I am.

Words are bubbling up in my chest, and I keep swallowing them back down again. It's like acid, the way they're burning their way to my lips.

The bus pulls up, and we climb out, then make our way home. Molly is cuddled into Seven's side, where I always used to be, and I know I could attach myself to the other, but I don't. I let the crappy feelings creep in deeper. Give them complete consent to ruin me. To make my heart feel like it's being flayed.

I'll never deserve a love like they have.

Then Madden's heavy arm wraps around my shoulders and pulls me in close. "I really am sorry. I don't know what I was thinking."

He wasn't thinking, that's the problem. At least, that's what my bitterness is telling me. It's cute that he thinks I'd have a chance with a guy like Derek, but he was only setting me up to fail, and I have to try really hard not to hold that against him.

"It's fine."

"You're sulking."

"Why would I be sulking? My dream man couldn't get away from me fast enough. That's not something to sulk about."

I can feel the three of them exchange looks over my head, and I hate that they can do that so easily, but I'm also not going to draw attention to it. If I do, it'll give them the opening to talk, and I don't do that with just anyone.

I'm heavy by the time we reach the house, and I can't stop

questioning whether Derek really did go home or if he's off hooking up with someone he's actually attracted to. I shouldn't be mad at Madden when I'm the one who came on too strong. I'm the one not good enough. I'm the one who failed. Like always. Maybe if I'd kept things light and breezy, we'd still be talking now. I have this deep hunger to know everything about him, and I actually had the chance.

I blew it.

"I'm going to paint," I say lifelessly as I leave the others in the foyer and make my way down the hall to my studio. I don't have the itch to paint, but I haven't all week. My last canvas was a fucking mess that someone paid four figures for because when it comes to art, people are stupid. They can't see the mistakes and horrible lines and the way I fucked up so much I had to smother my work in five layers of paint to get it to a passable level.

Acrylics are what I like to work with the most. Slightly abstract landscapes, mostly forest or woodsy with an other-worldly magic to them, but my cityscapes do the best.

The more realistic art, or the art I do when I'm in a fever pitch of emotion, doesn't see the light of day. It's stored against the wall in racks of canvas that I never have to face again.

I grab a smaller canvas, planning to sponge it with a gray, green, and pink color scheme before I decide what to add to the layers. My process is to sponge the background until I'm happy with it, layer and build the acrylics around it, and then paint in the details. Most of my followers love watching the time-lapse videos of a piece coming together, even though I fucking hate filming my process and usually cut out as many of the imperfections as I can.

I set up my phone and switch to the front camera. My makeup is intact despite the sweaty club, and I spend a moment trying to fix my hair, that weight on my chest deepening as it won't stay flat.

"You stupid fucking *fuck*," I grit out, attaching my phone to the tripod and starting again. The heat in the club has fucked with my pedantic straightening job, and the ends are all curling back like they're fighting me. I fucking *hate* my mousy poodle curls. I fucking *hate* my ugly gray eyes. I was born the most boring person in existence, so I really can't blame my parents for giving me away.

My dumb hair won't damn cooperate.

Instead of filming myself painting, I redirect the camera so that only the canvas is in frame. The video won't do as well as the ones that have me in them, but at this point, I doubt it will even be posted.

There's no passion driving me, only that deep-seated guilt brought on by a week of not working and the fear that if I don't regularly update, I'll become obsolete. All that luck I had will disappear, and I won't be able to pay my bills and make rent, and then everyone will get sick of me and kick me out of the house. It's going to happen eventually, and some days, I don't know why I keep fighting it.

I hit Play, then reach a shaky hand out to the brush with the googly eyes. "Make this one good for me, Paint-bruh."

With him held up to the camera, I put on his voice. "Can't wait, little Z. We're going to create a masterpiece."

I snort. "Way to oversell it, dickhead."

Paint-bruh is set down in favor of a sponge instead, and then I get to work. It's frustratingly tedious. The colors aren't blending out right. I'm trying to lay a background of light coming through trees, but I'm nowhere near talented enough to pull it off.

I really should have studied this, but the funny thing about foster parents is that none of them are all that eager to shell out a fuckload of money to send some random kid to a specialty college. In order for me to get the scholarships I would have needed, I actually had to finish high school, and while I could have tried for community college, by the time I *should* have been looking into it, my first piece went viral. Turns out that people online with money to spend don't give a shit about standardized education. I've been keeping myself afloat since, but having my high school diploma would have been nice.

It's been a long time since I learned that degrees are for healthy people.

As I work, I fall into that single-minded void of creativity that helps drown out the constant background noise of not being good enough. That void where all that exists is the colors and how they're working—or, in this case, not working—together.

I wet the sponge to bring the darker green further down, but it's looking less like a forest and more like the claggy boogers inside a nostril. Every time I start a new piece, all I can think about is how much easier this might be if I was actually good at it. If I had something beyond a detailed vision of the end result and a very rough framework to get me there.

Once the canvas is covered in paint, I take a step back and inspect it. The more I look, the deeper a sneer pulls at my face. I end the recording, delete the video, and toss the canvas into the stack of disappointments in the corner. The stack that's far outnumbering the ones good enough to sell.

Maybe if I become homeless, I can beg Aggy to let me stay with her. She's old now, and she doesn't have as long as everyone else to get sick of me, so I'd have a good chance there.

If my anxiety doesn't kill me, the smell of her potpourri would.

I meticulously wash up my equipment in the small sink in the corner and then plan to sneak out of the room to head upstairs and shower. The second I open my door, sunlight burns my eyeballs, and I have to blink rapidly to cool them the fuck down. What the hell time is it?

Past six.

Right.

I've blocked out all light coming through the windows into my room to make it feel like a den in there. Like a cozy, hidden cave for a scared little animal like me.

I hover in the hallway, straining my ears to see if anyone else is awake, but I don't pick up any noise. I know the sound of all my roommates' and their partners' footsteps, can place where they are in the house and the ways their walks change based on their moods. I'm tempted to go looking for company anyway but too terrified to find an empty house. No matter how desperately I need connection, how my heart feels bruised and raw, I ignore the urges.

Upstairs, I shower, scrubbing every inch of skin I can reach until it's red raw. Then I dry my hair, straighten every strand, and set to work putting on a light layer of makeup.

I'm hesitant to take out my contacts, but my eyes are feeling seriously dry and irritated, so I remove them reluctantly, then avoid looking in the mirror.

I'm not that person anymore. Not the boy with the brown hair and gray eyes. Not the unlovable, invisible child.

Back in my room, the giant, frumpy hoodie I stole from Christian is calling to me. I'm craving the warmth and the comfort, but I ignore it in favor of a midriff and cotton shorts. No comfort. Only cute. Imagine the disaster if I fell unconscious in my sleep, needed to be rushed to the hospital, and was wearing something five sizes too large for me? I doubt any of my roommates would think to stop and get me changed first.

So, I dress. And I curl up in bed. And I try not to mess up my hair and makeup while I fall into a fitful sleep.

# Chapter Eight

Derek

Not my finest moment. I wake up dusty-eyed and full of self-loathing. I'm not someone who does self-loathing usually, but last night was messed up. I let myself fall into Xander's vortex way too easily.

I stumble from my bedroom out into the kitchen to put the coffee machine on. I've got a whole day off today, followed by dance classes at the nursing home later. *If* I don't get a call. A loud yawn rips from me, and while I wait on the coffee, I head into my spare bedroom to check on the ants. They've almost decimated the apple I left them yesterday, and so far, it doesn't look as though queenie has snacked on any of her workers.

This colony might be a good one. I'm hopeful, at least.

It takes me a few minutes to head around the room, checking the little microenvironments I've set up for some of my insects. They're well looked after, and I genuinely care about every one of them, but as much as I love that I can have this, it's a hobby. Something I can keep busy doing that's within my control.

One day, I'll have my bees. Helping replenish the bee population is a passion of mine, and if I took Manny up on his offer of all that land, it's one of the first things I'd invest in. It's a big commitment though, and I'm not sure I'm ready for that until I've had a chance to travel.

After I've confirmed my bugs are fine, I make my coffee, get changed into gym clothes, and head down the street for a workout. Only a block away. Still within easy distance of the pharmacy. This is what my life has become.

I refuse to resent it, but I'm also worried that I won't always be in control of that. The protectiveness I feel over Xander isn't normal, and the last thing I want is for that to sour because I like liking him.

If only he wasn't my patient and I could actually do something about it.

*There's an easy way to change that*, a little voice in my ear reminds me. I'm not interested in giving myself false hope, and I wonder if I was actively dating, whether Xander would still have this hold over me.

Unfortunately, dates aren't usually understanding when you have to dip out midway. If I was a doctor, it would be totally fine. No questions asked. But nurses aren't seen as the medical professionals that we are.

So no dating. No traveling. No moving.

Just trapped here.

Fuck me. I'm definitely going to grow to resent him.

Still, I've managed to make it years without that side kicking in yet. Maybe it's my attraction to him that's saving our relationship while simultaneously making it impossible to be around him. I groan, realizing that I'm thinking about him again, and send a quick text to Constantine.

Do we sell anything to create memory loss?
Because I could use it.

CONSTANTINE:

I'm sure it's the side effect of something. Got
little Smurf boy on your brain?

ME:

It's so weird when you call him that.

CONSTANTINE:

I still maintain that as you're not a doctor and
you're not actually giving him treatment, just
reassurance, that the rules are loose in your
case and you should definitely take him out for
lunch.

ME:

Loose doesn't mean non-existent.

CONSTANTINE:

Then cut things off, I don't know. Tell him you
won't be around anymore and when enough
time has passed, ask him out.

The Xander I saw last night wouldn't be all that opposed to
it. The asking out part. The cutting things off … I can't see
that going well.

Even if I could do that, how long is enough time without
seeing him, and how do I force Xander to go cold turkey? That's
the real kicker. If I trusted that anyone could take over from me
and get Xander to calm down from his panic attacks, I'd stop
answering the calls. I'd stop making myself permanently available.

At least, I like to pretend I would.

But deep down, I don't think anyone can care for him the
way I do. There's no way anyone else at work would dedicate

their whole damn life to Xander because they're, you know, actual levelheaded humans. I've reached the point of no way out, and now, I have to suck it up and deal with my choices.

I head home and shower after the gym, wondering how last night could have turned out. If everything was ideal and I hadn't met Xander the way I met him—

*Fuck.*

I comb my fingers through my wet hair and tip my head back under the water. It's official. I hate myself. I hate that I can't separate work from everything else and that no matter how many fucking times I tell myself to shut up about him, my internal monologue won't listen. In a weak moment, I warned Madden that I'm dangerously close to overstepping and getting Xander the help he needs, and that thought haunts me every day. Because I know I'll do it.

I'm *that* stupid.

So what, I like caring for people? Maybe have a little bit of a hero complex? Maybe. The entire reason I became a nurse was so I could improve people's lives in whatever way I'm able to, and I'd like to think I'm improving Xander's.

Not mine, but that goes hand in hand with nursing.

I avoid the mirror when I climb out of the shower and tug on some jeans and a T-shirt. No matter what I set out to prove last night, I *am* getting old. Don't they say forty is when everything falls apart? Yet here I am, wasting the last of the best years of my life with no end in sight.

I snicker, imagining Mom's reaction if I told her that her best years were behind her. She's closing in on sixty and RVing around the country, doing menial tasks when she can find them to fill the gas tank, and constantly saying her best years are ahead.

She also *hates* that I'm stuck in the one place, and I sometimes wonder if the self-doubt is my voice or hers.

I leave for the nursing home, walking the three blocks to get there. It's a smaller facility and really well looked after. I've been in some before that were too big, too busy, and the people who lived there were treated like a number.

Heart and Home has a more personal feel to it.

I greet the front desk staff as I enter and grab my volunteer badge from them. Coming down here once a week helps give me that little bit of purpose I'm always craving, and if I did move away, it would be one of the things I missed. I'm a naturally social person, really love people, and the residents at the home are never short on stories.

After signing in, I head down the hall to the left. It's a familiar route to the room I use for dance classes, and all along here are various activities taking place. The flooring underfoot is shiny vinyl, the lights in the ceiling were recently replaced with LEDs, and different voices drift toward me from the rooms I pass.

Until one overly familiar voice makes me freeze. "For forking sake, Kevin. I said we're aiming for a tree. Not a turd."

There's muffled laughter, and I stiffly turn toward the open room, assuming I must be wrong. In all the years I've volunteered, I've never seen him here, so what the hell are the chances? I creep closer, and the quick glimpse of blue is all I need for my suspicions to be confirmed.

Xander.

The room is filled with large paper pads on easels and residents sitting at each one. Chancing another quick look around the doorframe, I watch as Xander paces between them, pausing at each artwork. There are too many people in the room clambering for his attention, so he doesn't notice me watching him.

Like a creeper.

Which definitely won't be people's first impression when I tell them I'm lost. Y'know, even after those hundreds of other times I've been here.

But it's not often I get to see Xander interacting and being himself, and I'm transfixed.

He takes Bethany's arm surprisingly gently and guides her stroke in a smooth line down the paper. "Like that. Push through the arthritis, girl, you can do it. You're my last hope at anything even remotely resembling a plant."

Kevin wheezes around his oxygen tubes. "Shit is organic."

"And also not part of the brief."

"Maybe I had my hearing aids turned down for that part."

Xander plants his paint-covered hands on his hips. "Let me guess, all your report cards as a child said you were highly distracting in class?"

"Don't remember that far back. But I bet yours said you were an uptight pain in the ass."

"Yeah, but I got a pass on account of not having parents. Abandonment works, folks."

"Who would abandon a sweet boy like you?" Genevieve asks.

"Assholes."

"Well, at least you inherited something from them," Kevin says.

I cringe at the comment, but Xander doesn't look bothered.

"Careful, or I'll unplug your oxygen. Don't test me."

"You would too." Kevin glances over his shoulder, and I try to follow his line of sight. "Aggy, where did you find this feral raccoon?"

"Rooting around in my trash."

"You're supposed to love me," Xander shoots back at her.

"I do, sweet one. But it doesn't mean you're not a feral raccoon."

This weird defensiveness rises up in my gut. A feral *raccoon*? Where the fuck do they get off calling him that? Don't they know that Xander has been through way too much for him to sit here and be called names?

My heart has taken on that indignant race that happens when I'm fighting to keep my words to myself. It's not something I do a lot. I'm an open and honest guy, and thankfully, at work, I have some seniority, so other than fucking Susan, I don't have much to bite my tongue about.

The urge to walk in there and sweep him away from their insults and negativity is strong. Too strong.

Which is why I need to walk away.

Hero complex or not, I'm not *Xander's* hero. I can't be.

Lines last night were blurred.

I can't let that happen again.

# Chapter Nine

Xander

What the *what*.

I race to the door and stick my head out into the hall. I'm sure I saw Derek walk past. Maybe it was wishful thinking, but as I watch the man walk away, that stride looks far too familiar. The way it instantly comforts me has to mean something, doesn't it?

Derek is here.

Does he have family he's visiting? Is he working?

I cut a quick look Aggy's way. She's still talking with Kevin and not paying me any attention. Theoretically, I could slip out and follow him. Just to make sure. I can't tell her that I want to go stalk my future husband when she's explicitly warned me off him, but considering these people don't need my help creating what I like to call works of fart, I see no reason why I can't slip off.

Just for a quick sec.

Then I'll slip back in. Half the people in this room have Alzheimer's and don't know who the fuck I am anyway. Why Aggy thought I'd like to teach an art class here is beyond me, but when she gets an idea in her head, there's no getting rid of it. Molly would be better at this than me. Or Seven. Or … literally anyone. Not only do they have the talent, but they have the patience to back it up. I'm one blue tree trunk away from upending the kiddie paints over my head.

Or maybe not.

Even though those little bottles *claim* they're nontoxic, I wouldn't be surprised to develop heatstroke, accidentally ingest some, and end up in emergency.

So really, stalking Derek is the safest option.

I check Aggy is still distracted and then slip smoothly into the hall.

My hands are a mess, and I probably should have washed them first, but there was no time. Plus, it's not like I'm going to let him see me anyway. My hair is done, I'm in a cute outfit, and I'm teaching a paint class, for fuck's sake. Obviously, I'm going to get a little messy. If he has an issue with that, then … then …

That crawly feeling climbs over my skin, and I glance around for a bathroom. When I come up empty, I resign myself to staying paint speckled, hurry to the end of the hall, and slip down the left he's just taken.

Then almost trip over my feet in an attempt to backpedal.

Derek's paused outside the room up ahead, but my rapid movements catch his attention.

He glances up as I'm mid-leap, and his wide eyes meet mine as I disappear back behind the wall.

Well. That probably looked weird.

I'm about to bolt, claim this never happened and he's imagining things—*"You thought you saw me, Derek, maybe you should look into the deeper meaning behind that"*—when he takes the choice out of my hands.

His sudden appearance knocks the breath from my lungs. Almost a full head taller than me, rugged features, and the kindest eyes of anyone I've ever seen.

"This isn't the bathroom," slips out before I can stop it.

Derek tries to fold down his smile, making his cheeks pop happily. "Were you following me, Xander?"

"Depends what your answer would be if I was."

"That it's incredibly inappropriate and a little odd."

Well, that wasn't the cute response I was hoping for. "Oh. Then in that case, no. Definitely was not."

Derek's laugh comes free, and it's so warm and full I want to wrap it around myself and live there. "You're a shitty liar."

"Isn't that a good thing?"

"A good thing would be not lying in the first place."

"Then how would I keep things interesting?"

His steady gaze sweeps over me. "I'm sure you'd find a way."

That *almost* sounds like a compliment. I cling to it, cheeks getting hotter and stomach all fluttery. "What are you doing here?"

"I'm about to teach a dance class. Or, more accurately, spend an hour spinning people around the room and pretending not to notice when the older ladies tap my butt in thanks."

"Awww, grandmas. The lil assaulters."

"Apparently, it's cute if you have wrinkles."

I lean against the wall, thankful that my stalking at least seems to be forgotten about. "So you're telling me I have a few years to wait?"

"I think I'll be dead before you have wrinkles."

Derek's face drops, I'm assuming because he's just realized he used the "D" word. And sure, I have fits where I think I'm dying, but unless I'm in that headspace, I know how ridiculous it is. Logically, I *know*. The last thing I want is Derek tripping over himself to apologize or making things suddenly weird between us, so I jump in before he gets that chance. "I might not have wrinkles, but if I took your class, would you let me tap your butt in thanks?"

"You're asking my permission?"

"Not geriatric enough to get away with anything else."

There's a war going on behind his eyes. I love those eyes. I assume they're hazel, but they have flecks of just about every color ever in them. Gold, brown, green, blue, black. If I had eyes like that, I'd never have to wear contacts.

"I saw you painting."

That throws me. "What?"

"Well, I saw you helping some of the residents paint. I didn't know you volunteered here."

"I don't."

He lifts his eyebrows like he wants me to go on. Talking about myself is a tricky line to manage because I don't usually know when to shut up. My trauma dump is more of an avalanche, and once I start, that mess keeps coming.

Which isn't a great thing when the more people learn about me, the faster they run.

"My neighbor Aggy thought running a class here would help."

"Help with what?"

I twirl a finger by my ear. "All this."

He clamps down on his lip, and I know what he's about to say before he says it.

"*No* therapy." I groan. "Don't bring it up. We're having a perfectly normal conversation, and I don't need the reminder that all you see when you look at me is how fucked-up I am."

Derek sighs, and the sound tugs at me. "You're not fucked-up."

"If you really thought that you wouldn't keep using the T-word on me."

He wants to fight back. I can read it all over his face, and if he pushes, I'll be ready for a fight. It's one of the things I'm good at. I'm always ready to go claws out.

He derails me with his next question. "How was it?"

At first, I think Derek is talking about therapy, and that's not at all a can of worms I want to open around him, but then it clicks. The class. He's not pushing the issue.

"Shit."

"You didn't like it?"

"I don't think I said that."

Derek lists his head. "If the class is shit, that sort of tells me that you didn't like it."

My instinct is to point out to him that everything is shit, but this is the first time we've had a conversation that he hasn't been reluctant about. Having his attention is the single greatest blast of light I've felt in a long time, and so I dig deeper.

I lean my shoulder against the wall and scratch at the paint on my hands. "Their paintings were shit. They had no idea what they were doing. A lot of them couldn't hear what I was saying, and Kevin is the rudest jerk I've ever met. The second I walked in, he asked if I'd dumped paint over my hair to make a point, and when I said no, he asked if I was one of those fairy types."

"He *what?*" Derek's whole posture stiffens, and I set a reassuring hand on his arm without even thinking about it. We both freeze at the contact, and it takes me a second to yank my hand away again.

"I don't care," I say. "Having my life … as my life, pretty much nothing gets a reaction out of me. He could call me the nastiest words he's ever learned, and it wouldn't have an impact."

"It doesn't mean he can say whatever he wants."

"Of course it does. We live in a free country. There's a thing called freedom of speech. If he wants to be a bigoted piece of crap, that's his right."

"Freedom of speech doesn't mean you're free from the consequences of what you say."

"Duh." He doesn't need to teach me that. I say fucked-up things all the time, and I have to deal with the aftereffects. "I'm sure he's run his mouth to the wrong people before, but he's a stranger, and I've dealt with worse, so if he wants to call me a fairy, I'll call him a crotchety has-been and move on."

"That's very cool of you."

Unlike Derek, who'd been prepared to storm the nursing home, apparently. It niggles something deep and longing in my gut. "Were you about to walk in there and defend my honor?"

"Not just yours, but yes."

Of course he was. When I look at Derek, I see a guardian angel. A protector. It makes absolute sense that he'd want to stand up for what's right and not let people get away with shitty behavior. I have enough shitty behavior of my own that calling someone else out feels hypocritical. Derek though? Derek's perfect.

"You're sweet."

He grunts. "I also heard them both call you a trash … panda?"

"Feral raccoon."

"What the fuck was up with that?"

Again, what the hell does it matter to me if someone calls me a feral raccoon? Raccoons are cute. I'm cute. "Aggy is my honorary grandmother, and she's as much of a pain in the ass as I am."

"You shouldn't talk about yourself like that."

I lean closer. "And *you* shouldn't tell people what to do."

"Sorry. I … you're right."

"You don't need to pretend to care though," I say, lightly

punching his chest. "I'm very tough. I can look out for myself. If someone pisses me off, they know about it."

That brings his laugh back. "I've found that out for myself."

"On many, many occasions."

There's still warm amusement in his eyes as he looks down at me. Then something shifts. "Xander ... I *do* ... care. You know that ... right?"

The heavy hesitation in his tone surprises me. Derek reminds me of one of those guys I used to watch in high school. The ones where everything came so effortlessly to them. Sports, schooling, friends. Nothing weighed them down. Nothing was unscalable.

I used to want to be one of those guys.

Now, I *want* one of those guys.

The fact that the kindest, sweetest, hottest, most caring man in the entire fucking world is in my life, that he fills me with the type of safe contentment I've never had and has zero interest in giving me more, feels like a sick joke.

I need him. He doesn't need me.

So he can say he cares all he likes. I know what he means.

"Of course you care. Everyone cares about the kicked puppy."

I shift, about to ready myself to leave, when Derek's big hand circles my wrist. His grip is soft, but his gaze is steady.

"Not like a puppy, Xander. You're so much more than you give yourself credit for." He lets go suddenly and nods, but I've swallowed my damn tongue. That actually sounded ... genuine.

"I'm going to set up," he says. "I'll probably see you around ... but I hope not."

# Chapter Ten

Derek

Sometimes I'm convinced that I'm deliberately self-sabotaging. Telling Xander that I care about him is so completely fucking counterproductive to, well, everything.

I caught him watching my dance class and had to pretend like I didn't notice him hovering right outside the door. If I didn't see him, I didn't have to invite him in, and if I didn't invite him in, I wouldn't have to spend more time with him.

It was airtight logic.

Except for how fucking distracted it made me that I kept stepping on feet and running into walking frames. It was a disaster of a class, and I owe these people better.

"I'm telling you," Manny says from where he's driving next to me. "Once you see the lot we're in the process of subdividing, you're going to lose your mind. You can turn the whole thing into a bug house if you want to."

The further we get from Seattle, the less settled I am. I've been to Manny's house for dinner and out this way to visit our old teammate Elias a couple of times too. Every visit is the same though, like a weight slowly pressing down on my chest the further I get from the city. Usually I make up some excuse not to go, but when Manny showed up earlier, he wouldn't take no for an answer. At least he's one person in my life who won't let me retreat into nothingness.

"Why are you quiet?" he asks, looking over at me through his huge black sunglasses.

"No reason." There is a reason. I'm on edge, waiting for my phone to ring.

"You really haven't been yourself lately, and I thought it was maybe something you were going through, but this mood has stuck. Should I be worried?"

Manny doesn't know about Xander, and I'm not about to tell him either. It's bad enough everyone I work with knows how my entire life is at a standstill. I wouldn't say I'm necessarily embarrassed by it, but I probably should be. There's a line between helping someone and becoming a doormat for them, and I've pole-vaulted right over into the latter.

All I can do is hope that this land Manny is showing me suddenly injects some goddamn life back into me.

"Work keeps me busy," I explain. "There's nothing to worry about."

He throws me a skeptical look. "There's more to life than work. I thought you got into nursing so you could travel and help people."

"You of all people should know plans change, Mr. Super Bowl."

"Yeah, but I was never close to being good enough to go all the way. That wasn't me changing my plans; it was me being shit. You, on the other hand, are already a nurse. That part's done."

"Almost sounds like you're trying to get rid of me."

Manny laughs, scenery speeding by outside his window. "You're my bestie, bestie. I want to make sure you're where you want to be in life. Where's that fun-loving guy I've always known?"

"Geez, get out of my head. I'm already well aware of how old I'm getting, thanks."

"Old? We're mid-thirties. That's not even close to being old."

"Feels it though."

Manny snaps his fingers. "There. See? That. Where did this grumbly old man come from?"

The fucking rut I'm stuck in. "Tell me, if I do end up buying this land from you, am I going to have to deal with you nosing into my life every other day?"

"You don't give me enough credit. I have no issues doing that *every* day. Whether you live by me or not."

"Not helping your case."

"But the *football field*, Derek. Remember the football field."

"And all those children I don't have."

"Now you're getting it."

I withhold rolling my eyes as he turns the car onto his property. We're well outside of the city, and I'm trying to turn off the reminder of how long it would take for us to get back there if I have a phone call come through. Definitely not fast enough to beat Xander to the pharmacy, and if he's there, sitting, waiting … if *Susan* tells him I'm not coming … I picture the way her offensively pink lipstick sinks into the lines in her lips whenever they strain under a smile. It'd give her a thrill to send Xander away.

The images are all false and made up in my head, but the irrational anger stoking at my rib cage is real.

Manny bypasses the big house and drives further down his land. It gets more overgrown as we put distance between ourselves and the main property, until at last, he pulls up on the edge of what's been maintained. There are marker pegs in the ground.

I follow Manny out of the car.

"This is it," he says. "It goes alllll the way down to that border fence. The wire one?"

I squint to see what he's talking about. "It's a lot."

"Yeah, and with work and wanting more kids, I don't have the time to look after it all."

"You'll have no issues selling it."

"I know." He plants his hands on his hips and turns to me. "But I don't want to sell it to any old stranger."

"You've said."

It's sort of perfect. Big, open, plenty of space for bees. The drive to and from work each day wouldn't be ideal, but it's not terrible. The land itself will probably fetch a decent price for Manny, but I'd have enough for the down payment. I could easily make this work. What I'm not expecting is how much I want it.

I can see myself here. With a real home. A memory of those endless summers, kicking at grass, getting sunburned, sweat and bruises marring my skin from too much football. It's quiet. *Me.* I hadn't realized how busy my brain had gotten until now. I'm standing here, and everything around us has stopped, taking me back to a time when I could breathe.

"What do you think?" he asks.

"It's incredible."

"Told youuuu."

"Yeah, yeah, get all smug. Doesn't mean I can take it."

Manny lets out a frustrated groan. "Come on, man. You're renting, and you can get to your job easily enough. There's nothing in the city holding you back."

Nothing except for Xander, who I can't walk away from. For someone so outwardly full of confidence, he has a lot of self-doubt. I hated the way he was talking about himself the other day, and I want to be able to help him with that too. I can't and won't. But I still want to. "I have my bugs," I finally say.

"Do you hear yourself when you say that?"

"What? I only just got the formicarium set up, and now you want me to move it?"

Manny makes a noise in his throat. "Be real. It'll be a while before this place is ready to build on and even longer before it's ready to live on. Is it me? Am I the problem? Would living here be too close?"

"No way." I won't tell him and let it go to his head, but living near Manny is a selling point. He and Hannah never fail to make me feel welcome and like part of the family, which would happen even more if I lived out there.

"Then ..." He kicks at some loose rock and sets his hands on his hips. "Sorry, I don't get it. Seattle's depressing you. You moved there, and I've had to watch you slowly become a hermit man."

"I'm not depressed. That's a serious illness. I'm ..." Frustrated? Antsy? Resentful? "Stuck."

"Stuck?"

Shit. I didn't mean to say that out loud. "It's a long story," I hedge. "Nothing all that exciting, but for the foreseeable future, I'm not leaving Seattle." I give the site one more longing look, then picture going home to my two-bedroom, right on the road, overshadowed by the two houses it's squashed between.

Before that image can get me down too much, I force myself to picture Xander. The sweet, fleeting smile, his shrewd eyes, and the defiance he wears like armor. To imagine never seeing him again.

I'm a selfish, selfish man. Obviously, seeing him again is bad if it means he's sick. But ... I think back to how he looked at the nursing home. A bright pop of color in the white halls. Big, pretty eyes. A little flirty. Holding himself more defensively than I'm used to seeing him, though I prefer that over him looking drained.

And he said—well, he didn't say he *liked* the class, but he sort of implied it. So if he enjoyed volunteering there, would he do it again? Will I see him next week? I shouldn't want to, but I fucking do. He's like a brightly colored bug, reminding me he's dangerous. If I had any kind of survival instincts, that would be enough to make me stay clear, but I'm like a fucking fly to his bright light.

So wildly, inappropriately attracted. Especially after the other day.

"Derek …"

I blink back to the now. I'd almost forgotten Manny was with me.

He clears his throat. "I'm here if you need anything. Right?"

I sling my arm around his shoulders, wanting to reassure him. The Xander part of my life might be a mess, but otherwise, I have no complaints. "I know. You're the fucking greatest, and I really appreciate you showing this to me first. You have no idea how much I want to say yes—"

"Then do it."

*Don't fucking tempt me, dammit.* "I can't." I'm firm about that. "But one day, I might be able to move up this way."

"Or finally take off doing all that nurse stuff you want to do."

That's one thing I'm confident will never happen. "Maybe that too," I lie. Hypocritical of me, considering I told Xander he should be truthful, but no matter what people think of me, I'm far from perfect. Which includes the lying. Sue me.

Manny hooks a thumb back over his shoulder. "Want to stay for lunch?"

After him insisting he'd pick me up, I really should stay for a while before he has to drop me home, but then I picture my phone ringing. Having to explain to him why I need to get back. Trying to justify my inappropriate attachment to a patient.

But worse than all of that is Xander. Xander showing up to the pharmacy and me not being there to help him.

I give Manny a tight smile, already dreading the words I'm about to say. I *want* to stay, but I can't.

"I can't today."

"Damn, huh?" He sweeps a hand over his face. "Maybe next time?"

"For sure."

That's a lie as well.

# Chapter Eleven

Xander

"So … why is this a secret again?" Seven asks, pulling his car up out the front of the nursing home.

"Because I don't want Aggy to be mad at me."

Seven splutters. "I don't want her mad with *me* either. Tell me you're not going to try and muscle her into a place like this. You know she'll never go."

"If she keeps annoying me, she will." I chew on my bottom lip, not sure how much to tell Seven. Knowing my luck, he'll tattle to Molly, who'll say something to Aggy during their weekly baking. "I really like spending time with the old people."

"The … old people. Do you call them that?"

"Sometimes."

"Do they hate you?"

"Probably, but not for that." I grin at him innocently.

"Here's an idea." He reaches across me to pop open my

door. "Don't insult their age and try to get to know them. We should be so lucky to live the lives they have."

"*You* will." He and Molly will have long, happy lives. "I'm fully committed to dying in my thirties."

"You shouldn't put that out into the universe."

"I'm not. The universe is putting it on me." Besides, as far as I'm concerned, my Bertha brothers will likely be sick of me by then, so it's as good of a time as any to go. If nothing else gets me, heartache can. It sounds morbidly romantic. Maybe if I have it etched onto my tombstone, someone in fifty years will read it and be sad for me.

"You get yearly blood tests, and you're always perfectly fine. Stop talking yourself into it."

"My white blood cells were up last time."

"Only from your previous test." Seven laughs. "They were still within range."

That's what he thinks. They might be in the average range, but the elevated levels weren't average *for me*. Which means there's something going on with me, and the doctor wouldn't sign off on the extra testing I requested. If I drop dead tomorrow, I've given Seven strict instructions to sue him.

"I'm going to die one day, and you'll all be sorry."

"Very sorry. I'll have to hear Molly sobbing over it for the rest of our lives."

I pause, then slowly lift my eyes to his. "You'd be sad too … right?"

"I'd be devastated, you ninny. Stop talking about this."

He would, but he'd get over it. Molly would help him, and he'd help Molly, and soon enough, they'd forget about me. They'll go on to have their own family and vaguely remember that guy they used to live with that one time.

Seven's scowling at me, and it's maybe my favorite expression to see him wear. He's trying to hide his hurt, and that goes a long way to reminding me that he does love me. For now. No matter what my brain tries to tell me.

Maybe being loved for right now is enough.

Before I can get out, I lean over the center console and squeeze him in a hug. Seven squeezes me back, lips pressing hard against my temple, and I want to crawl into his lap and live there forever. Seven is my safety. The thought of losing him makes my throat close over, and it would be so easy to slip into that headspace where I'm choking, can't breathe, where that existential dread sinks down into me.

"Z?"

I jolt back. "I'm fine. I'm okay."

He watches me for a moment, then whispers, "I love you."

In an ideal world, he always would. He, Molly, and I would have our little family and be happy together. And in an even idealer world, Derek would be there too.

I came back here with Aggy last week, at the same time, and found Derek teaching his class again. This time, I'm planning to hang around until he finishes in the hope of some more alone time, and I can't have Aggy getting in the way of that. I wish I could make her understand. I wish she knew that this isn't some stupid crush. There aren't a lot of people who make me feel safe, but Derek is one of them, and if it was up to me, I'd get to have him always. As mine. All mine. It would be ideal, really, because then I wouldn't have to race off to the pharmacy every time there's something wrong.

Then maybe I wouldn't need Seven and Molly as much as I do now, and it would take them longer to regret having me in their lives.

"Pick me up in two hours?" I check, even though he's already agreed.

"I'll be here."

I jump out and slam the door behind me, then hurry into

the building. The front desk lady, Mary, recognizes me instantly, and her face lights up with a smile.

"Bethany was hoping you'd be back," Mary says, grabbing a volunteer badge for me.

My face wrinkles. "Really?"

"Yes, she's talked of nothing else except your class for the last week."

I'm speechless for a moment. Maybe Seven might have a teeny-weeny point that these old people are more than just reminders of my mortality. Bethany doesn't talk much, and her movements are limited, but even with the arthritis, I can tell she had a steady hand and good eye once upon a time. Besides, Aggy is older than most of them, and I love her.

I clip the badge to my T-shirt, shaking my guilt over the reminder that the only reason I came back was for Derek.

"I can't wait," I tell Mary. Then, I head down the hall and get ready.

It's not until halfway into the class that I get that first glimpse of Derek, those stunning, curious eyes gazing around the doorframe and into the room. He's too slow to look away, and I catch him watching me, holding on to the hope that he's been doing that for a while now.

My face splits into a grin, and I beeline straight for the door. "You're here early."

"I've got to set up." There's a slight pause and then, "I haven't seen you this week."

"Careful, you almost sound disappointed about that."

The way amusement lights up his whole face has me swooning. "If it means you're good, then I'm good."

At least he didn't say something shitty about being happy about it. Pushing my luck, I give his sleeve a tug. "Come on, I set up a station for you too."

Derek blinks rapidly. "Me?"

77

"Yep." This time, I tug his sleeve and don't let go until he takes a reluctant step into the room.

"I can't paint."

"Damn, you'll really be a fish out of water amongst these masterpieces." I wave my hand toward where Kevin has somehow managed to turn his dog into a turd this week.

Derek stamps down his smile. "I need to set up."

"We'll wrap up five minutes early, and I'll come and help you. It's just shifting a few tables."

"You'll help me move tables?"

The skepticism in his tone makes me narrow my eyes at him. "I'm a lot stronger than I look."

"I don't doubt that."

"Then stay," I say, not above injecting some pleading into my voice. "I haven't seen you all week. If you don't stay, I might start to miss you, and then my brain will play tricks on me so I can see you at the pharmacy instead."

It's not until the humor drains from Derek's face that I realize I've said the wrong thing. Joking about my mental health is something that comes naturally to me, so half of the time, I don't even know what fucked-up things I'm saying.

The way Derek immediately closes off makes it clear I've crossed lines with him though. He pulls gently from my grip and steps back. "I'll decide whether or not to join your class on my own. You don't need to guilt me into it."

Then he turns on his heel and leaves me with a big, fat lump of anxious energy burning through my gut.

"Struck out, did you?" Kevin grunts.

"Go back to your scat play," I snap before returning to the front of the room and ignoring them for the rest of the class.

I DON'T KNOW why I'm here again. I barely say a word to Mary as I collect my badge and storm into the room to set up for this week's class. All the easels, all the paints, all the supplies are things I bring with me. Things I pay for. I'm still not sure why I'm wasting my money.

I've just set the last art pad in place when I turn to plant myself in a chair as I wait for the residents. My eyes brush over the seat by the door, and I jolt at finding someone sitting there.

"Derek?"

He doesn't completely meet my eye as he picks up a paintbrush. "Got here early enough this week."

Considering I assumed he'd avoid me like his life depended on it, I'm not prepared for this. Seeing him. Talking.

"You … did." I creep a little closer. After last week, I know that I owe him an apology, but it refuses to come out. Even my inside voice is stubborn. "I thought you hated me."

He manages a small smile. "I told you the other night that I didn't."

"That wasn't on purpose." The whole way to the pharmacy, that terrifying dread had only been disrupted by the fear that Derek would think I was faking it. That he'd think I was there to make him feel bad and follow through on the joke I'd made. Sure, I'm petty enough to do that, but I didn't.

"I know." He runs his thumb over the bristles of the paintbrush and nods at the paper. "So what do I do?"

"You paint."

That makes him laugh, and pride ripples through my chest. "Unlike you, most people aren't a natural at this. What do I paint? What colors do I use? How … how do I make it actually look like a thing?"

"Just … pick something. Picture it, how it moves, how the shape of it flows. Think of how the light captures it and keep building. Keep layering."

"I can't work out whether it's a sign of optimism that you

think anyone is capable of it or if you devalue yourself and what you do *that* much."

I don't want to think about that question. "Pick an animal."

"A … bird."

"Okay, what sort of bird? A swan? An eagle? A red-footed booby?"

He snorts. "You wanted to say booby, didn't you?"

"Little bit. So … do you like boobies?"

"The birds or the part of a woman's anatomy?"

I know I'm being cheeky by even asking, but I answer, "Both."

"The bird I have no opinion on. The anatomy … does nothing for me. I'm completely gay."

I don't remember how or when I learned that Derek's queer, but it's good to have it confirmed officially. I've always low-key suspected, the same way I'm sure he's always suspected about me as well, but that doesn't stop me from confirming it. "Me too."

"Let's paint a raven," he says.

I want to wave that suggestion off and get us back to more personal topics, but I'm afraid to scare him away like I did last week, so instead, I pull a chair up beside him. "Okay, what colors do we need for a raven?"

"Black."

"And?"

Derek's brow rumples. "Umm … I dunno? Maybe brown for a nest."

"And yellow, orange, red? For the features, white, blue, we'll make some gray." I squeeze out some colors across the round board. We don't have long, but I want to show Derek how things work together. How, when you look closer, the little details build to create an overall image. I start simple, with a wing. I lay the base color, create the shape, then layer the blacks and blues and whites. I add volume to the paints, and while they might not be as easy to work with as my acrylics, the wing takes shape. I move quickly, wanting at least a decent enough one down before everyone else gets here, and it's not until I'm adding texture, making it more three-dimensional, that I glance over and find Derek's still gripping the clean paintbrush loosely between his fingers.

I glance from it up to his face, immediately finding his eyes on me.

"You're not doing anything."

One corner of his lips gives the tiniest kick. "I'm watching."

"You won't learn much from that."

"Actually, I'd argue that I'm learning a lot." His voice is a smooth, deep whisper. The kind that pools in my belly and makes me warm all over. He's got these tiny lines by his eyes that I can only see up close, and they make his whole face friendlier. "You're really good."

I frown, turning back to the wing. I haven't let any of the paints dry since I was rushing, and they haven't blended together well at all. The shape isn't working, and the feathers don't look all that feathery. I smudge out one particularly bad edge with my thumb, but it only ends up looking worse. "Sorry," I say. "I ruined your paper."

Before Derek can respond, the door opens, and I turn to find Kevin, Bethany, and Toni walking in.

"What bullshit are we painting this week?" Kevin grumbles.

The quiet bubble between me and Derek snaps, and I reluctantly get up to help them.

Derek stays for the whole class.

## Chapter Twelve

Derek

There's something about seeing Xander create that has me transfixed. He sees things in a way most people don't, and watching him turn nothing into something breathtaking only reminds me of how much deeper Xander goes. That's not supposed to be something I know about him; I promised myself I'd keep my distance, but every week is a new nail in my coffin. I get there earlier and earlier until one week, I arrive before he does.

In an effort not to feel completely pathetic, I collect the supplies he has stacked in a cupboard and set up the room the way he normally has it. The look on his face when he walks in makes it all worth it.

It's only been a few weeks, but I'm scarily starting to live for these moments.

I reason with myself that it's healthier than living for the moments when I have to see him professionally, so … improvement? Maybe?

I'm doing my best to separate those two sides of him. The one I treat and the one I see running these classes. And that second man is something else. Getting to see him like that only deepens the hurt that he won't see a professional and try to get better.

This creative, snarky, passionate man deserves so much more than he lets himself have. It's hard not to get pissy about that.

Every week, I watch him interact with people. Every week, he gives me hell about how terrible I am at painting, and every week, I learn a new thing about him. A dangerous, wonderful new thing. Like how fall is his favorite time of year.

How he hates nail polish because he can never get it exactly right.

When he gets excited about something, his gaze sort of lifts, and his whole face lights up.

Insults are definitely his love language.

And whatever issues Xander needs to work through have left him with chronic emotional regulation problems.

"You painted a beetle," he says, amusement lacing his words as he looks at the paper I'm working on.

"You figured it out this time."

"Lucky guess." He grins at me, and it's rare I get that smile without something darker behind it. It hits right in my gut.

I poke his hand with my paintbrush and smear the grayish color over his pale skin. "Or maybe I'm getting better."

"If anything, I think you're getting worse."

He plucks the paintbrush from my grip and moves closer to the paper. Unfortunately, that also puts him closer to me. His hip is an inch from my thigh, and I'm transfixed by the way his hand moves as he adds more details to the legs.

"Why a beetle?" he asks.

I'm not embarrassed by how cool I think bugs are, but I do know that they give some people an ick. Personally, I don't get it, but I'm also the type of guy who gets excited learning about pollination, so I'm probably not the best judge of what's cool.

Telling Xander about my little passion is harder than I thought it would be. He's let me in a lot recently, and I want to do the same, but I'm suddenly wishing I was into car racing or competitive chess.

Even *that* has to be better than bugs.

"I think they're interesting," I say carefully.

He nods. "Is it a specific type of beetle or a general one?"

"It's a citrus long-horned beetle."

"Nice. Tell me … are long-horned beetles supposed to have a sheep face?"

It's so completely not what I'm expecting him to say that a laugh bursts out of me. "Now that you mention it, no."

He glances over his shoulder at me, a teasing expression all over his features. Then, with a quick flourish, he scrawls "Baa!" across the top.

I'm not thinking when I grab his wrist and steal my paint-brush back, but damn, his skin is soft. The warmth from his wrist wraps deliciously around my palm, and when I glance up, I've somehow tugged him closer. That stunning face holds nothing but surprise, and the *thud* of my heart gets more insistent.

I'm stuck in his gravity, and it takes me way too long to let go.

Xander's throat clears with a sharp snap before he walks off.

Usually once class wraps up, I'm the first one out the door, but today, I stall. It's always hard to leave when I crave more time with him, but it's doubly hard today, and once the residents start talking amongst themselves and getting ready to leave, I jump up and help Xander pack everything away.

He glances over at where I'm stacking things in the cupboard. "Don't you have people waiting for you to sweep them off their feet?"

"Yep." I stuff my paint-covered hands into my pockets. "I thought ..."

He flicks on the tap in the corner and holds out some soap to me. "Yeah?"

I have to move closer to take the soap, and he doesn't step away from the sink as I wash up. Instead, a moment later, he moves closer, shoulder to mine as he washes the paint from his hands as well. "I've been taking your class ... you want to take mine?"

I feel his eyes flick toward me. "You're trying to share the booty grabs around, aren't you?"

"So what if I am?"

He turns off the flowing water and dries his hands before passing the towel to me. "Sure. I'll do it."

"Okay."

"And so you know ..." He steps in so my towel-covered hands are pressed between us. "I won't say no to a thank-you booty tap. In case you get the urge."

Motherfucker. I've got the urge. I've got the urge good.

I *should not* have the urge because having the urge is very bad, but fuck me, tell that to my dick. I hurry to step back and get some distance before the stupid thing gets ideas.

"Right. Well. I'll see you over there."

I scramble from the room like Xander might bite me. Honestly, I'm not so sure I'd put it past him. I'm also definitely sure I wouldn't hate it.

There are ten residents I dance with each week, and it's less of me teaching them how and more of them teaching me. Dancing socially used to be a big thing before it became all fist pumps and twerking and—well, fuck. There I go, sounding like an old man again. I might as well book my room here now.

Since I'm late, Carla has taken it upon herself to get the music started, and I watch as they bop along to the beat. There are eight women and two men, and watching them laugh and get into it without any hint of self-consciousness makes me smile. Maybe getting old isn't so bad.

"Here he is," Carla says, lifting her hands. "We were beginning to think you'd forgotten about us."

"Never." I shift the table nearest me out of the way. "Did you scissors paper rock for who gets to dance with me first?"

"I won!" Jessie says.

"Hey, no fair." Nerves hit me at the familiar voice, and I glance back in time to watch Xander walk into the room. "I wasn't here for that."

Conversation breaks out, and I sigh. "Xander's here to help me."

His cute nose wrinkles his freckles together. "*Help* you?"

"Looks like you need another scissors paper rock to see who dances with him first," I tell them.

Carla, Mabel, and Josie immediately start a best of three, and I lower my voice so only Xander can hear me.

"Don't worry, I made sure they all know you're pro booty tap. You'll feel very thanked once this class is over."

The glare he sends me is adorable, and I move away before he can reply.

Throughout the whole hour, I can't help but track where he is in the room. As much as I want him to be having fun, I also want to make sure he's being politer than he usually is. Carla isn't the kind who'd take being insulted as a good thing, and she probably wouldn't hide her distaste either.

I love these people. We've been dancing together for well over a year now, and I've gotten to know them and sometimes their families well. I know their stories, and it's so interesting to hear about how every one of them has lived an amazingly different life.

It hurts sometimes too. Not long after I started, we lost Alana. Then Adam broke his hip. Josie is forgetting more than she's remembering lately, but dancing is one of those things that's holding strong.

"Where did you find the little cutie?" Carla asks when it's my turn with her.

"He … runs the art class." Not a complete lie.

Her eyes cut to Xander and back to me. "The art class?"

"He's very talented."

"He's a terrible dancer. Didn't even know what the two-step is."

"Neither did I until you taught it to me."

Her lips quirk. "I hope he comes back."

Me too, Carla. Get in line.

She suddenly lets out a warbly "*Ohhh*."

"Shit, are you okay?"

"Fine, fine, dear. Just quite tired all at once. Quick, Paul, help me to a chair. Xander, dear, take over for me."

I stiffen slightly as Paul leaves Xander, and Xander smoothly slides in front of me. He holds up his hand, and after a second of debating with myself and failing, I take it.

My free hand settles high on his waist, which I assume will take some of the temptation away, but I've underestimated Xander. Touching him like this, where it's casual, not clinical, is more than I'm prepared for.

Those unnerving purple eyes meet mine as his hand rests on the side of my shoulder. "Hi."

"What a coincidence that you were closest when Carla suddenly needed to sit down."

He's not even trying to hold back his smile. "I hope you're not accusing my new best friend of anything."

"Like what?" I play dumb.

"Like helping me orchestrate getting to be your partner for a dance."

"I'd never suspect anything like that from you."

His smile takes on a wicked edge. "You should."

"You're too sweet to be sneaky."

"And you clearly know nothing about me. You should fix that."

A few weeks ago, I might have agreed. I've gotten snapshots into his life, seen him at his most vulnerable, been witness to him accidentally letting things slip in weak moments, but real conversation has been slim.

I didn't know how badly I was craving it until we started, and somehow, I need to let it go. Everything is friendly enough for right now, but I know how I'm feeling. I know how that little ball of care and concern is slowly changing, and I know that I'm not doing a damn thing to stop it from happening.

This fucked-up ride isn't going to end well.

But then I look into his face, feel his warmth through his shirt, his slim side under my hand, and my craving for him deepens.

"You're a much better dancer than painter," he says.

We're not doing anything more than rocking side to side because, as Carla pointed out, Xander has no idea what he's doing. "And you're a much better painter than dancer."

His eyes light up, and then he slowly steps forward, one foot resting on top of mine, and then the other does the same. "Teach me."

He's flush against me, angles slotted with my grooves, and all my energy goes into controlling my cock rather than telling him to move the hell back. There's something beautifully at war on his face that's impossible to look away from. So I go with it.

I bounce my left leg. "This one first."

"I'm ready."

He might not be able to dance, but he has no issues staying in time with my steps. My pulse is racing in my ears, and he's all around me. His scent, the cute freckles, the way he's gripping me tight. Every step has my groin skimming against him, and I'm dangerously close to getting hard. Just his proximity is doing it. Somehow, he's even more stunning up close. Up close where I can make out the guardedness in his eyes, the way one side of his face holds tension, like he's biting the inside of his cheek maybe, how the bow in his top lip is more pronounced on the left, and above it, in the middle of his cheek, an eyelash has fallen out to rest beside his freckles.

I'm drinking in every fucking detail.

Swallowing back the want it's bringing out in me.

This is a platonic dance.

Because it has to be.

The music playing comes to a gentle end, and Xander steps down off my feet. It takes me a second to release him.

Then the clapping starts, and it's like all my good sense switches back on at once. I glance around to find everyone has stopped dancing to watch us, and heat rushes to my cheeks.

"Yeah, yeah, back to it," I say, trying to brush off how I'd forgotten any of them were even here.

Xander cuts me a sly look. "No booty tap?"

I harden my jaw and stalk off without a word.

---

# Chapter Thirteen

---

Xander

I love dancing. It's the single greatest thing I've ever experienced in my life. Fuck art, fuck dying, fuck everything except spending the rest of my life plastered against Derek.

I drift inside after Seven has picked me up and head straight to my room. I don't want to see anyone or talk to anyone or do anything except keep reliving that moment over.

I'll wrap it around me and live there forever.

Derek's eyes are my weakness. Every time I look into them, I'm convinced he sees me. They're sweet and welcoming and fill me with so many messy nerves it's like I'm going to vibrate out of my skin.

Why can't he want me the same way I want him? Why can't he feel this same body-prickling need? All I could think about with his hands on me was him ducking his head to bring our lips together, and even imagining that has such violent butterflies taking off in my stomach that I worry I'm going to throw up.

But it eases, and when I step inside my room, I lock my door.

This isn't something I do often. Despite what I tell my roommates, I'm not constantly horny. Sometimes listening to them go at it will be enough to get me there, especially if I pick up murmured, loving words, but my dick is always triggered by something. Some*one*. Spontaneous horniness is rare.

I'm hard now though.

Dancing up close, getting the hint of a slightly citrusy cologne, watching those sweet eyes watch me, it short-circuited my brain. I barely made it through the end of the dance hour.

And now ... now Derek and I have a date with my fantasies.

I pushed my luck today, and he one hundred percent let me get away with it. He should never have let that happen because I know me. With every little inch he gives me, I'll go after two more. I'm greedy when it comes to what I want, and I've never wanted anyone the way I want Derek.

I don't think I've ever wanted anyone at all.

I strip my shirt over my head and toss it to the floor, then my shorts and underwear go next. Even with how turned on I am, there's an edge of sadness to it too. I'm desperately lonely, and I wonder if, one day, I'll ever get to do this with another person. If I'll ever feel hands on me and a cock against my cock and not feel anxious or used or like it's all going to slip away.

Maybe one day, I'll feel wanted.

Until then, I can only imagine what it will be like.

My gaze snags on my reflection in the huge mirror I have set against the opposite wall. I see myself too much, and none of it is worth looking at. I'm too thin. Too short. My dick is nothing special.

*Better stick to those memories, Z. There's no way a man like Derek could ever want all this.*

My eyes squeeze tight, and I fight against the voice. The voice that sounds too much like Seven's, saying words he'd never say. I rock on my feet, that dark impulse trying to get me to stay put while I fight against it. My dick is flagging, but I want this. I want so badly to remember Derek and how he felt and have this split moment in time where I enjoy myself and nothing else.

I take a weak step forward, then another. Just focus on moving until my knees hit my bed and I collapse down onto it.

*"And you're a much better painter than dancer."*

*"Teach me."*

That moment swims back to life in my memories. The way I'd wanted to know what Derek's stubble would feel like. How safe it was in his hands. How I'd counted the colors in his eyes and knew I'd never be able to paint them all.

I slide my hand down and wrap it loosely around my dick. It's thickening again, and relief washes over me. I didn't lose it.

The memory of me and Derek dancing switches from the room full of people to the middle of my bedroom. His hand moves from my waist and slides down, down until it settles on my lower back. He pulls me closer, firmer against him, and I chance a quick stroke over my cock. It's nowhere near enough, but *fuck*, it feels good.

I sink into the memory, morphing it and twisting it to be everything my dreams are made of. Derek's hands dipping under my shirt, pressing it up over my head. I shiver at how his hands would feel on me. Soft? Scratchy? I can't decide, but it doesn't matter either way as long as it's Derek. I remove his shirt next, exposing that body I drooled over at the club. The body I never would have been able to imagine myself.

The memory makes me shivery. What would it have felt like if we'd danced then? Pressed together. Overheated bodies with no space between them. His chest hair tickling my skin, our sweat slick together, hot, heavy breaths by my ear.

A soft sigh falls from my lips as I scramble for the lube in my bedside table and finally give in to the urges. My hand slips up and down my shaft, bringing out the deep kind of ache that only Derek can give me. I've tried too many times, with so many men, and no one gets me hard the way he does.

Maybe I should get myself tested for impotence?

But there's none of that going on now. The angry vein along the underside of my dick is stark against my pale skin, and what feels like all the blood in my body is pooling in my reddened tip.

It's not often I get to experience being this worked up, and I love the addictive, overwhelming desperation. The way my brain empties of everything except images that make me feel good. Wanted. Needed.

I want this feeling to last forever. I'll never understand how guys with dicks that work properly don't become sex addicts. If I could get horny like this, every day, I'd never leave my bed.

Dream Derek shoves down my pants, then lifts me into his beefy arms before stalking closer to my bed. He sets me on the edge of it. I imagine him kneeling between my legs, firmly pushing my thighs open, while his kind eyes look deep into mine.

Nerves rattle around deep in my stomach, and my hand moves faster over my shaft. In my mind, Derek dips his head and presses his lips to mine. Soft, sweet, an electrifying ghost of skin on skin.

Then, he bends down and wraps his mouth around my cock.

I don't get further than that before I shoot. My balls tighten as I throb out ropes of cum onto my stomach and sink into that mind-spinning high where nothing else can touch me.

But the high never lasts. Bit by bit, it slips away, and as I glance down at the mess, as I catch sight of my hip bones and lack of abs, something deep in my chest twists.

I pant as I catch my breath, gaze redirected to the ceiling, reminding myself to appreciate these moments because they sure as hell will never be real.

———

THE FEW TIMES I see him at the pharmacy, Derek is the same as he's always been, and I hate it. Now that I've seen him without the professional mask on, I want more of that, but he refuses to budge. Just gently inspects me, then softly talks me down.

I want to kick him. Or throw something.

Anything to startle him out of this bland version of who he really is.

It makes me even more grateful for our time together at the nursing home.

I'm way too excited to get to the painting classes that week that I'm snappish and impatient, waiting for Seven to get his shit together to drive me. He'd tried to teach me how to drive once, but the first time I got behind the wheel, this immense responsibility pressed down on me, and I couldn't even bring myself to turn the car on. What if I fell asleep randomly on a busy highway? Hit ice? Experienced a mechanical failure that sent me careening into a tree?

Not to mention that these days, it feels like if Seven's not driving me somewhere, I don't get to spend time with him. I hate having to fight for people's attention. Hate having to remind them I exist too.

"Back in two hours?" he checks.

I nod and climb out, throat too sticky to answer him. The whole time I'm stomping across the grass to the entrance, I'm torn between trying to be happy for him that he has Molly in his life and angry that he only has time for Molly in his life. Seven was supposed to be the one person who was all mine, and I love him so much that I want him to be happy, but since he started therapy, something's changed. That person has been messing with his brain.

Seven was perfect exactly how he was, and now he's becoming a different person. A grown-up person.

And grown-ups have never had time for me.

I need Derek more than ever today. I need his distraction and his time and his attention and his terrible art.

Maybe Carla will help me dance with him again.

Maybe I can convince him to hang out after this, just the two of us.

The nerves are bubbling happily in my gut as I check in and head down to the room. He's not here yet, which isn't unusual, but I know it won't be long. He always shows up before the others so we can sneak a couple of moments together.

Until he doesn't.

During the whole class, I'm watching the door, waiting, growing slowly more confused as time creeps on. It's moments like these where I wish I had his number and could check he's all right, but it's always felt weird to ask. We're not technically friends.

I don't trust myself not to abuse the privilege.

Five minutes before I'm due to wrap things up, he strides straight past the door. My gut almost shoots out of my mouth in excitement, and I dart out into the hall, calling out his name to catch him before he can turn the corner.

He stops but doesn't turn around.

"Running late today," I tease.

"Yeah." He still doesn't glance back. "I've got to get going."

"I'll come help."

"No." Finally, Derek looks back over his shoulder, and even

with the length of the hallway between us, I can tell there's none of his usual warmth there. "I've got this. You focus on your class, and I'll focus on mine."

"You ..." My throat is closing over. "You don't want me ... to ... to ..."

Something in his expression shifts, and he paces back toward me. "I'm sorry, but I have to focus on the residents. They're who I'm here for. Thank you for teaching me that I'm a terrible painter. Now, I'll leave it for the masters." He goes to reach for me but stops. "I'm here for you if you need me, but I don't think it's a good idea to be friends."

For maybe the first time in my life, I'm stunned stupid. There are so many things I want to say to him, but I've forgotten what words are. The sparky little gremlin wants to rage at him. Wants to swear and stomp and tell him he was a shitty friend anyway, but for the first time ever, there's something more powerful holding it back. The sadness wraps around my chest and renders me silent.

I stand there, and he stands there, and after a moment of soul-searching eye contact, he swallows thickly and walks away. Like everyone always does.

You'd think I'd be used to it by now.

I'm not.

# Chapter Fourteen

Derek

It's official. I'm a fucking asshole. The best thing for me to do is go set up a tent on Manny's property and fuck the hell off out of Seattle. Quit my job, quit volunteering, just remove myself completely from Xander's life.

I *know* it's the right thing to do.

Then I remember the look on his face, how helpless he'd seemed, and I want to take it all back. I could easily find his address in our system and head over there. Apologize. Give him the hard truth that I'm a worthless fucking man who's growing feelings for him that I really fucking shouldn't be. That I'm not worth whatever it is he sees in me.

And then where would we end up?

Nowhere fucking good is the only answer I have for that.

My frustration is brimming over, making me desperate to lose myself in the wrong end of a bottle, staring down at my hands in my steadily darkening living room. Xander deserves the goddamn world, and after how easily I blurred my professional boundaries, I'm not the guy to give it to him. He won't let me talk to him about therapy. His roommates won't push him toward it.

It … it feels like we're giving up on him. But how the hell else are we supposed to react when he gave up on himself a long time ago?

Even after the hardest moment of my life, he still owns me. Otherwise, I'd be pass-out-drunk by now.

Dancing with him, seeing hope in his eyes for the first time ever, it scared the hell out of me. I can't be Xander's hope. It's way too much pressure to put on one person. Then, add in that I'm the one he turns to during his panic attacks, and it's a relationship made in toxic heaven.

As much as I'm feeling for him, it's not something I'd ever want for myself.

It wouldn't take much to tip me over that point though.

The blast of my ringtone fills the small, dark room. I don't need to look to know who it is. I've been waiting for this call, trying to convince myself that I won't take it.

With a sigh, I reach over and answer it anyway.

"Yeah?"

"Xander's on his way," Susan snaps with clear disgust in her voice.

"Thank you." I hang up because I don't have the energy for any of her shit tonight. Then I get up, get changed, and start a slow walk to work. I easily beat him there, and for the first time ever, I'm dreading each step. This used to be my one time to see him. My favorite and most hated part of the week.

Now that I've had that glimpse of the real Xander, the thought of seeing him so broken down is nauseating. He deserves so much better than this.

So I slip on my professional mask, unlock the treatment room, and wait.

It doesn't take long.

"Can't … can't … breathe …" he gasps out as Seven helps him into the room and closes the door behind them. "Lungs … won't work …"

Xander's clammy, eyes unfocused and body trembling. I try to lock down the protective feelings that threaten to take over, but it's harder today.

"On the bed."

He's trembling as he climbs up, close to tears and unsteady on his feet.

"The first thing I need," I say, struggling to keep my voice even, "is for you to focus on breathing. Can you do that for me? Can you breathe along with me, Xander?"

He shakes his head. "C-can't … Gonna … p-pass … out."

"All I need is for you to try. One in. Let's go." I count him through it. Normally, it's easier than this. Normally, being in the building is enough for him to let go of whatever panic has kicked in, but this time, it's clinging to him. This time, the more I try to have him breathe, the more he panics.

"I know your lungs hurt," I confirm. Whether they do or they don't, in his mind, it's real. I have to make sure he knows that I'm listening and not brushing him off, but while I hate that doubtful little voice telling me it's always a possibility, I also know he does not have lung cancer. Or pneumonia. Or whatever issue his brain is projecting on him. I listen to his breathing every other week, and there's nothing irregular there.

"I need to listen to your lungs," I explain as calmly as I can through my growing frustration. "You need to take a deep breath for me, Xander."

It's like he can't hear me.

"Hey!" I move so I'm right in his line of sight, and slowly, gradually, his eyes focus. "That's it," I reassure him. "I'm here. You're okay."

He sways a little.

"Deep breath. To three. Go."

Finally, he makes an effort, and as his breathing steadies and his heart rate calms, I'm able to check his vitals. Lungs are clear, oxygen saturation is good, blood pressure within his normal range after an episode. No temperature. No irregularities. No other symptoms.

I repeat the information to him until it sinks in, and the tension leaves him. He slumps back onto the bed.

Somehow, my hand finds his, and I give it a squeeze. "There you are."

Instead of the exhausted or sullen look I'm expecting, Xander sits up and turns an angry glare on me.

He snatches his hand away. "Yeah, fine. Good. Seven, let's go."

Seven's mouth tightens, and we exchange a look.

I step between the two of them and drop my voice. "Are you okay?"

"Don't act like you actually give a shit."

*Act*? The urge to bite back is strong. "I know this is hard for you—"

"Fuck off. You don't know anything."

"I know you need help." Keeping my voice level is getting harder by the minute. "I know you don't want to be here multiple times a week—"

"You don't know anything about me."

"I've been treating you for years. I know plenty."

"Treating." He crosses his arm. "Just a stupid, sick patient to you."

"You *are* my patient. The stupid and sick part comes and goes." I'd never normally say that, but all week, he's had my nerves on end, and the usual patience I have for him isn't there.

Despite saying he was leaving, Xander doesn't make a

move, just redirects his glare to the wall. Then … a tear drops onto his cheek.

*Shit.*

I move closer. "Xander, it's okay."

Wrong thing to say, apparently. "Fuck. You."

"Excuse me?"

"Stop trying to act like you actually give a fuck about me. Stop trying to act like you care. I'm a job to you, I get it— message received loud and fucking clear. I won't bother you with my friendship anymore, and in fact, I'll stop coming here. You're not the only nurse in the entire goddamn fucking world."

"Xander," Seven snaps.

"Oh, fuck you too," he shouts. "You think it's some secret that you don't want to be here? You think I don't know that everyone in the house thinks I'm a giant fucking inconvenience?"

"That's enough." My voice is louder than I expect it to be, but this is it. I've hit my fuck it moment. It's been simmering there for a while now, and even if I wanted to hold it back, I can't. He thinks I don't *care*? Like I haven't somehow spent the last few years of my fucking life centered around him and what he needs?

He goes to argue, but I drag a chair over and plonk myself in it, then lean right into his space.

"I don't fucking *care*?" I echo. "Why don't you pull that pretty head out of your fucking ass for a goddamn minute. Why do you think I'm always here, Xander? I don't live in this goddamn pharmacy. I saw a lease on a place around the corner shortly after you started coming here, and I decided it made sense. I moved. Into the city. All because of *you*. Every time you're in trouble, I show up for you. Your brothers show up for you. So this fucking tantrum is so far out of line, and I'm done. I'm not going to be spoken to like that. I'm not going to be told I don't care. My whole fucking life is on hold while I wait for you to get better, and you won't do a single thing to make it happen."

His glare has deepened. "You don't get to blame me for your shitty life choices."

"I do when you're one of them."

His jaw drops.

"Hurts, doesn't it? When people say mean things? Now, I don't know what the hell you've been through, and I've reached the point where it doesn't matter. You need help. And as much as it kills me, this is where I draw the line." My throat tries to close over, but I'm in it now. I can't back down. "The next time you call, it won't be me waiting here. I'll make sure someone is … but it can't be me."

The glare blinks away as tears take over, and that's enough to make my eyes water too.

"D-Derek."

I shake my head and stand. Fighting the urge to hug him is easier than I thought it would be. The fact that after years of this, he can still possibly think I don't care has rubbed me raw. "I care, Xander." My voice lowers. "Too much."

I turn on my heel, and his begging fucking wrecks me.

"You can't. Please. Don't go. I need you. I'm sorry. I didn't mean to say any of it. I was mad, please …"

I'm not hearing those words as his nurse though. I'm hearing them through the lens of a relationship and exactly how things will be if I let my feelings lead. I've already given them too much leeway.

Seven's panicked expression makes me pause. "You're not going to be here anymore?"

"I can't."

"But—"

"*No.*" I'm fucking pissed with him too. "I warned Madden. I told him what would happen if you continued to enable him, and since none of you will convince Xander to get the help he needs, I have to do this."

"What are we supposed to do?"

"Get. Him. In. Therapy." I'm fucking shaking. I know they think they're doing their best, but we're past that. It's not good enough anymore.

"I can't."

"The fucked-up thing, Seven, is that you can. Out of everyone, *you* can. He'll do anything you want him to do, and if you need to goddamn exploit that, then do it already."

"It would kill me." He looks ready to cry too, which isn't something I thought I would ever see. "I'm sorry."

I huff. This is it, then. Holding back my tears is getting too hard, and I need to get the hell out of here. "Then fuck you too."

## Chapter Fifteen

Xander

I can't breathe.
   I can't breathe.
   My panic attack won't end.
   I need him.
   I need Derek.
   We get to the pharmacy.
   I know he'll be here.
   He's always here.
   Derek …
   Derek …
   Derek …
   He never shows.

# Chapter Sixteen

Xander

I'm at the table working on the family puzzle when Seven walks in. His face is almost as red as his hair, and his hands flex like he wants to tighten them around my throat.

I smile. "Nice morning?"

"Where the frogging hell were you?"

I adopt the most patronizing tone I can manage. "What's wrong, Seven? The hour session didn't magically fix you?"

"You promised me you'd be there."

That almost makes me laugh. "I promised Molly last week as well. Considering how mad you both were about going to therapy, it's a touch hypocritical that you're trying to get me there."

"Because the appointment wasn't *for* us!" He's almost shouting.

"Maybe it should be." I eye him. "Any unchecked anger issues you should be working on?"

"Only with you." He kicks out a chair and throws himself into it. "We're not giving up."

I turn back to the puzzle. "Yippee."

"I told you I'd be there to support you, and I will. Stop pushing me away."

"*I'm* not the one who locked you out of his room last night."

He groans. "Dude, we were having sex. Come on."

If he'd told me that beforehand, I wouldn't have spent the night in my studio, convinced that everyone wants me out of their life. I'm ... exhausted. So tired of being tired. So over being alone. I almost convinced myself to go today. To therapy. Fucking therapy. I was one foot out the door.

Then I remembered the cold eyes, the pointed questions, the call for me to be admitted.

Therapists can't do a single goddamn thing for anyone. None of them care. None of them are actually invested in people getting better; they're only in it for the paycheck until it gets too hard.

But what if ... no. The scared little boy inside me hoped for too much for too long. He doesn't get to trick me with that anymore. I talked to more than enough psychologists when I was younger to know that it's all bullshit. Just a way to check a box on their mental health programs to make it look like they care. So I stopped talking. They assumed I was fine.

Then they tried to take Seven away from me, and I lost all fucking control. A *psychologist* did that. The pain hasn't ever gone away. How I'd finally found someone I could trust. Who kept me safe. Who had the same mess living in his soul to what I had in mine. The year we were together, I never let him out of my sight. He welcomed my neediness; he didn't try to take advantage of it. He was just ... there. The first person in my entire life who *wanted* to be there.

Seven's mine. And when he turned eighteen and moved

into his own place, I wasn't allowed to see him. Words like "unhealthy" and "suspicious" got thrown around. People I didn't know asked if he'd taken advantage of me. If we'd had sex. If he'd forced things. The sickness those words infected me with couldn't be controlled.

I don't remember when I stopped functioning, but my memories get really hazy after that. I know I ended up on some kind of medication to make me eat and sleep since I refused to do it myself, but even the medication couldn't get rid of that deep fucking dread. The one that sits in my gut and refuses to shift. That convinces me everything is about to end.

That same dread that's trying to take over now.

Seven moves closer to kneel beside me and pull me into his arms. "Push me away. I don't care. I'm not going anywhere."

"That's what you think. One day, you and Molly will want to move out. Or have kids. Or travel. Or do generally anything without me."

"Nope."

His denial is frustrating. "Might as well come to terms with it now."

*"Come to terms with what?"*

I stiffen at Molly's voice.

Seven rests his head against mine. "This pork chop thinks we're going to get sick of him."

"Not possible," Molly says. "You're not Seven without Xander."

"Exactly," Seven agrees.

And while I know they're trying to make me feel better, it doesn't work. "You should see someone about that," I say flippantly. "Sounds unhealthy."

Molly leans against the table in front of me, cutting me off from the puzzle. "How was therapy?" The suspicion in his tone makes it obvious he suspects I pulled the same trick on Seven that I did with him.

"It was great," I lie. "All fixed. Five gold stars."

"For fuck's sake, Xander." Molly points at Seven, whose arms are still around me. "Let him go. He doesn't deserve hugs right now."

Seven releases me. "But he was sad."

"*I'm* sad, dammit. You promised."

Ooohh, I don't like cranky Molly. Cranky Molly isn't like cranky Seven.

"Sorry," I mutter.

"Don't apologize to me. Apologize to Seven."

I shoot Seven a *don't make me* look, and he smirks back, waiting. "Fine. Sorry."

"I'm even going to pretend to believe you mean that," Molly says. "Why are you doing this, Z?"

"With zero context, I can only assume you're talking about the puzzle, and I'm doing it because we all do it."

"Wrong answer." Molly gives my hair a sharp tug.

"Hey. *Ouch.*"

"I have been way too invested in you and Derek since I met him for you to give up now."

"Do you have a brain bleed? I didn't give up on anything. He got sick of me, and now I'll never see him again. Don't worry, you'll get used to people walking out on me. Y'know, if you don't walk out first."

"If you think you're not every bit a part of my life as Seven is, maybe you're the one with a brain bleed."

Seven groans. "Don't give him ideas."

*Lack of sleep ... zero appetite ...* "You know, a brain bleed would explain a lot."

Molly gives me a flat look. "You *don't* have a brain bleed."

"How would you know?"

"Because you're still talking. About a lot of bullshit."

"We'll see, I guess. At least if I die in my sleep, you won't have to play dad anymore."

"It would save us from conversations like this too. Don't you want a chance with Derek?"

"I don't have a chance with Derek."

"What was the last thing he said to you?"

I ignore Molly's question, so he turns to Seven instead. "Well …?"

Seven hesitates before carding his fingers together. "He said he cares about you too much."

"Exactly." I roll my eyes. "Too much. Too much is a bad thing. No one wants too much of anything."

Molly pulls my hair again. "Too much, because he's not supposed to care at all. It's against the rules or the law or something."

We've been over this so many times. If he cared—even a little bit, not even too much—he would have been there or reached out. Made sure I'm okay.

"When you think about it, it's really romantic," Molly says, his eyes getting all big like they always do when he's especially sunshiny.

Seven pulls a face. "Doctor and patient. I'm sure I've seen horror movies about that before."

Molly scowls at Seven. "And what did Derek say to *you* last?"

I throw Seven a *suck shit now you're in trouble* look.

"He swore at me."

Molly waves the answer away. "Before that."

"Oh, when he thought it would be awesome to tell me to manipulate Z into doing what I want."

"Exactly." Molly crosses his arms. "Now would be a good time to do it."

*Excuse me?* I swing my attention up to Molly, expecting to find him joking. But that's his serious face.

"Oh yes," Molly says. "This *is* my serious face."

"I can't do that," Seven says.

"Why? Don't you love him?"

I scowl. "I'm pretty sure you're not supposed to manipulate people. Like, that isn't a good thing."

"Neither is codependency, but we're doing that reasonably well if you ask me." Molly turns to Seven and tilts his head my way. "When you're ready."

"But—"

"The three of us need you to do this."

"*Three?*" Seven scoffs. "I don't need to push him into it."

"Not you. Me, Xander, and Derek."

"Derek?" I echo. "There is no Derek."

Seven's face goes blank. "He's part of this now, huh?"

"I don't remember a time when he wasn't," Molly replies. "I would do it for you, but I don't think it will be as effective."

Molly and Seven stare at each other while I wait to see who breaks first. It's Seven, and I really should have guessed that. He turns to me, and there's regret on his face.

"Z ..."

"It's not going to work."

He huffs and turns back to Molly. "See? Pointless."

"Fine." I'm surprised by how easily Molly relents. Until he keeps talking. "I guess you don't want to make me happy."

"Of course I do, you muppet."

"Well, I can't be happy if Xander's not happy, and he won't be happy unless he has Derek, and *Derek* won't be happy if Z's not in therapy. Do you see the problem here?"

"You're relying on far too many people to make you happy instead of finding that inner well of happiness and tranquility?" I throw back.

"You're starting to sound like Madden."

"Well, you're starting to sound like me," I tell Molly. "And there's only enough room for one emotionally stunted, chronically needy person in this relationship."

"Exactly." Molly gives Seven his pleading eyes. "Help him."

Seven lets out a long, drawn-out sigh. Then he does something I never, ever thought he'd do in our entire lives.

"If you don't go to therapy, you don't really care about me."

"What?" I recoil. "Fuck you."

He shrugs. "Say whatever you want. There's only one way to prove it. Go or don't go. That'll give me my answer."

"You know I love you."

"I don't know that at all."

I glare from him to Molly and back again. "Well, if you love me, you won't make me go."

"I'm not making you do anything."

He is though. He knows he is. I could easily be an asshole and not go and point this out for the stupid ultimatum that it is. But I know Seven. I know his messy center, and I know that he's always scraped for love the same way I have.

Seven deserves to know he's loved.

"I hate you," I tell him, then turn to Molly. "And I hate you."

Molly doesn't back down.

They're actually fucking serious this time.

Serious about putting me in the most uncomfortable position they ever have. Talking to one of those people, having them mess with my head, trying to take away my personality and the pieces that make me who I am, makes me physically nauseous.

But then I replay Seven's words. He didn't actually specify that I had to be *involved* in the session, just that I had to go.

So fine. I will fucking go. I'll waste my time and money and sit there silent for an entire hour. Then I'll prove I love him and never have to go back again.

I hope everyone is happy.

Because I sure as hell won't be.

# Chapter Seventeen

Xander

"Your couch is uncomfortable," I tell Sherwin.

My psychologist smiles at me. "Feel free to move to another one, then."

I glance at the armchair opposite me. "It's offensively green."

"You don't like green couches?"

"Does it matter? It's not like they're a metaphor for my neglectful parents, who I don't even remember."

"Is that what you want to talk about?"

Fuck. I forgot I wasn't supposed to be talking. That's enough of that. I get up off the couch that feels like it's made out of screws and pace to the bookshelf. Lines of fancy-looking books stare back at me with random nonsensical ornaments plonked in between. None of it tells me much of anything about Sherwin.

"Does your office depress you?"

"No. I find it calming."

That's hard to believe. "It depresses me."

"Actually depressed, or trying to engage me in negative emotions depressed?"

"Is there a difference?" I glance over, and he's watching me. "*Don't* ask me if I think there's a difference."

Dr. Sherwin laughs. "I wasn't going to. But I am getting the feeling that you don't want to be here."

"Your big ol' framed certificate told me you were a smart one."

"I am." He nods slowly. "But if you don't want to be here, I can't help you."

"You couldn't help me even if I did want to be here."

He's still doing the annoying watching thing.

I scowl. "Stop psychoanalyzing me."

"But that's what you're here for."

"No, I'm here so Seven will know that I love him and I'm willing to put myself through this shit to prove it."

"Seven's your boyfriend?"

I frown, hating that assumption. "My foster brother."

"You're close."

"Duh." I wouldn't be here for just anyone.

"Well, you've proved that you love him by being here. Now, why don't you prove you love yourself by letting me help you?"

That makes me pause. "But I don't love myself. No one does. It's no big deal. I'm not a very nice person."

"Interesting you think that."

"You're telling me that you don't?" I snort. "I've walked in here and insulted everything you have."

"Not true. You haven't said a thing about my desk yet."

"Big and wooden. What a cliché."

He goes on smiling at me. "We have a whole hour. Now, I get paid either way. Are you really going to waste your money by using this hour to talk about my decor? I have a lot of experience, and I'd like to put it to good use."

"I'll pass."

"Your choice." There's a pause. "It's very quiet in here though. If you don't want to talk about yourself, tell me about Seven."

"*He's* the one who goes to therapy." I fold my arms and lean against the bookshelf. "Actual fucked-up things happened to him as a kid."

"I'm sure he didn't deserve that."

He really didn't. Who would he be if he'd never had to go through what he did? If he'd got to have an easy life, the type we both should have been allowed to experience. "People are assholes. Nothing will change that."

"I'm a firm believer that anyone can change. If they want to."

"It must be nice to be an optimist. Molly's one too, though I probably would be if I had a DILF for a dad like he does."

"You remember your parents?"

"Nope." Not that it's a real loss. "Better off without them though. I was taken as a toddler. They passed out high in the park, and someone called the cops because I was crying."

"Where are they now?"

Sure, because I've really gone looking for them. "No clue. Maybe if I hadn't cried that night, we'd still be one big, fucked-up family together."

"Or maybe not."

"Or maybe not."

He watches me kindly. Eyes like Derek's and also not like Derek's. "Children cry, Xander. And adults make their own choices."

I yawn, obnoxiously loud. "Gotta say, you made some shit choices along the line, having to listen to people whine all day."

"I like talking to people."

"Are all your clients as big of a pain in the ass as me, or am I a special case?"

"I think you're interesting."

"Poor you."

His cheeks dimple. "I also think you have a lot to say, if you'd let yourself say it."

I clamp my mouth shut, uncomfortably aware that I've given him too much.

I talk all I need to. At home, especially. If Sherwin thinks I'm going to walk in here and trust him with every little thought I've ever had, he's an idiot. He's done nothing to gain access to that side of me, and it's not something I like talking about anyway. He already knows more than most people.

"You've had to be strong your whole life, haven't you?" he asks.

I hum, not willing to give much away. "Ah, *that's* why my brain has cracked it."

"Cracked it?"

"Gone fucking cuckoo."

"Right. Tell me one thing you like about yourself."

Like? About me? I don't know how talking about that is supposed to solve all of my first-world issues, but I'll humor him. "My hair."

"And the second."

It takes me slightly longer on that. "My eyes. No, my freckles. No. Eyes."

He squints up into them. "They're very purple."

"Doc … are you hitting on me?" I pretend to curl my hair around my finger.

"It's a fact, Xander. Is that your natural hair color?"

"Natural hair color. You're *so* funny."

He doesn't bite.

"What do you like about your hair?"

"It's bright."

"And your eyes?"

"People always comment on them."

He takes a moment. "Do people comment on your hair?"

"Sometimes."

"Have you had any other color than blue?"

"Sometimes."

"When was the last time it was your natural color?"

Before I met Seven, for sure. Maybe the foster family before him? No. It would have been the one before that. The family's eldest daughter was always dying her hair black and did mine for me. I liked her. "Dunno. Maybe fourteen."

"I applaud your dedication." He runs a hand over his salt-and-pepper hair. "I don't have the same level of commitment, I'm afraid."

"You should get Botox. It's not too late."

"Thank you for that advice."

Something in his tone makes me smile before I catch myself. "You're not going to take it, are you?"

"It's unlikely. Sometimes I get insecure about things because I'm human. That's part of us. But I'm generally happy with who I am, and if I have a few wrinkles, that's all part of life."

"Philosophical of you. You'd get along great with Madden."

"Another foster brother?"

"Roommate. But he's basically my brother. He's a nudist."

"Brave of him."

"S'pose."

Dr. Sherwin crosses his legs at the ankles. "Are you comfortable standing there, or did you want to try the green chair?"

I cast my eyes over the ugly color. "Fine. But I won't like it."

"That's up to you."

At least this chair doesn't feel like I'm sitting on nails.

"Have you been in therapy before?"

"Yep." I lean back and cross my hands over my stomach. "They told me I was crazy."

"They said those exact words?"

Does it matter if they didn't actually use the word "crazy"? It was implied, and I'm not an idiot. I knew what they were all thinking. "More or less."

"So you don't want to talk to me because you think I'll think you're crazy?"

"No. I don't want to talk to you because I know it won't work. Nothing personal, just some people can't be helped."

"Well, I don't believe that at all. And out of the two of us, I'd say my experience makes me slightly more qualified."

More quack talk. He's the same as all of the shrinks I've ever met before him. They all think they're smarter than me and that they know more about me than I do. They're not the ones who have to live in my head; they're not the ones who have to exist in this flesh packet day in and day out. Sherwin is slightly nerdy but still good-looking. He suits his old-person hair. And his wrinkles.

He doesn't understand what it's like to be so completely unloved and unwanted that even the sight of you irritates people. Including yourself.

"What's next? Are you going to throw me on meds? Tell me what I can and can't do? Diagnose me with a list of letters and call it a day?"

Dr. Sherwin uncrosses his ankles and stands. "Actually, I want to talk. Out of the two of us, you're the one who's an expert on Xander, but sometimes it helps to talk things over with someone who can get your thoughts into order. To see them from another point of view. The only thing I want to achieve out of these sessions is to help you help yourself, in whatever way you deem necessary. You're the one in control here."

The words take a really fucking long time to sink in. If there's one thing I've never had in my life, it's control, and I'm too scared to believe I have it now. It's a trick. It has to be.

"I don't want to be here at all," I say, testing him.

"Then it's very possible you're not ready. And that's okay. Healing is something that can only be done on your own time-line, Xander, but your first step is accepting that you deserve it. Because you do."

"I don't deserve anything."

"I'm sorry that you feel that way."

I watch him, waiting for him to deny it or to go on. He doesn't, and it's like I accidentally skipped a step. Like the script in my mind wasn't followed. Panic flares up in my mind, and I trip over what to say next.

He beats me to it. "Can I ask you something?"

"Yes," I say, like I'm latching onto anything.

"Aren't you tired of fighting?"

A rush of emotion prickles behind my nose. I can't answer him.

"On your intake forms, you said the one thing you want to get out of therapy is Derek. Now, it's up to you. If you're not ready, you can leave. But if you are … do you want to tell me about him?"

This is my cue to go. The thing I've been waiting all session for. Something keeps me in that chair though. Something thick, and restricting, and annoying. And almost hopeful.

# PART TWO

SIX MONTHS LATER

# Chapter Eighteen

Derek

Maybe I shouldn't be this nervous. It doesn't make sense.

A lot has changed since I last saw Xander, and I don't even know if he volunteers here anymore. Knowing him, probably not. I'm nervous over nothing. Being ridiculous.

It's been six months, and it wasn't until yesterday, when the jet lag started to wear off, that I let myself think of him, and as soon as I did that, it's like no time passed at all.

Ghana was … an experience. Amazing and humbling, and for the first time in years, I switched everything off and focused on other people.

Xander was a distant memory.

I should have known that wouldn't last.

My guilt at the way I left things has come back strong, and I'm dreading seeing him again. I'm dreading not seeing him again but for so many other reasons. I know his visits to the pharmacy have lessened, but I have no clue if that's because he's doing better or not, and it kills me to think that I might have made everything so much worse. If I hadn't gotten on that plane when I did, I wouldn't have been able to stay strong.

Before I left, I made sure to brief the other two nurses at the pharmacy on how to handle his attacks. Every second of running them through it felt like a betrayal, and I know that once I go back to work, if I'm on shift, I'll need to be the one to see him.

My only consolation is that at least his visits aren't as frequent anymore. Constantine's been keeping me updated because even out of the country, I had to make sure he was okay.

Apparently, Xander means more to me than I thought.

"Derek!" Mary's face splits into an enormous grin as I approach reception. "I thought your name was an error when I saw it on my list."

As much as I loved Ghana and the people there, being back feels right.

"Nope, I landed two days ago and couldn't wait to get here."

"You'd think spending four months volunteering overseas would give you a breather from volunteering for a while."

I shrug and take the badge she hands to me. "I missed everyone." Which isn't a lie, but I also hate how much "everyone" mostly means Xander.

"Well, I know Carla will be happy you're back. Another volunteer, Xander, stepped in to cover for you, but I think she ended up teaching him."

My head snaps toward her so fast I swear I almost break my neck. "Xander?"

"Yeah, you know him?"

I'm right on the cusp of asking her if he's here, if he's been volunteering the whole time, how he's been … but I swallow it all down. "Vaguely."

She fills me in on how some of the residents are doing, but my brain has already checked out of the conversation. Normally I'm not this rude, but I'm desperate to head up the hall and poke my head into the art room.

"Thanks, I'm going to set up," I say the second there's a large enough gap in her updates.

"Of course. I'll see you later."

I walk too fast as I head up the hall. My guts are in fucking knots as I approach the door, and when I glance around the frame, it's like I take a punch right to my middle. He's here, only feet away, crouched beside Bethany as they laugh over something.

Xander.

Laughing.

It looks real, too, and not some snide snicker over a joke that only he's in on.

I want to go over there and ask what's made him so happy, but the anxious balloon inside me snaps, and I step back out of sight. He's the happiest I've ever seen him, and something tells me that going in there will ruin all that.

The reality sets in like a slow trickle that Xander … he's better off without me.

All this time, I've been missing him and hating how I left, and he moved on. I'm selfishly torn between being thrilled for him and hurt that he didn't miss me. Not like I missed him. I guess what I'd been feeling build between us was only on my end after all.

At least I can take comfort in the proof that I made the right choice. Even if it fucking sucks to lose him.

And sure, one laugh isn't enough to base a whole fucking opinion of a person on, but even his panic attacks are getting better. None of that can be a coincidence.

So I do the last thing I want to do.

Instead of stopping in to say hello, I duck my head and keep walking.

I'm about to turn the corner when—

"*Derek?*"

I should have given him more credit. Preparing myself for his anger, his disgust, or his total lack of care that I'm back, I turn around.

"Fuck …" slips from his lips.

Then he's running.

I get my arms open in time to catch him.

Xander hits me with a soft *ooof*, arms latching around my neck and body pressed tightly to mine. I hold him back, knowing I shouldn't, but I can't stop myself. It's *Xander*. Here. After months of being scared to face him again. He smells like paint and feels exactly how I always imagined he'd feel against me.

I don't deserve this.

But I need it.

I soak every second in until he pulls away before I'm ready.

"Shit. Sorry, I … You're back."

I nod, wanting to tell him I missed him and I'm sorry, but then he looks up, and my whole train of thought is derailed.

"Your eyes are gray," slips out before I can think it through.

Xander immediately drops his gaze, but I tilt his face back up to mine like I've done countless times before. Our eyes lock, and while the purple was pretty, this is *real*.

I want to tell him that his eyes are perfect. That I can't look away. But I lock up those thoughts and manage a cowardly half smile instead. "That was a welcome back I wasn't expecting. And don't think I deserved."

His answering laugh is soft and fast as he breaks contact. "You caught me by surprise, I guess."

"I can tell." What I really want to say is that I hope I can do that more often, but I'm not going to push my luck here. I know how much I hurt him to leave like that, but I'm hopeful it might have gotten him to wake up about some things. Needing people the way he does isn't good for him.

"So ..." He focuses somewhere mid-chest. "Are you back for good?"

"I haven't figured that out yet. I think I'll volunteer again because I really loved it, but maybe not for so long next time."

"Why so long this time, then?"

It's a brave question since I'm sure he already knows the answer. So I'll be brave right back. "Needed some space from you."

A familiar resignation crosses his face. "You wouldn't be the first."

"Not like that," I whisper.

"Then like what?"

"I know you didn't want to hear me the last time we spoke, and I don't blame you. That ... that wasn't my best moment." I'm still so embarrassed that I lost my cool and exploded like that. "I couldn't have been more unprofessional if I tried. So I'm really sorry. I know that doesn't make up for it, but getting mad at you over something you can't control ... urggg, I hate myself."

"Yeah, stop that. I hate myself enough for the both of us." He flicks me a look. "At least that's what my shrink says."

I try not to let the way I get excited over that show. "You're seeing someone?"

"Apparently, if I didn't want to be a manipulative little shit anymore, I had to." He picks at some of the paint on his thumb. "I need to say sorry too, I guess."

"Hey ..." I nudge his arm gently. "That was almost an apology."

"See? Therapy changes you. Maybe I don't want to be a good person, Derek."

"Suits you though."

We smile at each other, but it takes me a moment to notice.

"Mary told me you've been running my class?"

"Your class has been running me. Unlike you, I'm appreciative of all the unsolicited butt taps. Almost feels like I'm in my jock era."

"As a former jock, those taps aren't anywhere near as erotic as people make them out to be."

He presses his hands to his ears. "All I heard was that the jock rooms are an erotic fuck fest, and you had the time of your life in college."

I humor him. "Yep, that's exactly what I said."

His grin slowly slides from his face. "Is it okay if I still come to your class? Only, I sort of owe Carla five bucks for stepping on her toes last week. I'm still not very good."

And this is where I should draw some lines.

It's been six months. As a past, long-term patient, it's against all kinds of ethics to even consider pursuing a friendship with him, let alone anything else. It's the main reason I ran away in the first place.

This whole thing with Xander was supposed to be that my feelings came about because of our proximity. The time apart was supposed to drive in how wrong it was and how many lines I crossed.

It didn't work though.

The distance killed me.

During a weak moment, I may have looked up the rules surrounding dating former patients, and they … weren't good. Well, no. They're good. I agree with them. I only wish that I'd met Xander literally any other way.

Six months wasn't long enough. I should have gone for the full two years that's recommended as the minimum time distance between treating someone and seeing them outside of work. Not that waiting two years is some magical guarantee of it being okay anyway. Maybe the distance would have been good for me though. Maybe then I wouldn't want him more now than before I left. Maybe he'd have found a partner, and none of it would be an option anyway.

But I didn't.

And it is.

He's biting the corner of his lip, waiting for me to reply, and I can't say what I'm supposed to. I deserve to lose my fucking license for this.

"I … well, if you want, maybe after this, we could catch up?"

His entire face brightens. "Yeah?"

"Want to grab a coffee?" There's nothing wrong with coffee. Somewhere public. Purely platonic. Everyone likes coffee.

There is a guardedness in his eyes as he studies me. "I'd like that."

"You better get back to your class."

He keeps watching me, walking backward, and it's not until he disappears inside the room that I turn and thump my head against the wall.

I need to leave again.

Because I can see exactly where this is heading.

# Chapter Nineteen

### Xander

Dr. Sherwin isn't totally terrible. I could even argue that he's semi-okay, and I don't dread having to see him as often as I do. It's not fun, I test him and push him all the time, and he hasn't fixed me or given me some magical cure, but I've got coping strategies in place that I sometimes remember to use.

Having to face that I was willingly being a burden to the people I love most was the hardest part of our sessions, and while being my abrasive shithead self fits like a well-worn pair of jeans, I loosened my hold on it. I try not to make lashing out my default.

But I'm also careful about not losing who I am. Some might call this progress, but it's exhausting and has me frayed down to the bone some days.

Dr. Sherwin is also getting me to see that asking for help from people is okay, but needing it the way I do isn't healthy and will only hurt me in the long run.

He can pry Seven and Molly out of my cold, dead fingers, but I'm trying to apply more healthy boundaries with everyone else in my life.

Which, unfortunately, includes Derek. If it was up to me, he'd be on Seven's level, and we'd be equally obsessed with each other. Even with my boundaries in place, I don't think that will ever change, but Sherwin has me working on *empathy* and seeing things from other people's perspectives. I guess, for normal people, I can understand how being the focus of someone else's obsession could be uncomfortable.

Sounds like heaven to me though.

And all that work with Sherwin is proving a success with facing Derek today.

I don't push my luck by trying to dance with him in his class. The residents are all too busy wanting to hear about his travels anyway, and being in the same room with Derek after him being gone for months is doing things to me that I'm not prepared for.

He's a lot more tanned than he was when he left, his face is scruffier, his hair is longer, and he's somehow the same Derek I knew, but not. The unkempt look suits him.

"Our boy's back," Carla says. "Where's my five dollars?"

I hand over the bill, not able to look away. "Is he hotter, do you think?"

"Oh, yes," she says. "Derek's seen some things. You can tell by his eyes."

"Really?" I squint, tilting my head and trying to see if I can pick anything different.

"Of course not. I'm messing with you."

"Gee. Thanks. Very helpful."

"You should dance with him again. Want me to make it happen?"

Of course I do, but I'm all mature and well-adjusted now.

At least, I pretend to be. So I shake my head instead. "I'm good. You go dance."

Derek and I don't interact much, but once class wraps up, he approaches. I know it's impossible, but I swear he's gotten taller too. My toes scraped the ground when I hugged him.

"Ready to go?" he asks, and relief surges through me. I'd been prepared for him to make up an excuse and change his mind.

"Yeah. Can I grab a lift? I told Seven not to pick me up."

"Of course." We head for the reception desk to drop off our badges. "You don't drive?"

"Nope."

One side of his lips hitches up. "Any reason?"

"Scared of getting into a massive accident and having my brain leak out onto the pavement."

"Of course."

"I want to die in a pretty way, you know. It's more tragic."

I make him laugh, and it feels amazing. "That's complete bullshit, Xander."

"Excuse me, I'm trying to have *standards*. Sherwin says it's important."

"And this is the thing you've decided to have standards for, is it?"

It's as good a place as any to start. We don't know when we're going to bite the dust, so fuck it. When I go out, I want to look good doing it.

"I think you're going to live to a very old age," Derek says.

I pretend to gasp. "Are you wishing colostomy bags and cataracts on me?"

"You've volunteered here for months, and that's how you see these people?"

I drop the act, and a small smile breaks out. No. That isn't how I see them at all. Sure, at first, they were all gnarled hands and fake teeth and wispy hair, but I know where that disdain comes from.

I'm terrified of death.

Go figure.

"They're okay, I guess." I hand over my badge to Mary and lead the way out of the front doors. "Except for Kevin. Kevin sucks."

Derek chuckles. "Still painting poop?"

"Yup. Somehow, he's even worse at it than when he started."

I follow Derek to his car. It's a newer-model black Toyota and somehow looks like the perfect car for him. It's instantly my favorite car ever.

"I love spring," I say, climbing into the hot cab.

"I thought fall was your favorite?"

Wow. I glance his way, wondering how the hell he remembered that. "It is, but since it still feels like forever away, I'm pretending it's not." I watch his beefy forearm as he starts the car. "What's your favorite season?"

He thinks it over as he backs out of the parking lot. "I don't think I have one. In summer, it gets too hot, and I want it to be winter. Then in winter, it's the same in reverse."

That's a good answer. "Molly loves summer."

"I could have guessed that."

"Because he's always so happy and gets stupidly excited over squirrels?"

"Well, I didn't know about the squirrel thing, but yeah. He seems like a summery guy."

I'm not sure what a summery guy is like, and I wonder what Derek means by that. "He's pretty too," I bait, hating how easily I drop back into bad habits.

"He is. He and Seven look good together."

"I look good with them too," I insist.

"Sorry. I didn't know you were dating them."

I don't know if he's being a smart-ass or not, but that comment makes me groan. "He's my brother, don't be gross."

"You said it." The teasing in his tone is everything I've been missing. Then, he gets overly focused on the road. "So … *are* you seeing anyone?"

It's the first time I've gotten the temptation to lie. How would Derek react if he thought there was someone else in my life? The fact I can't tell whether he'd get jealous or not care doesn't help make up my mind. "Are you?" I ask instead.

"Nope. Other than my host family, most of the people in Ghana who I met were patients. And you know the law between patients and the medical professionals treating them."

Unfortunately, I know about those rules way too well. "That it's not allowed."

He takes his eyes off the road for long enough to meet my gaze. "They'd take my license."

Well, I guess that's that. Coffee really is just coffee and not a euphemism for him wanting to take my virginity. At this stage, I'd gladly yeet the damn thing because I want it gone. I'm almost thirty and still haven't had sex.

Dr. Sherwin hasn't even begun to work with me on my weirdness to sex when we have so much else to unpack, like my catastrophizing, anxiety, and apparent OCD—while I repel people, apparently, I collect mental illnesses like trading cards —but apparently, it makes sense. To him. Which, yippee for me. I've been neglected so many times, and sexualized so many others, that I need trust before I can go there.

I'd told him his theory was stupid and went out that night in an attempt to hook up, which led to me hyperventilating and passing out in the middle of the dance floor.

*Ah … the memories.*

But that leaves us at one point to Sherwin. Zero points to me.

Maybe I need to stick my dick into a glory hole and get it over with, but my mind won't let me go there. All I can think about is whether the person on the other side has bad breath or funky teeth or … or … *thrush* or something.

There's also the potential he'll chomp off my dick and leave me bleeding out on a seedy bathroom floor—not ideal circumstances for getting it up.

Derek doesn't have funky teeth though. Derek smells nice. I bet he uses breath mints and brushes twice a day.

I want to have sex with him. I want to have sex with him a lot.

We get to the cafe, place our orders, then settle at a table in the back. He takes the booth side, and I sort of want to join him there, but instead, I remind myself that a friend would take the opposite seat.

Derek takes a tentative sip of his black coffee while I dump sugar in my hazelnut latte.

"Sweet tooth?" he asks.

"Sometimes." I nod to his coffee. "Old man?"

He laughs. "Sometimes."

While this might be friendly catch-up coffee, I need to clear up a few things. "Did you really go to Ghana to get away from me?"

"Sure did."

I'm not expecting him to admit it again. "I don't understand."

Derek drums his fingers against the mug handle. "I've wanted to volunteer for Nursing International since I completed my degree, so it wasn't totally because of you. It's something I needed to cross off the bucket list and actually experience."

"And you did it."

"I did. It was amazing. Really helped open up my perspective of the world. But you are the reason I decided to go now."

"You're welcome."

His eyes spark. "Am I?"

"Yes. It's basically because of me that you achieved your dreams. I'm an inspiration. A voice of the generation, you might say."

"If you're the voice of my generation, I'm worried we're going to be greatly misrepresented."

"I think the Kardashians already have that covered." I prop my chin in my hand. "Why did you need space from me?"

He sighs and meets my eyes. "You know why."

A bucketload of hope dumps over my head. "You care about me? Or ... cared? Care?"

"Stop fishing."

I give him my evilest grin. "Then answer the question."

"I treated you for years. It doesn't matter how I feel or how I felt because nothing can happen, even if we were both on the same page."

"That's the dumbest shit I've ever heard."

"Actually, the rules are there for a very good reason."

Fuck the rules. The rules can go to hell. Though I can say that because I'm not the one who would have to deal with the fallout if we hooked up and he got into trouble for it.

But ... "Does that mean ... are you saying ... so if you'd never treated me, I'd have a chance with you?"

"I ..."

"Yes or no?"

He watches me warily. "I have no idea what your thoughts are—"

"My thoughts are that I want this coffee date to be an actual date."

Derek laughs, sunlight catching in his messy hair and clean, clean teeth. When he answers, lines around his eyes creased and voice dipped low, I can barely hear him over the other people around us. "You're all I can think about."

"Then—"

"No." He doesn't leave a break for me to argue back. "I love being a nurse, and I want to volunteer overseas again. There's a placement in Cambodia that I think I'm going to apply for."

My heart sinks with every word. "So you don't care about me at all."

His hand crosses the table to cover the one I'm not leaning on. "Please try to see where I'm coming from. This isn't easy for me."

"Then why did you come back?"

"Because you were here."

"But—"

"I know." He clears his throat and lets my hand go. "I can't offer much, and I get it if you say no, but I'd really like to be friends with you."

Friends. He wants to be *friends*? I stare him down, trying to get a read on his expression and whether he knows what he's doing to me.

*Not good enough. Not wanted. Second best.*

All my fears and insecurities come rushing forward as Derek confirms that he won't even try. It's been six months— we could easily keep things a secret.

Doesn't he get that I *need* him?

My eyes prickle as I whisper pathetically, "I want to own you."

Something deep in his eyes shifts, and I worry that I've scared him off. That he's going to tell me I'm too far gone for anyone to help. That it's creepy and obsessive and—

His foot slips between mine under the table and then links behind my ankle. Derek leans over the table toward me, and this time when his hand covers mine, there's a possessive grip to it.

"I'm trying to be a good person. At least let me pretend."

I know all about pretending to be a good person. I know all about the lies I have to tell myself to do it.

So I tell one more.

"Friends," I agree. "Nothing more."

# Chapter Twenty

Derek

> We're hanging out today.

The text doesn't surprise me. It's been two days since I've seen Xander, and I'd been either expecting him to show up once I finished work or to get a message like this.

Ever since I got back, Xander's been using our friendship as an excuse to spend as much time as possible together. Between volunteering at the nursing home, grabbing lunch or dinner, and the constant texting, he makes sure he's never far from my mind.

It's embarrassing how much I love it.

ME:
> How do you know I don't have plans?

XANDER:
> If you do, cancel them.

ME:

You're very demanding, you know that?

XANDER:

Yeah, I know. It's part of my charm.

I can't argue with him there. One of the things about Xander that's really growing on me is how he's unapologetically himself.

Except it's been a month now, and while I don't want any space from Xander, I need it. My balls are fucking blue. I'm trying really hard to be good and do the right thing, but it's not going to take long for my resolve to crack.

Xander's gorgeous. Contacts or no contacts, cute clothes or sweatpants, lip gloss or bare face, I'm constantly blown away by how stunning he is. But it's not only his looks that I'm attracted to. Xander is an old soul. I can see it in his wary eyes, how sometimes he turns so introspective I lose him for a moment. He jokes about what he's been through and has no issue saying some messed-up things about himself that make me die a little inside. I can't imagine he means them or that saying those things is good for him, but I'm no psychologist, so what would I know?

All I know is that I really enjoy spending time with him.

ME:

Think of something we can do. I'll pick you up once I'm done here.

The hours can't slip away fast enough, and by the time six o'clock hits, I'm out the door. Xander's had a few panic attacks since I got back, but I've held fast in not being the one to treat him, even when it meant telling Seven there was no one at the pharmacy for them to see. It ate at me all day until I got a message from Xander, letting me know he was okay, but I hate that it's something I have to do.

If we're going to be friends for right now, it's important to me. I can't go back to being his carer, not when I look at Xander and everything I want to do to him inundates me.

Turning my professionalism on and ignoring how I feel would be next to impossible now.

Besides, I just really don't want to.

He's waiting out in front of his place when I pull up to collect him. He invited me to something called Monopoly Monday last night, and even though I'd wanted to go, I'm chickenshit. I have no idea what the others think. There are blurred ethical lines between me and Xander, but having someone else point them out will cheapen this friendship we're building.

His hair is freshly dyed, and he's wearing large, gold-framed sunglasses.

"Where to?"

"The park."

"The … park?"

"Yup. I figure that I missed out on a childhood, and you want to relive yours, so let's begin there."

I choke on my inhale. "Who says I want to relive mine?"

He wriggles his fingers in the grays by my temples. "No clue where I got that idea."

"Okay, okay." I bat his hand away. "We both know that was an excuse to touch me."

"Am I that easy to read?"

"When you want to be."

I can feel his satisfied smile from here. "I only had one blood clot this week," he comments, like he's telling me about what he had for lunch.

"Correction: you had zero blood clots."

"One. In my brain. I couldn't see or anything. It was touch and go for a while there."

A flash of Xander, mid-panic attack, threatens to overwhelm me. "Sorry I couldn't help."

"It's fine. I get it."

"There are a lot of things I want to be for you, but I can't be that as well."

"I *know*." He sets his hand on my thigh, higher than he needs to. "Stop stressing."

I send a smirk his way. "Hand, Xander."

"Ooops. When did that get there?"

"Total accident, I bet."

He squeezes my leg before releasing it, and the feeling goes straight to my cock. I ignore it. I have to ignore it.

"Turn right here," he says, and I do.

"What did you do today?"

"Smashed some clay."

"Uh-huh …"

He shrugs. "I should have been working on a painting since I have about ten thousand people waiting to buy one off me, but …"

I almost drive us off the fucking road. "Excuse me, how many?"

"Ten thousand. Well, that's a guess based on my serious mailing list. My other one is closer to two hundred thousand."

Holy shit … he's not exaggerating. My face falls into a frown. "I've seen you in class, and I know you're good, but … why haven't I seen any of your work? The stuff you sell?"

His expression is pure confusion. "Why would you want to?"

"Because I'm a bit fucking overwhelmed that you have that many people just *waiting* to buy something from you."

He shifts and turns his attention to his hands. "Some of them might have lost interest, I don't know. But the second I send something out, it sells. Then I get a whole flood of angry emails from people who missed out. They range from disappointment and making me feel bad to people saying I'm a scam artist who isn't actually selling anything. Sounds like a weak scam to me, but what would I know?"

I pull the car up out the front of the park. "People get mad at you about that?"

"People get mad about anything."

My jaw aches at how tight I clench it, caught by surprise at the anger that bubbles up. "I don't like that."

He unclips his seat belt and turns toward me, leaning closer. "What are you gonna do, Daddy Derek? Gonna message them all to leave your poor little Xander alone?"

I groan and swipe a hand down my face. "I'm not that bad."

"You sure? You're sounding very overprotective. Gonna spank them all?"

I burst out laughing. "Of course I'm fucking not. But I'm not going to act happy that people are being dicks to you."

"Ehh. That's how people are. Not giving a shit about the things they say to me is one lesson I can thank the universe for learning early."

"I wish you didn't learn it at all."

"There are lots of things I wish for. Lots and lots and …" His gaze drops to my mouth. "Lots …"

"Stop that."

His devilish grin comes out. "Make me."

Instead of setting myself up to fail, I release my seat belt and climb out of the car.

Xander follows, and when he's close enough, he nudges me in the direction of the swings. "They're both free, come on."

Other than a mom with two young kids, the playground is empty. Xander and I take the swings side by side, and I push off the ground. It's been … well, forever since I did this. I'm sure I loved it as a kid, but it was so goddamn long ago that I don't remember now.

The slow creak of the chains eases us back and forth, him forward, me backward, until we switch.

"What's your favorite word?" he asks.

Him randomly asking my favorite anything threw me off at first, but I'm ready for him this time. "Formicarium."

"Formi-*what?*"

I laugh because I knew he'd react like that. "It's a man-made ants' nest."

"Right …"

"I have one."

"Wait, *what?*" He drags his platform sneaker in the mulch to stop and turns to stare at me. "Ants? You keep ants? Is this your way of breaking it to me that you have a really dirty house? Because that's not a formi-whatsit—I'm pretty sure that's just a hovel. And unhygienic. Our first time cannot be there, so if it's going to happen at my place, you'll have to deal with my roommates listening in."

"No first time. No any time."

"Sure."

I don't call him on the obvious brush-off because if I do, I might start thinking about sex. "It's an actual thing. They're my pets. All very contained in my formicarium, and my place is not at all a hovel."

"Noted. Your place, it is."

"I got a queen ant before I left for Ghana, and my friend looked after them while I was gone. They're thriving."

Xander wrinkles his cute nose. "You're … actually excited about them. You like ants."

"I like bugs."

"Oh my god." Xander holds on to the chains and hangs himself right back. "I'm going to marry a freaky little bug man. Why, cruel world, *why?*"

I drag myself to a stop as well. "You'd be fucking lucky to marry me."

"Derry, are you proposing? In a *park*? The same place I was ruthlessly stolen from my parents? I never knew you were so romantic."

It's an effort not to roll my eyes. At one point, I might have worried about offending him, but Xander wasn't lying when he said he gives zero fucks about what anyone says to him. Though, it's more than that. He's completely desensitized to what happened in his life, but if Seven, Molly, or one of his roommates upset him, he'd feel it more than the average person would.

Across the park, the mom and her kids leave.

"Come on, that slide has your name on it."

Xander goes down a few times before peer pressuring me into trying it too. Unfortunately, I'm a lot bigger than he is, and my hips are so lodged in there it takes a painfully long time to reach the bottom, which makes him laugh like an idiot. I spin him on the thing that goes around too quickly until I'm worried it's going to end up in a head injury, and then he drags me back to the swings.

We watch the sun go down before he stops again, and I slow as well.

Xander turns to look at me, and I have another one of those moments where I'm stunned stupid for a whole second, just by the sight of him.

"Come here." He loops his arms around both of his swing's chains and holds them out to me.

I take his hands. "What are we doing?"

"Twist our swings together, then when we let go, we'll go flying."

"That sounds dangerous."

"Okay, Grandpa."

Fuck it. I'd wanted to be more fun and remember that age

is only a number, and here's Xander helping me find that side of myself again. "Let's go."

We twist our swings together around and around and around until the tension on the old chains gets so tight I'm sure they're going to snap. My feet barely reach the ground, and Xander's definitely don't. Our knees are crushed between each other's. Xander's so close he could lean in and bump our noses together.

"I'm ninety percent sure one of us is going to hurt ourselves," I say.

He lifts a slight shoulder. "I'm not scared. I don't think I've stopped hurting a day in my life."

"That's ... *Xander* ..."

His eyes are purple again. I haven't seen the gray since the day I got home, and he watches me for a long moment. "It's always so weird seeing people react to the things I say."

"Why?"

"Because it means nothing to me. I don't feel it. I don't connect with it. But you do. That's ... *so weird*."

"It's called empathy."

"I don't know if I have that," he whispers. "I know I'm supposed to."

There he goes, underestimating himself again. "How would you feel if Molly was sad?"

"Angry. I'd want to fix it."

"Because you care about him."

Xander nods. "Sometimes more than Seven."

That's surprising. "I thought Seven was everything to you."

"He is. But Seven can look after himself. Molly's ... precious. Too breakable."

"Molly seems like a very capable man, not that I know him well."

Xander thinks for a long moment. "They're mine, you know. Both of them."

"I know."

"And if anything happens between ... I know I joke, but, like, us or ... whoever. If I ever find someone who doesn't get sick of me one day, they'll be his as well."

It's like a knife to my fucking chest every time he says things like that. Sick of him? No one can get sick of Xander. I've seen the way his friends love him. The way the residents love him. How much Seven and Molly care. And I know how I feel about him as well.

My fingers find his cheek, and *fuck me*, it's so soft. His eyes drift closed, and my heart is beating out of my chest.

"Xander, I—"

Xander's eyes snap open. "Now!" He lets go and flings away from me. The chains untangle in an aggressive twist that shoots me one way and yanks me the other. I nearly lose it backward off the seat, and when I'm sure it's stopped trying to murder me, I suck down a breath and look over at him.

Xander's whole face is flushed bright.

"Never again."

He cracks up laughing as I'm still trying to orient myself.

I'm never going to survive him.

# Chapter Twenty-One

Xander

I have exactly one iota of willpower left, and it's almost depleted. I fully expect it will be gone by the end of the night, which is why I'm finally going to show Derek my "art." He's going to be woefully unimpressed, but if that somehow still leads to sympathy sex, I'll take it.

Going to a club and dirty dancing all over him briefly crossed my mind instead, but that would have been a terrible idea.

I can't dance, and I hate going out. The stares, the pressure to drink and be sexy. I'm more of a homebody. A few drinks and a game night with my friends is my idea of heaven— except when all of their boyfriends stop by and I'm the pitiful extra.

I wish Derek could be that for me, and I understand why it's not possible, but I also think it's really, really stupid. In our case, anyway. He hasn't taken advantage, there haven't been lines crossed, all Derek ever does is make me feel good, and I don't understand how someone else gets to have an opinion on what could be an amazing relationship.

Does it kill me that he's not around during the moments when I can't get my brain to brain right? More than I'll ever tell him. But if the trade-off is a shot with him, it'll be worth all the pain.

Hopefully.

To tip the odds in my favor, I've dressed super fucking slutty tonight.

I don't want to leave anything to the imagination. I don't want Derek to be able to keep his hands off me.

I'm so fucking sick of being a virgin.

It's not even the label. If it was only about getting it over with, I would have done it already. Probably. If I'd found someone who wasn't a complete turnoff.

It's about the fact that I want to feel hands on me. I want to know what another naked body is like against mine. I want real fucking intimacy. And I want to experience that with Derek.

There's something deep in my consciousness that trusts him, and I try to tell myself to cut that shit out because it's exactly how I'll end up left and alone, but I don't fucking learn.

I want him. I'm sure he wants me. I don't understand why we have to jump through so many fucking hoops to make us happen. It was *last year* that he last treated me; why isn't that enough?

A text comes through to my phone, and I grin at Molly and Seven. "He's here."

"I guess we're doing this," Seven mutters while Molly lights up.

"Would you dim it?" I snap at him.

"What? I'm excited."

"I know, stop it. You'll get my hopes up, and they're already doing a great job of being overinflated on their own."

"Sorry." He doesn't dim. Just goes on smiling.

It'll be a miracle if between Molly's sunshine, Seven's grumpy, and my horrible paintings that Derek manages to last long enough to show him my room. I'm going to hold out hope, though, because it's not like there are any other hot men I want to drag up there.

Molly gets to the door first, and he immediately pulls Derek into a hug. I try not to be annoyed that I didn't get to do that first, but when Molly releases him—after way too fucking long —Seven takes over before I can.

Derek's whole face turns to shock when Seven hugs him too.

That's almost enough to make the wait worth it.

"Ah … hey," Derek says as they pull away. "I was expecting more of a punch to the face in greeting, but I'll take it."

Seven holds up his hands. "Despite how I look, I'm harmless."

"I wouldn't have blamed you being pissed after what I said last time I saw you."

Seven glances my way. "Ehh. You were right."

"Didn't make it easy though."

"Which is exactly why I didn't punch you."

Derek laughs. "I thought you said you're harmless?"

"And I am. Unless someone messes with Molly or Z, and then I'll flipping kill a birch."

This is exactly why I love him. Not that I'd let him commit murder for me. Probably. It's just sweet to know that he would.

"Do I get a turn yet?"

Derek's attention lands on me, and I get a split second of that gorgeous smile before he catches what I'm wearing: one of Rush's work shirts with only one button done up at the front and very thin cotton booty shorts. Derek's eyes widen a second before I push onto my toes and hug him. His arms close around me, and I get that familiar feeling of being so happy I could burst.

"We need to get out of the doorway before someone comes trampling through it," Molly says. "Ooh, Derek brought wine. What a gentleman." He sends a teasing look back over his shoulder as he drags Seven down the hall after him.

Derek lets me go, and his fingers dip into his neat hair. "I was so scared to see Seven."

"Why?"

"Because I really thought he was going to have words for me after I told him to fuck off."

I play with the bottom of my shirt. "He'd never. Yeah, I went off the deep end pretty fucking dramatically after you walked out, but we all know that you didn't do it to hurt me. And I think they—and me, *I guess*—can see that maybe, possibly therapy hasn't been a completely bad thing for me."

"Maybe possibly?" His lips twitch.

"That's the best you'll ever get out of me, so take it or leave it." I turn to leave when he grabs the back of my shirt and tugs me backward.

Derek steps in close, all body warmth and a fresh wash of citrusy cologne as he leans down by my ear. "I really hope you're planning to put clothes on before dinner."

"I don't know what you mean. I'm wearing clothes."

His groan is rough. "Let me rephrase. I'm going to need you to put on something where I can't see the outline of your cock."

"Why?" I turn my head so we're nose to nose. "Does it make you uncomfortable?"

"Only one part of me."

Excitement chases the nerves away. "I like my choices, then. I guess that *one part* of you will have to find a way to make itself feel better."

I head for the kitchen, and as I go, I slowly lift the back of the shirt, showing off how these shorts don't cover my ass. It could be my imagination, but I swear he chokes back a sob.

This is looking very promising.

"Dinner's ready," Molly says as soon as we walk into the kitchen. He's completely oblivious as he plates everything up, but Seven's watching us suspiciously. He can play the big brother role all he likes; there is no way in hell he'd cockblock me.

He might not know how weird I am about sex, but he does know that I never stop talking about Derek. No matter what his feelings are, he wouldn't get between me and my happiness.

But as we sit down to eat, a new kind of nerves kick in. Not for what happens next but for *this*. Them. Unlike me, they've only ever spoken to Derek at work, and the thought of the three of them not getting along makes me nauseous.

"You cooked this?" Derek asks Molly.

"Yeah, I've learned a lot since moving in here. Our neighbor Aggy cooks with me once or twice a week."

"Aggy?" Derek glances at me. "She was with you at the nursing home that one time?"

Seven's face twists in distaste. "Aggy was at a nursing home? She's not planning to move, is she?"

"Hell, no." Aggy will be stubborn enough to die in that house. Probably on an expensive piece of furniture too. Then we'll have to lie about the whole dead body thing when we sell it. I wouldn't put it past her to haunt the place either.

Seven visibly relaxes. "Good. She's too young for one of those places."

If that's the lie he needs to tell himself, I'll let him. Pretty sure when the inevitable happens, neither of us is going to handle it well. There are some things therapy can't fix, and losing the only motherly figure we've ever had will be one of those things.

"You're all close with her, then?" Derek asks, turning to me. "I might have to meet her properly."

"Hmm … yeah, that won't be happening."

It takes me a moment around chewing to realize the three of them are waiting for me to go on.

"Not because of you," I say. "Well, sort of because of you. But mostly her. She made me promise that I wasn't going to try anything with you and risk your job." I throw my hands up. "She's a meddlesome old bat."

"Tell me you didn't *promise* her," Seven says.

"Of course I did. If I tried to gag her, she would have fought back, and let's face it, she'd win. How else was I going to make her shut up about it?"

Derek fixes me with a look. "Probably not like that."

"Oh well, it's done now."

Thankfully, they let it go, and dinner is … *great*. Turns out one of Seven's regular clients is a friend of Derek's, and Seven monopolizes way too much of Derek's time talking about some person I don't even know. Derek shows way too much interest in Molly's move here and how Molly likes it in Seattle, and if he'll ever go back, and if he misses his dad—

"Molly has a perfectly wonderful father, and he's very loved, blah blah blah, we get it," I finally cut in.

"Really, Z?" Seven asks flatly.

"Sorry." Molly's bouncing in his seat. "I'm a talker."

Derek doesn't even look at me as he picks up his empty plate and then stacks mine on top. "It was delicious, and I'm glad we finally got to know each other."

"Me too."

I make *back off* eyes at Molly's enthusiasm.

"I think I need to give Xander my attention now though," Derek says, and my bad mood evaporates.

Seven takes the plates from Derek. "I got this."

"You sure? I feel bad not cleaning up."

"Trust me." Seven's eyes flick my way. "We only have so long before he turns needy."

"Noted."

Well, fuck them both very much. I'm not *that* bad.

Derek stands up, and I hurry after him. It's not until we're out of the room that he looks at me, and thankfully, he looks amused. "Next time you want my attention, just ask. Don't get annoyed with your friends."

"I wasn't … annoyed." Even I don't believe that, so I drop the lie. "*Fine.* Molly's very pretty and nice and sweet, and I'm none of those things, and clearly, you were enjoying that."

His eyes light up as he steps closer. "Were you jealous of Molly?"

"No. I love Molly. But did you need to show him *that* much attention?"

"Yes." Derek reaches up and gently tucks my hair behind my ear. Soft fingers skim against skin, and all the annoyance drains out of me. "He means a lot to you, so one day, he might mean a lot to me."

I'm trying very hard—and failing—not to read into those words. "And … do *I* mean a lot to you?"

He avoids the question. "Time for you to show me your art."

Urg. *That.* "I can show you my room instead."

His lips twitch. "Art."

"*Fine.*" I take his hand and pull him after me. "Might as well lose all respect you have for me up front."

"I'm not worried."

"You should be."

"I can barely paint a tree. I'm confident anything you can do will blow me away."

That's not the compliment he thinks it is, but I open the

door to my studio and lead him inside. The room is as chaotic as ever, but I try to see things from his point of view.

Admittedly, it probably looks even worse like that.

There's a paint-stained couch next to my abandoned stack of canvases, tables with half-finished busts and pots and metal works. All things I dabble in and have no real clue about. There's a whole workstation of paints and paintbrushes, random jars of dirty water, and the heavy curtains over the window are about the only surface in here that hasn't been attacked when I'm freaking out and spiraling and need to paint something. The floors and walls hold too many of those stories.

"Wow." Derek swallows. "This is ... wow."

"Yeah, I maybe should have cleaned up first."

"No, I love it. It's like ... beautiful chaos. Like I can feel you in here." He points at the canvas propped on the easel by the window. "Is this what you're working on?"

"Unfortunately."

He walks closer, and I wish I could tell him to stop. That it's not a big deal and we can go literally anywhere other than here.

"Is it finished?" he asks.

Of course it's not fucking finished. I huff and join him. "No. That's the background, and I'm building and layering here to be the forest floor, and this is a stream cascading down over the rocks. Then I'm going to paint a large misty-looking tree kinda leaning through the middle here, with some animals, and *then* it will be finished. Maybe. If I don't get sick of it before then."

He's staring for a really long time. "Yeah, I can see it. That's going to look incredible."

I hate compliments. I never know what to do with them. There are only so many times you can tell someone that your work is shit before you both start to look stupid. And thanking him for something I don't believe doesn't feel right either.

"*You're* incredible, Xander."

I slowly look up and find him watching me.

Derek's warm fingers find my cheek like they belong there. "You're so fucking incredible it kills me."

## Chapter Twenty-Two

Derek

His expression doesn't hold the hope I once saw in it, but there's something close. Something almost afraid to be there, and in my gut, I feel it too. I don't know what I'm doing, and I probably shouldn't be heading down this path, but fuck me. Xander *is* incredible, and he deserves to know it. He deserves to be told every single day.

"What ... what if it didn't?" he whispers.

"What?"

"What if it didn't kill you? What if you were just you, and I'm just me, and we're in a room together with no one else?"

I wish it was that easy. "Ethics are still ethics, even if no one else knows about your choices."

Xander's expression darkens. "I understand why they have those rules. I get it. But we both know that we didn't do anything wrong. None of this is wrong." His tone has a begging edge that's getting me right behind the ribs. "Please. I want to kiss you. Just one time."

Fuck, there are no words for how much I want that too. For how easy it would be to cup his face and taste his lips. I've been half-hard all through dinner with what he's wearing, but I can resist that. I could resist him dancing naked in front of me. Not easily, definitely not fucking easily, but I'm sure I could.

This though? Xander begging for something I *want* to give him?

This is my limit.

"If anyone found out …"

"They wouldn't." Xander steps closer. "I know we can't have a relationship. I know it can't mean anything. But this once. What if this doesn't kill us? What if it's everything we ever wanted?"

Doesn't he know that's exactly what I'm afraid of? "What we have isn't enough for you?"

"I don't think I can be friends. I never could."

"Xander … that's all a relationship is. Friends who have sex and care about each other. Isn't two of those things good enough? Sex isn't everything."

He's quiet for a moment before he looks up and meets my eyes. "Maybe it is when you've never had it before."

It takes me a second. "What? You're a—"

"If you freak out over that, I'm going to scream."

"No, I'm not … freaking out. I'm … *how*?" Xander is one of the sexiest men I've ever seen. There's no way it's from a lack of options.

He taps his temple. "Don't know if you've heard, but I'm a little fucked-up."

Instead of telling him he shouldn't say that, I take his hand and press a kiss to his pointer finger instead.

A breath hisses between his teeth. "Good, but not where I want it."

I give myself a whole moment to think it through. To assess whether letting myself do this will be worth risking everything. My job. My respect. My license. The potential volunteer trip to Cambodia.

All it takes is one word from him. "*Please?*"

He's worth all that and more.

My mouth slams down over his, and it's exactly what I dreamed it would be. Soft, willing, a heady mix of nervousness and excitement and way too much lust to contain. He's gripping the front of my shirt like I'm going to disappear on him, but there's no way in hell I'm stepping back now. It's already too late.

I need this as much as he does.

My tongue sweeps into his mouth, hungrily meeting his. Xander's following my lead, almost hesitant, making me question how many people he's kissed. How many other men have gotten to share this with him. And how many other men stupidly let him slip through their fingers.

We kiss for what feels like the better part of my life. I lose myself in him.

He still pulls away too soon. I can't focus, my dick is so hard, and I'm craving to touch, but after finding out he's never done this before, I'm hesitant to push for more.

"Wow," Xander whispers. "That was ... I don't think one kiss is enough."

"I agree."

His surprised eyes find mine. "Really?"

I can't believe he's even asking me that question. "You seriously underestimate how attracted to you I am."

"Yeah, well ..." He waves a hand over himself. "There's not much to look at."

The fact he said that and actually believes it almost makes me see red. It takes me a moment to settle down the need to rage, and instead, I reach for the button on the front of his shirt. "Can I?"

He curiously holds my gaze as he nods.

I undo the button, then slowly reach for where the shirt is sitting on his shoulders. I give him plenty of time to stop me as I slide the material off and down his arms until it lands on the floor at his feet.

Then, I take a minute to look. I've seen Xander shirtless before, but I didn't actually *see* him. I wasn't looking at him like that. I had my nurse glasses on, and there was nothing specific I paid attention to.

But fuck, I'm paying attention now. He's on the thinner side, with prominent collarbones, but he's got a nice-sized chest that tapers down into a narrow waist and those sinful shorts.

My teeth bury into my bottom lip.

Then Xander blows my fucking mind by hooking his thumbs into the front of his shorts and, with the same tortuously slow speed I used, pushes them down his legs. He's not wearing underwear, so I'm left with the sight of what might be the prettiest cock I've ever seen.

He's hard, head flushed a deep red that's tempting me to taste it.

My own dick is filling with blood and straining against my fly. I'm so desperate to grab hold and try to stop the excitement, but it's already too late. I wet my dried lips with one goal in mind.

"What … what do you want? What are you comfortable with?" I ask, trying to be conscious of the fact this is all new to him, when all I want is to get carried away in the moment.

"Anything when it comes to you."

I reach for my shirt and pull it over my head, getting a small, choked sound from him. I grin. "Still comfortable?"

"I'd be more comfortable with you naked too." I don't miss the wicked glint to his eye.

But I do it anyway because both of us naked sounds like a good idea to me. "This better?"

Xander exhales deeply. "Worse. So much worse. So, so much worse because I already think I'm going to come."

"If we only get this one time together, we can't have that."

Proving how fucking brave he is, he moves closer until we're almost toe to toe. "Are we going to have sex?"

"If you want to."

"I want. I want to finally know what it's like."

"Then kiss me."

Xander's mouth finds mine, and it's less desperate than our first one. This kiss is pure relief, a mix of this beginning and us never wanting it to end. My hand finds his lower back, and I guide him in close until we're standing there, skin on skin, and all my fucking dreams have been answered.

But if this is his first time, I want him to remember it. Before he can ask what I'm doing, I reach down and lift him off his feet. His legs immediately lock around my waist as I carry him to the couch.

"You're a natural," I mutter into his mouth as I turn and collapse back onto the cushion. Xander straddles my lap, and I slide my hands further down to grip his ass. "It blows my mind that you don't know how sexy you are."

"It's your lust goggles." He grins against my lips. "You just keep them there until you've made me come."

"Xander ..."

"How do we do this?"

I guess that's the end of that, then, but it's okay. He might not want to hear about how fucking perfect he is, but I can show him instead. "I'm going to spit in my hand so it's nice and wet, then I'm going to jerk us both off together."

His eyes widen. "At the same time?"

"Yep." Something niggles at me. "Have you seen it in porn?"

"A few times, but …"

"Yeah?"

"Well, I don't really like it that much. The professional stuff, at least. I've found some amateur stuff where it's like they know each other or they're a real couple or whatever, but …"

What would you know? Abrasive, impulsive Xander is a romantic at heart. "Just kiss me and let me do the rest."

Relief crosses his face. "Okay."

He leans in until his lips meet mine, and I reach between us and close my hand around our cocks. Xander isn't overly large, but having his cock gripped against mine is fucking ecstasy.

He moans into my mouth as I run my hand over us. I'm fully expecting this to be short and sweet since it's his first time and I've been blue balling it for months now, but I'll take every second I can get.

I hold the back of Xander's head with one hand and jerk us off slowly with the other. All I can concentrate on is him. I'm holding and touching and kissing *Xander*.

I'm leaking a whole hell of a fucking lot, balls aching with the feel of him against me. Our kissing gets deeper, and I'm struggling to keep up with breathing through my nose. I'd fucking devour him if I could.

Ruin him.

Leave him begging for more.

Exactly how I will be once this is over.

# Chapter Twenty-Three

Xander

Derek has big hands. Enormous hands. The largest hands of anyone I've ever met.

At least that's how they feel wrapped around my dick.

My entire body is flushed, face feeling overheated as my mouth hungrily takes everything he's giving me. The sensations on my cock are more than I ever imagined, and even though I was fully prepared for discomfort or aversion to kick in, the opposite has happened. The want I felt for Derek before has exploded. I need his hands all over me, need to press closer, while knowing it will never be close enough.

I'm trying to hold in the needy sounds wanting to escape me, and it's a real effort not to thrust into his fist. Derek's steely cock is rigid against mine, and I don't think my brain has completely caught up that this is actually happening. It's too swamped in this fuzzy, buzzing high.

His mouth breaks from mine, and I chase it for a moment until he speaks.

"Touch me, Xander."

It's not until he says it that I realize my hands are locked on his shoulders, where they've stayed since he picked me up. "Where?"

"Everywhere," he groans.

Seeing Derek like this, knowing that I'm the one turning him on, has shivery need flooding my limbs. Our mouths slot together, and I let my hands drop, reveling in the smooth, warm skin under my palms. He's got chest hair, which apparently is a massive turn-on for me, and I run my hands over it before I reach his chest. That gorgeous chest I was drooling over when I saw him dancing in that cage.

Broad and strong, my hands linger on his pecs, thumb gently stroking his nipple.

A hiss sucks between Derek's teeth. "That feels so good," he says into my mouth.

I keep doing it, proud that I could make him sound that way.

As I explore, his free hand grips the back of my neck while the other keeps working our cocks. His hands are smoother than I was expecting, and his hold is tight. Every downstroke makes me see stars, and every upstroke has me leaking. Not as much as him though. Derek is something else.

I'm panting as I look down, needing to actually witness this. To burn this moment into my mind. That sexy chest, his softer belly, the hair that runs down it and into his pubes. That large hand with prominent veins wrapped around us in a tight fist. The way the flushed head of my cock disappears and reappears with every stroke. Derek's only a little longer than me, but his cock is thick, and watching it pressed against mine has my mouth watering. I want to taste him. Lick the shiny tip and make his eyes roll back in pleasure.

But doing that would mean putting distance between us, and there's nothing in this fucking world that could make me stop what we're doing.

His lips press desperately to my jaw. "Tell me you're close."

I give in to the urge to thrust and almost whimper. "So good."

"That's it. Fuck my fist. Make yourself feel good."

I thrust again, and Derek's groan fills me with the confidence to keep going. I ride his fist like nothing else matters.

My balls are tight and almost painful, and I'm clinging to Derek like he might slip away. I'm not convinced I won't wake up and work out this was all a dream, but there's no way my imagination is this good.

The sweat is cool on my back, his lips are hot on my neck, and I've lost track of what's happening. I'm chasing the type of high I've never had before, and judging by the sounds Derek's making, he's not far off either.

I test out a moan, and it feels so good leaving my lips.

Derek nips my collarbone. "You're going to make me come, sounding like that."

I'd laugh, but I'm too close to the edge. I wrap my arms around his neck, face pressed against his hair, needing to be as close as humanly possible. I want Derek wrapped around me, engulfing me, for our bodies to meld together and never let go.

His stubble scrapes my skin, and I want more. More of his groans, more of his scent, more of the way he touches me. I've never felt safety and care like this. Never been so overwhelmingly consumed by another person.

But after years of wanting, I finally get this. I'm not an idiot to think it'll happen again or that Derek's worry about his job has magically gone, so I'm going to do what I do best. Get everything out of a moment before it abandons me.

Derek's warm tongue runs over my collarbone before he drags it up my throat.

"*Fuck.*"

My dick jerks in his hold as my orgasm smashes into me. I'm a panting, shivery mess, sinking into the waves of bliss passing over me before Derek stiffens and cum floods into his fist.

The satisfied sigh that passes his lips gives me hope.

Still pressed against him, I ease back so I can see his face. His wonderfully disastrous eyes are bright, cheeks red, hair damp and messy.

"Was that okay?"

The lines by his eyes crinkle. "I think I'm supposed to be asking that question."

"Too bad I beat you to it." Even if I'm sick with nerves that it might only have been okay for him.

"It was … wow, Xander. That was every bit as amazing as you are."

My eyebrows flex with a frown I fight against. Fucking compliments.

"No." He pulls me down to kiss my forehead. "You don't get to disagree with me. You might not have enjoyed it, but you don't get to argue that I'm wrong."

"I wasn't going to."

He gives me an *I know you* look, and it's hard not to believe it.

My gaze drops to where my hand is resting on his chest. "It was … I don't think I have words. I guess I'm not a virgin now."

"Was that important to you?"

"No. I get that it's all a construct and not a real thing, so I didn't care about being a virgin. I cared about … about the fact that I'd never had someone want me that badly. I've never had someone want me in their lives at all, let alone be sexually attracted to me."

"I'm struggling to believe *no one* has been sexually attracted to you."

The fact I have to explain this isn't something I want to do, but it's either explain or sound like an idiot. "No, well, they have. That's the issue. Surface-level attraction, it sort of, well, I don't like it. Strangers looking at me ..." My gut twists up in familiar knots. I don't even really know where the aversion has come from, but my whole life, I've kind of had this instinct. This deep knowledge of who's good and can be trusted and who will probably hurt me.

Derek's a mixture of both, but at least I know his hurt won't be intentional. At least I know what I'm walking into with him.

"It makes you uncomfortable?"

I swallow roughly. "Yeah. I'm not someone who can do one-night stands, I guess, and there aren't a lot of people who'd get involved with someone like me. I'm high-maintenance."

"You're n—"

"*Don't* lie." It's sweet he was going to, but I don't need that. It's empty. "You pointed out that your whole life revolved around me, and that's shitty as hell." My voice loses some of its confidence. "I've never told anyone this before. Not even Seven. Sometimes I worry that I'll say or do the wrong thing or put too much on him, and then he'll decide he's done. And he'll take Molly with him. That terrifies the fuck out of me."

"Has he ever done anything to make you feel that way?"

My smile is tight when I look up at him. "Haven't you got it yet? My brain doesn't run on logic. It runs on catastrophizing, negativity, and throws in the sheer terror of mortality every now and then to keep things interesting."

"We both see you very differently."

"We ... do?" I'm a self-aware guy, and I know there aren't many other ways to think of me. I'm either being annoying by thinking I'm dying or annoying by needing too much attention.

I can't turn off either of those sides of me, especially because they feed into each other. Seven and Molly are the only two people on Earth I've ever felt love me so fucking deeply that I can trust they won't go anywhere, but a day or two without their full attention, and I lose it. I'm working on my coping strategies, but I don't think anyone knows how deep that well goes. How convincing my brain can be.

Derek nods, running his nose over my jaw. "You're someone who so badly wants to do the right thing. You'd go out of your way for the people you love, and you lash out sometimes because you're scared. People haven't been kind to you, but you so badly want to trust them anyway. That's huge, Xander."

"Or delusional."

"I have a serious question that I don't want a snarky answer for."

I almost roll my eyes. "No guarantees."

"Then no question."

My glare doesn't work on him. "What if I don't want to answer you?"

"Then say that."

The truth? Kill me now. "Fine. Go."

"Do you actually like putting yourself down all the time? At first, I didn't think you knew that you were doing it, but I'm getting the feeling it's on purpose."

That's an easy one. "It helps to think of myself the way everyone else does."

"Right. And who is everyone?"

"I thought medical professionals were supposed to be smart. Everyone is *everyone*."

"Is Seven everyone?"

"Probably."

"And Molly."

Does he not know what everyone means? "Of course Molly."

"So everyone thinks you're annoying and worthless?"

"Yup."

He lets that sink in for a moment. "What if I told you that I don't?"

"Then I'd ask why you're bothering to lie to me. I'm not offended by people thinking I'm a shitty person. It is what it is."

Derek pinches my chin and steers my face until it's right in front of mine. "You're not a shitty person. Sometimes you act like it when you remember to, but I've seen your guard down way too many times to believe it. I'm sorry we can't have a relationship. I'm sorry this can't be more for us. But if we're going to continue to hang out and try to stay friends, I need that to stop."

"You want me to change my whole personality for you?"

"No. I want you to stop forcing this mean-boy persona *for you*. I'm sorry people have hurt you. You don't deserve any of it. But that also doesn't mean you should keep hurting yourself. All I can see is an *incredible* person punishing himself for something that wasn't his fault."

"Stop using that word."

"*No.*"

The finality in his tone hits something behind my ribs. "You won't?"

"I won't."

"Even though I don't like it?"

"Why does it make you so uncomfortable?"

"Because it's not true."

Derek pulls me down against his chest, and I melt into his arms. Our cum is dried to his stomach, and the scent of sex is strong. I think I'm already addicted to it. "It's true. And one day, I'm determined to make you believe it."

# Chapter Twenty-Four

Derek

Hanging out with Xander is the hardest thing I've ever fucking done. He said he couldn't ever be friends with me, and I know what he means, but for now, we're existing in this weird sort of limbo where we both want each other and we both want more, but we're pretending that side of us doesn't exist.

Xander glances up from where he's snuggled under my arm. "You're finally going to show me your house?"

Okay, we're *sort of* pretending it doesn't exist. Or, more accurately, we're ignoring the fact that we know it exists and will take every opportunity to touch each other platonically. Xander craves being touched. He craves being close. I've noticed it with Seven and Molly, too, when we all hang out together, and I figure if he can snuggle up to them and it not mean anything sexual, then there's no reason why he can't snuggle up to me.

"You're going to judge me," I warn him.

"Duh. That's the whole point of seeing someone else's house. To make a snap judgment about them and their whole personality."

"You're not doing a single thing to make me feel better about this decision."

"Good, because I'm not trying to. Now, show me. I can't wait to be right about it being a hovel."

"It's not a fucking hovel," I grumble, unwrapping my arm from his shoulders to unlock the door.

"We'll see." He gives me one of his smiles. The kind that would look adorable if his eyes didn't scream mischief.

"Your fake innocence doesn't work on me."

"That's what you think."

He follows me inside, and even though I spent the morning cleaning up, it isn't much to look at. A leather couch, a TV, a stark white kitchen, and a small dining table that's never used. There isn't much clutter because there isn't much of anything.

Bertha house feels alive, and while I like that my place is clean and open, I can admit it lacks the soul of their chaotic household.

"See? No hovel?"

Xander doesn't say much as he walks across the living space and looks around. "This is like ... a proper grown-up house."

"It's pretty basic."

"There's nothing on the floors. Or clothes thrown over the back of the couch. Or shoes cluttered around the door so that when you walk in, you almost trip over them and break your neck."

"Anyone ever told you that you're dramatic?"

"It could happen. The hall table is *right* there and super heavy. Knock your head on that and it's good night."

"I suggest you stay on your feet, then."

Xander moves around, looking way too good in my space,

and tugs on the corner of a cushion resting on the couch. "These are fancy."

"Hannah bought them for me."

His purple glare snaps up to me. "*Who?*"

I almost laugh. "My best friend's wife."

"Manny?" he confirms. I don't know how many times I've mentioned Manny before, but Xander still has a wariness there.

"Yup."

He twists his lips from one side to the other. "I think I should be your best friend instead. I spend more time with you."

He spends all his time with me. It's not something I'm going to complain about either. In the few weeks since we had sex, Xander's decided that boundaries don't exist anymore. His texts are constant, he meets me after work or has me go to his place, and when we can't meet up, we end up talking on the phone until late. Too late. I fell asleep during our conversation last night, and I can only imagine what shit I spewed in my sleep.

"Manny's been my best friend since high school."

"People change."

It's hard not to tease him when he's being ridiculous. "What if I have two best friends?"

"That's not how *best* works, but nice try."

I cross over so that I'm standing at the back of the couch, right in front of him. I tug the cushion from his hold. "You're cute when you're jealous."

"I'll have to be jealous more often, then."

"Or you could believe me when I say that I don't want to be best friends with you. Keeping that little bit of distance between us is needed. For my goddamn sanity."

Xander slowly drags his bottom lip between his teeth and leans forward. "Have you ever jerked *Manny* off?"

"Nope."

He lets out a satisfied *hmm*. "Guess that means I win, then."

"Exactly." And even though I shouldn't, I add, "It's no competition."

He tries to hold down his smile. "Can I see your ants?"

Well, I guess we're not putting that off any longer. I probably shouldn't have mentioned them to him in the first place, but imagine if he'd come over and randomly walked into my bug room. It's a fast way to scare the hell out of someone.

"Might as well see what you really think of me. Who knows? Maybe it'll scare you off, and we won't have to worry about, well, anything."

I turn for the hall, and Xander catches up, wrapping himself around my arm. "You're severely overestimating my standards."

"And you're undervaluing yourself again."

"Hey, if I say it's what I'm good at, does that mean I'm complimenting myself and therefore saying something positive?"

I struggle to follow his twisted logic. "No. Because at the heart of it, you're still being mean about yourself."

"I'll stop recognizing my strengths, then."

"Or maybe you could start."

It's a common conversation for us since I first went over to his place. I don't look into it too deeply or try to force him or anything, but I'm hoping the constant reminders might sink in one day. Xander's used to putting himself down, and I think it's a way of protecting himself, but I hate that he doesn't know any other way to be.

With any luck, his psychologist will help him through it. I'm not bluffing when I say that I won't play doctor to him anymore.

"In here," I say and push the door open ahead of us, and then I follow Xander into the room.

It's a standard-sized bedroom with lots of natural light, the formicarium taking up one wall and cages of bugs stacked on shelves on the other. Most of the cages are empty, but I've been slowly adding interesting species to my collection since I got back.

"Fuck, me, the thing is taller than I am," he says, approaching the formicarium. If I had to guess, I'd say he's about five eight or five nine, which I happen to think is the perfect height for someone who's six one. Like me.

I need to stop thinking that way, but I can't convince my common sense of that. The smart thing would be for us to end this stupid pretend friendship and go our separate ways. To move on. Forget the other person exists.

But when I'm with Xander, I don't want to be smart. He feels like mine. He acts like mine. In another universe, we met at random and are already dating. In that universe, I can touch him whenever I want.

Which is always. The mixture of sweet, snarky, and sexy is too much for my small brain. The defensive set to his shoulders, the curve of his back, the pop of that mouthwatering ass ...

"There's so many in there," he says.

I shake off my building lust and go join him. "Yep. The queen took well."

"What if she didn't?"

"The colony would have died out like my others ... or she would have eaten her workers."

"Cannibalism. Cool."

"If you think so."

He wrinkles his cute nose, and it's something I've noticed him do a lot. I'm not sure if it's linked to any kind of emotion, but it really draws attention to his freckles, and it makes me wonder. Is the nose wrinkling a habit or specifically calculated to be cute?

It brings something back to mind.

"You said that it makes you uncomfortable when people check you out?"

"Yep."

"I'm curious why you always dress like you want people to notice you, then?" Xander's clothes are a mixture of cute and sexy, and I don't think I've seen him in anything casual. Even during winter, all covered up, there's something about him that drags your attention in. "I don't mean that in a slut-shaming way, more, like, your hair color, for example. Or those thigh-high socks you like to wear. Those things get attention."

"It's … complicated. I want the attention. I want people to look at me and think I'm pretty but not get the chance to look too closely."

"Those things are more of a distraction?"

"Maybe? Sherwin talked about it once, and it was so boring I almost fell asleep."

The flippant tone catches my attention. "You weren't bored at all, were you?"

He shrugs. "Doesn't matter. He was wrong."

I remind myself that's something for Sherwin to deal with. "It sounds like you want people to be in awe of you but not attracted to you?"

"I … yeah. I think so? Kinda conceited, am I right?"

With what Xander's been through? After a whole lifetime of neglect, it's reasonable to think he'd crave attention but not want people to get too close.

Every day I spend with him reminds me of how lucky I am that he trusts me. That Xander chose to let me in.

"The most brightly colored bugs are usually the most dangerous."

Xander tilts his head, blue bangs drifting over his forehead. "What do you mean?"

"Well, in nature, it's either camouflage and not be eaten or be so brightly colored that it's a warning to any creature who might try to eat you that it's a bad idea."

His gaze drifts down, and when it snaps back up, I can already tell he's going to test me. "Are you saying you want to eat me, Derek?"

I set myself up for that. "That question is off the table."

"Why?"

Before I can stop myself, I pull him in, cradling him in my arms as my lips dip to his ear. "Because I already know it's a bad idea. I know how dangerous you are, little bug, and I'm still trying to pretend I'm a good person."

He shivers in my arms, making my heart pound harder. "Am I your little bug?"

I refuse to answer that. You don't name a pet unless you want to get attached, and I figure you don't pet name a person unless you want to fuck yourself over.

"It works, you know," he says, not letting it drop. "Because you like bugs, and I'm scared of catching them. Not bugs like insects—bugs like flesh-eating viruses that corrode your lungs and make your brain bleed out of your ears, but same thing."

That's not the same thing at all. "And now you've ruined it."

"Nuh-uh." He pulls back so he can see me. "It's mine now. And I'll always remember the sexy way you whispered it in my ear."

"Fuck." I release him and step back, dick thickening against my will. "And that's enough overstepping for one day."

"You're such a flirt."

"Barely. I'm just a guy who likes bugs and apparently lacks self-control."

"You have too much self-control for my liking."

*Mine too, bug. Mine too.* "You agreed to be good."

"You should know not to trust me." He gets his evil smile.

"The second you ask to have sex again, I won't even pretend to think about it."

"Then I *really* need to work on that self-control."

"Maybe. Then again, there's no one else here either. Just you … me——"

I cover his mouth and fix him with the sternest look I'm capable of, while an "I'm fucked" warning tugs at my mind. "It's only been a few weeks. I think my willpower can last longer than that."

"A few weeks, huh?" Xander's gaze travels over me. "I can wait."

I wish he wouldn't. I wish he'd give up on me and realize that anything between us is a lost cause. I wish I could disappear for a year and trust that he'd be here waiting. For me. I'd wait forever for him.

The flirting is cute and fun for the time being, but it's getting difficult. How can I simultaneously love his attention and want it to continue while knowing it would be better for us both if he got sick of me and moved on?

Xander deserves someone who'll make him their whole world. Who'll give him all the attention and love he deserves.

I can't be that person. Not right now.

But damn if I don't wish every day that I could be.

# Chapter Twenty-Five

Xander

"… meeting up with my football buddies."

That sentence does something to me. First, Derek playing football is hot as fuck, and I need to see that, but second—"With *Manny*?" I ask, switching my phone to the other ear.

He chuckles, and thankfully, he finds my jealousy amusing. For now. I'm not an idiot to think he'll always be like that, but knowing he's ditching me for them has a pit burrowing deep in my gut. "Of course he'll be there."

There's a pause while I try to work out how the hell a normal person would respond to this. How to tell him it sounds fun and I hope he wins, without it sounding like I'm speaking through dirt.

He gets in first. "Did you, uh, wanna come?"

"And play football?" Does he want me to be murdered?

Derek laughs properly, and I'm glad he finds that idea as

ridiculous as it is. "You can play if you want to, but I meant to meet my friends."

The pit eases. "You want that?"

"Of course. I've met yours."

The fact he's even suggesting it lessens the stabby rage I wanted to fly into, but now I'm faced with the complete opposite. Anxiety. These are his friends. His friends who he's been friends with for a very long time and are of the jock variety that I never vibed with in high school.

Derek might have his lust goggles on, but none of them will.

They'll see right through me.

They'll know I'm not good enough for him, and then what if they tell him that?

Is it so bad I want Derek to be deluded for a little longer?

"If that's too much—"

I cut off that train of thought. "No, I ... I want to, obviously, but ..."

"What's wrong?"

*I'm a hot mess, and you picked wrong, and you really should move on with your life and find someone who's worth your time and won't drag you down into their shit.*

"Xander?"

"I'm ..."

"Are you nervous?"

I guess that's a mild way of putting it that won't terrify him. "Yes."

His voice softens. "They're going to love you. I've ... told Manny a lot about you."

I'm not sure why that surprises me, but it isn't something I'd thought about before. "What did you say?"

"That we've been hanging out a lot. That you're really cool, and I love spending time with you." Derek sighs. "I wish I could have said more."

I draw a circle on the carpet with my foot and shift the phone back to the other ear. "What more would you have said?"

This is one of those moments. One where we get close to Derek telling me what's on his mind right before he pulls back again. The little tease of him telling me he wants more without him actually saying the words. I'm not so sure I'd survive Derek telling me he wants to be with me, so that's something. No dying from spontaneous cardiac arrest before I even have a chance to find a boyfriend.

Like every other time, Derek's self-control holds out.

"Can I come and pick you up?"

I glance down at what I'm wearing. "I don't really have an outfit appropriate for standing in a field."

"I got you."

He hangs up, and I'm left wondering what the fuck that means.

Rush does a double take as he passes my room. "Are you okay? You're very still. Is this a petit mal seizure?"

"This is meeting the boyfriend's friends shock."

He glances around again. "You have a boyfriend? Is he in the room with us?"

"Urg, you're as bad as Seven. And Molly. *And* Derek."

"I'm lost."

"Fine, Derek isn't technically my boyfriend."

Rush crosses his arms and leans against the wall in thought. "If he's *not* technically your boyfriend, then it means he isn't your boyfriend, so therefore, you don't have a boyfriend, so how on earth are you meeting the friends of someone who doesn't exist?"

"Do any of us really exist? There's a theory that the world ended in 2020, and our consciousness is refusing to let go of existing."

"That's true. It's impossible to know, really. The other theory is that the barrier between multiverses is weakening, and we're slipping in and out. Which would explain why I keep losing my chia pet."

I glance over at the clay unicorn on my windowsill. Madden gifted a different one to each member of the house. "Why do you move it?"

"I don't. But somehow, it ended up in the downstairs bathroom."

"Maybe you took it down there to water it?"

He thinks for a moment. "That actually makes perfect sense."

My phone lights up with a text from Derek, letting me know he's out the front.

"Shit, I have to go."

Rush straightens and turns to leave. "I hope your consciousness has fun with your imaginary boyfriend's not-real friends."

"Thanks. I hope your chia pet is done playing hide-and-seek."

Even though Derek's waiting, I pause to check my reflection. My reflection made up of fragments of a person. My hair. My eyes. My skin. Focusing on each little piece is easier than trying to look at my whole self because it disappoints me every time. Too short. Too skinny. Hair too harsh for my skin or too faded to be cute. My clothes too loose or too tight or too long or too short.

*My freckles need a touch-up.*

Some of them have faded, and the thought of meeting Derek's friends, of them not being able to see the tattoos, not coming to the conclusion that I'm cute and sweet and worthy of him ... I swallow the taste of panic and try to remember what Sherwin said. Something about refocus. About remembering what I do like. About taking back my agency. My eyes drift closed, and I try to remember. I'm here. I'm alive. There's something about me that Derek likes enough to keep coming back.

"Hey, you ready?"

I jump at Derek's voice in the doorway.

Holy fuck, how long have I been standing here?

"Yes. Yes. I'm good. I'm ready."

His lips kick up at the corner, and he holds something out to me.

"What's that?"

"My JV sweater from high school."

I hold my hands out, and Derek hands it over. It's soft and smells like him.

"I was going to bring an old jersey," he explains. "But with it being big enough for the pads and everything, you would have swum in it."

"You were junior varsity?" I ask.

Derek winks. "Our school wasn't very good."

"And you want me to wear this. Around your friends?"

"You don't have to," he hurries to add. "You were worried about what to wear, and I thought … well, it sort of fits and— shit. This is dumb and weird, I get it. Don't worry. I don't know what I was—"

I tug the sweater over my head, and I'm immediately surrounded by him. "You know you're never getting this back now."

"You're gonna steal my sweater?"

"Yup."

His eyes look extra green today. "Do I get a hug hello?"

I jump into his arms, and Derek catches me, like he needs that as much as I do. I bury my face into his shoulder, glad that Derek at least is giving me this. He lets me be needy. He lets me be just that bit too much.

"Come on, we're going to be late."

I reluctantly set my feet back on the ground and then pull on some sneakers before following him out to the car. It's already warm, and the sweater is too hot to be wearing, but no way in hell am I going to take it off.

Derek drives us north, and it takes about an hour before we're pulling up at a park where we're meeting his friends.

Being this far from home, surrounded by strangers, gives me a solid moment of feeling completely displaced.

"Take however long you need to," he says.

I turn to glance over at him. He's wearing an old football T-shirt, stretched across his chest, and athletic shorts that hug his hairy thighs. His hair is messy, and his jaw is scruffy, and he looks like he's begging me to crawl into his lap and hide there forever.

"These guys think we're friends?" I clarify, focusing on them and not on all the ways I'm deficient.

"We *are* friends."

I send Derek a glare out of the corner of my eye, which only makes his smile wider.

"Whatever assumptions they jump to about us are on them. We know what this is."

"A two-year unnecessary torture session?"

"Exactly." He grabs my hand and kisses the back of it. "Now, stop overthinking it and be yourself."

I don't point out that Derek is the only one dumb enough to actually like that person. But I'm going to fucking try.

I climb out, feeling like I might vomit, and follow him across the park to where a whole bunch of really tall guys are standing. Some of them are still in shape like Derek, others have dad bods or scrawny legs, and one of them has a cuddly belly spilling over his gym shorts.

And all of them are happy to see him.

I step slightly behind Derek, hoping they won't pay me any attention, until one says, "Hey, this must be Xander?"

I glance up at a Black guy with perfect teeth and a fade hairstyle. "Umm, hi."

"Derek will *not* shut up about you. It's embarrassing. He's an embarrassment."

My eyes cut to Derek, and my brain abandons me on what to say. How do I act around these giants? How do I guarantee that they like me and don't pull him aside and tell him to ditch the loser?

I remember how jocks treated me in high school. I remember how they'd look at the scrawny kid with dyed hair and whisper slurs behind my back.

Derek steps closer, and his proximity is enough to remind me that whatever it was like back then, Derek would never let his friends be cruel. "I tell him he's an embarrassment frequently," I say, quieter than I want to, but the man laughs.

"I'm Manny. That's Cherry, Dongo, Flipper, and Tim."

"Tim doesn't get a nickname?"

"Who says the others do?"

The teasing helps release some of the anxiousness throttling me. "Poor them if they don't."

"Hey," protests the guy with the big belly. "I can't help that my mom thought Flipper was a good idea."

Flipper? *Flipper*? Before I can tell him that's the dumbest thing I've ever heard and remind him that he can legally change his own name, Derek tilts his head by my ear. "Don't believe a word that comes out of his mouth. He'll tell you that he saw aliens land in his backyard and kidnap his dog with a straight face."

"That really happened," Flipper insists, tossing a ball Derek's way.

"And your name is really Pat." Derek throws the ball back, harder. "Stop trying to scare off my friend."

"But then how else will we know he's good enough for you?" Dad-bod Dongo asks.

"You trust me when I say that he is."

It's like my heart gets little wings as Derek and his friends head toward a bigger group further across the field.

Manny nudges me with his elbow as he passes. "Nice sweater. Now, I could be wrong, but I swear I've seen it before …"

My cheeks heat because I'm not sure if Derek wanted people to know or not. That said, it's from high school—surely Derek knew these guys would recognize it.

I scramble for an excuse, trying not to give myself away. "I was cold."

"Makes sense. I always have my JV sweater on the back seat, waiting for the day someone is cold at the start of summer."

"Stop calling me on my shit. It isn't cute."

Manny laughs. "Hannah steals my clothes all the time too."

"I have no idea what you're implying."

"Just … go easy on him. Derek hasn't dated in a really long time, and I was worried about him there for a bit. Got real down about … I dunno. Something. Kind of lost himself for the last year or two. Just be good to him."

I'm uncomfortably aware that I might have been the reason for the last few years. "I don't know how to be good to anyone."

Manny pulls me into step with him. "Clearly, Derek disagrees. My man doesn't date just anybody."

"We're not dating."

"Really?" He looks legitimately surprised. "I dunno, man. It looks a whole lot like it to me."

Me too, Manny. Me too. Unfortunately I get the feeling that Derek hasn't explained the whole situation, and so I have no idea how Manny would feel knowing that I used to be one of Derek's patients. That I still would be if he wasn't such a good person who actually has morals.

We might look like we're dating. We might want to be dating. I might be growing more sure with every day that he's the man I'm falling for.

But we're not dating. And when my brain isn't playing tricks on me, I know reality is the only thing that counts.

# Chapter Twenty-Six

Derek

"You remind me of a little boy I used to foster."

I freeze in the doorway to the art room and yank myself out of sight. My dance class has been called off because stomach flu has hit the nursing home, and I thought I'd see if Xander wanted to go somewhere instead. Now, I'm worried that I've stumbled into the wrong end of a conversation.

"I wish someone like you had fostered me," he says.

I need to walk away, but I can't bring myself to do it.

"I miss those days," she says. "Oooh, Toby used to want to kill some people over what those babies went through."

I glance around the doorframe and find Xander and Bethany sitting side by side, painting.

"Why did you foster kids?" he asks. "We're hard work. Most of us are so fucking messed up and impossible to deal with."

"Impossible is a lie people tell themselves when they don't

want to put in the work. In all our years, only one child had to be removed, and it broke my heart."

"What happened?"

"She was violent toward the others. It was one of the hardest decisions I ever made." Bethany lifts a shaky arm to paint some more. "I had five other children in my care though, and I couldn't give her the one-on-one time she needed. I think about her a lot."

He shoots her one of those side-eye looks he's perfected. "You do?"

"Yes, I think about all of them a lot. Still remember every name. Kept a notebook with the thing I liked most about each child."

I can tell he's debating whether to continue the conversation. "What sorts of things?"

"Javier was seven. Used to be very particular about his teeth and would remind us all, morning and night without fail, to make sure we'd brushed so we didn't get cavities. Lauren had this one doll she always sang 'Once Upon a Dream' to as she was falling asleep. Nevaeh would cry when someone picked a flower because it meant the flower would die. And Rose—she was the one I had to have removed—I remember seeing her braid Lauren's hair one day when they didn't know I was watching. Told Lauren she could be a doctor if she wanted to."

"No one ever wrote notes like that about me."

"How do you know?"

Xander shrugs. "They all hated me."

"How many foster homes were you in?"

Xander huffs. "If that's supposed to be a farmhouse, you need to get your eyesight tested."

"They do it here frequently, thank you very much. Your frog looks like a goat."

"What goats do you know that are green?"

"You're the one painting it."

With them moved on to safer topics, I tap on the door-frame and walk in. "I think the farmhouse and the frog both look amazing."

Xander looks at Bethany, and they share a look about my lack of art skills, something the residents love to remind me about.

I throw up my hands. "Sorry. They're both terrible. Happy?"

"Much." Xander stands and gathers all the equipment up.

"You don't have to stop because I'm here."

"Bethany needs a nap," he says, and at first, I assume he's being his snarky self, but she nods.

"I'm dead on my feet this week. That damn stomach flu better not get me as well." She squeezes Xander's shoulder and leaves.

As he packs up, I debate whether to bring up what I heard, but it feels like being a sneaky liar not to.

"I eavesdropped on some of your conversation," I tell him.

"I know. You think I didn't see you lurking at the doorway?"

I catch my laugh in time. "I thought I was being sneaky."

"You weren't."

"Damn. There goes my life in crime," I mutter, helping him carry the paintbrushes to the sink.

The only sound is the rush of water from the tap and the paintbrushes knocking the side of the glass jar. "Go on. What did you want to ask me?"

"Nothing specific, but ... could you tell me about it? Any of it?"

He smirks. "I could, but once I get started, I tend to trauma dump. Then you'll want to give me sympathy, which isn't something I want because I don't connect with any of it anymore."

"I think … well, it's part of you. I've been, umm, reading up on neglect."

His head shoots toward me. "Why?"

"Because I want to know you. I want to support you—*not* be your carer, just support—with anything you need. And I think the more I know about you, the better I can do it."

"I don't need support though."

"Lie." He shoots me a glare. "Everyone needs support."

"Even you?"

I want to talk about him, not me, but he does this a lot. Challenges me to share something with him first before he feels comfortable enough to share right back. The problem is, I'm not sure what to share. It needs to be personal so he knows I'm letting him in, but I don't want to try and make my life sound bad because it wasn't.

"When my grandad died, I needed a lot of support. I was eighteen, but we were close from the minute I was born, and then suddenly, he wasn't there anymore, and it took a lot to adjust to. That's the biggest example I can think of, but there are always moments of doubt. Always moments where I question if I've made the right decisions, especially when it comes to you."

"Why me?"

"I don't want to hurt you. I … feel … a lot. For you. And I can't show you that, but I also don't want you to think it's because I'm playing with you or that I don't care. Every day, I go back and forth on whether we should even be friends or if I should leave you alone. Am I taking advantage of your neglect without me even realizing it?"

"No." His answer is fast. "If you were, you wouldn't be questioning yourself. Besides, I might have my issues, but I'm not a pushover. I happen to have a really fucking good bullshit radar and don't trust people easily. My brain plays tricks on me sometimes, but that doesn't mean I'm an idiot. I know what I want." He drops his eyes to the floor and whispers, "I've been waiting my whole life for you. Just you. I'm not going anywhere."

Somehow, that both makes me feel amazing and like fucking shit. I swallow around the lump building in my throat, nose oddly prickly. Instead of fighting myself on it, I reach for him. Xander folds into my arms like he's always meant to be there.

"I'm sorry I can't give you more right now. You deserve everything."

"And who says you're not already giving me that?"

I squeeze him tighter, and he squeezes me back.

Then he talks, and I'm not expecting what he says next. "I was in seventeen different homes. Five were where my nightmares came from. The other twelve ranged from okay to really good, but by the time I got to experience the really good, I think I was broken. I made them move me twice before I got too attached."

I uselessly want to apologize, but then I remind myself he doesn't want the sympathy. "Is seventeen normal?"

"Nope. I think three is standard. My parents tried to get me back a couple of times but couldn't stay clean long enough. I was in short-term places and care homes in between, plus there were ten long-term arrangements. Two of those, my parents— I don't even know why—complained and had me moved. Five, like I said, were awful. Two were amazing, and the last one … the last one was this super-educated and well-off couple who took in older foster kids to help set them up with the skills they need. Driving, bank accounts, college applications, that kind of thing."

"That sounds helpful."

"They also separated me from Seven."

The weight in those words leaves me speechless.

"When I was five, my foster brothers tied me in a thick

plastic bag and laughed as I tried to get out. When I was eight, I put on a lot of weight, and my foster parents put me on a strict diet, locked the cupboards and fridge, and would make me run around the neighborhood every afternoon, and I couldn't come back until it was dark. At thirteen, I counted how many days I could go without talking before someone noticed. One hundred and eighteen, by the way, and it was only after the fourth visit from my caseworker that she realized something was going on. But none of those things hurt as much as losing Seven did."

"Why?"

"Seven was really angry when I met him, but something changed, and he got his act together because he was determined to look after me. It wasn't good on him, either, when we were separated. They worried he'd done … things. To me. But the only thing he ever did was love me when no one else would. I'd had the health anxiety plenty before that, but those months are where it got really bad. He was the only reason worth living, and I knew that if I was struggling without him, then he was struggling without me. They wouldn't let me contact him. They wouldn't tell me if he was okay. I had panic attacks every single night, thinking he'd been arrested, or stabbed, or was living on the street. I thought I'd leave there and never be able to find him again, and the thought of that was so paralyzing I couldn't breathe."

I hold him closer, tears pricking at my eyes. "Seven's everything to you."

"Yeah." He pulls back, and no matter what he says about being unaffected by it all, I can tell it still haunts him. "I don't think I'm capable of letting him go. I'm sorry."

"Nope. If I can't be sad for you, then you don't get to be sorry about that." I cup his face and tilt it up until he's looking at me. "How did you find him?"

"I didn't get better. Even with meds and psychiatric visits

and appointment after appointment with psychologists. They even put me in a goddamn psych ward. When nothing worked, my caseworker stopped fighting it. I was almost eighteen, so it's not like they could hold me forever. She called Seven, and he came and picked me up. He'd found a tiny one-bedroom, and he was working at a fast food place during the day, a bar at night, and building his tattoo portfolio with every spare moment in between. He said that he knew I'd need him and made sure he was ready."

"I think Seven just became my favorite person."

Xander scowls, and I can't help it.

I lean down and brush my lips softly over his.

He chases me for more, and it hurts not to let him. His eyes flutter open, and when that bright purple hue appears, I hate it. I overwhelmingly, unreasonably, flare with hatred over it.

"Seven, Molly, Madden, Rush, Christian, Gabe. Those men are all in your life. You're not alone anymore, Xander. You're not waiting for your person. You've found them."

His pink tongue swipes over his lips. "And you?"

"I'm already yours in all the ways I can be."

# Chapter Twenty-Seven

Xander

"What would your reaction be if I told you that I wanted you to put some distance between yourself and Seven?"

Dr. Sherwin's question immediately makes me seize up. "You wouldn't."

"I might."

"I'd tell you to fuck off and that I'm never coming back again."

Dr. Sherwin laughs. "I appreciate the honesty. Does your closeness to him bother you? Even the smallest amount?"

"No." It's everyone else who seems to have an issue with it. If Seven's happy and I'm happy, I don't get why anyone else should care, but of course they do. Of course they look at our connection and want to make judgment calls on something they don't understand.

"Do you think your connection to him will affect you having future relationships?"

"I lost my virginity." I say it so fast it takes a moment for Sherwin to pivot.

"Really? That was something on your mind a lot."

"Yeah, it was, but it couldn't have been more perfect."

"Perfect is an … interesting word."

"It describes Derek."

"Derek. The thing you wanted to get out of our sessions?"

"Yeah, he's my boyfriend." Actually, it's probably bad karma to lie to your shrink. "Well, he's *not* my boyfriend, but he wants to be."

"And you're open to it?"

"Yes."

"So is there a reason you're not in a relationship?"

I bite my tongue. Our relationship isn't exactly illegal—I don't think—but is it the type of thing he'd have to report? I'm pretty sure I can't confess to killing someone in here without him needing to report it, and with how some people react about me and Derek, you'd think it's on the same level. I've told him about who Derek is as a person but nothing about our relationship.

"You've gone quiet," he says.

"Just trying to figure out how much to tell you."

He hums, and I narrow my eyes his way.

"What's that supposed to mean?"

"The hesitance has made me curious."

Of course it has. And this is why I don't like shrinks. Instead of assuming that maybe it's private and I don't want to talk about Derek, he's piecing together some far-fetched theory of his own.

"You don't need to tell me anything you're not comfortable with—"

"I know."

"But all I'm going to say is that if you're with someone who isn't available for a relationship, consider why that might be.

Whether this man is telling you the truth or not, the reality is that you're not in a relationship you both apparently want. Oftentimes, people who don't feel worthy of love will self-sabotage in this way."

I groan and hang my head back. "It's not like that at all."

"I'm glad to hear it. I'd still recommend thinking about the hurdle between you and why you're so content to accept it."

I think I already know the answer to that. That niggling, fluttery happiness that hits my chest every time Derek's around can only mean one thing. Like hell am I going to bring that up here when he already thinks I'm self-sabotaging. I don't have the words to explain it to Sherwin though. I've met a lot of shitty people in my life. I've seen what it looks like when people aren't interested. Or when they're telling you what you want to hear. Or when they think you can benefit them.

Derek is none of that. Derek is stability and honesty, and I trust him as much as I trust Seven.

He's the only person I've ever trusted that much.

And I still think they're both going to leave me.

I rub at where my chest is getting tight.

"How are the panic attacks going?"

Urg. Another subject I hate. "I'm using your coping strategies."

"When was your last episode?"

I chew on my tongue, not wanting to say.

"Was it recent?"

"Last night. Twice this week."

"They've picked up again."

"I'm not doing it on purpose!" And I don't like his tone. See? Fucking shrinks, man. They think they know everything and try to convince you of things that are just plain wrong. He doesn't know what it's like to show up at that pharmacy and get a random stranger and wish with my whole heart that Derek would walk in and hold me. None of them understand.

Going to the pharmacy isn't working anymore.

That building used to be enough to ease the panic, but not anymore. My emotional support person is gone.

And yes, I can recognize the need for an emotional support person is kinda fucked-up, but I'm trying. I don't mention my episodes to Derek. We don't talk about it at all. If I brought them up, I know that he'd feel guilty, and the anniversary of him walking out of the pharmacy that day is only a month away. We've made it through a year. One more to go.

I just need him not to get sick of me before then.

A smell tickles my nose. A familiar scent that reminds me of something nonspecific from my past. Something terrifying and lonely that throws me back into helplessness. Reality is a black rush of crushing pressure as it barrels away from me, and I lose grip.

The darkness hits me so quickly I'm powerless to stop it. And I'm back there. Before Seven and Molly and before all of my brothers. A completely insignificant speck. A nothing.

*If I go missing tomorrow, who the fuck would care?*

I try to remind myself Derek would, but then I see our future.

Derek getting annoyed. Derek getting distant. Derek giving me that taste of us and then taking it all away.

A deep pressure settles over my chest, making it hard to breathe, and fuck. Why? Why now?

Why this?

My lungs struggle to expand, and the harder it gets to inhale, the quicker I spiral.

A sudden pain slices through my chest, and I hunch forward, trying to breathe, trying to remember my fucking strategies to make it all go away, but Derek isn't here. Derek might never be here.

Each inhale makes my chest tighter. My vision takes on that loopy haze that almost sends me toppling sideways. My heart is racing, racing, racing out of control, and my face is getting so hot my brain is going to boil.

But fuck. The pain. It's deep in my chest and crippling, sharp and sudden every time I try to inhale.

Holy fuck.

I'm having a heart attack.

It's actually happening. It's actually goddamn happening. Shards of pressure radiate through my chest, a spike of agony that comes back and comes back and comes back.

"Fuck. Ah, fuck."

The room has disappeared, but gentle hands ease me forward, and a strong hand rests on my back.

"You're safe, Xander. You're in Sherwin's office."

"Call an ambulance."

"All you need to do right now is breathe."

"I'm ... heart attack. Pain ... call. Please call."

"You're having a panic attack."

His words are coming to me through water. An echoey drip of nonsense. My whole head is burning, and I'm trembling so hard I'm sure I've got a fever. Is that what's causing this pain? The bolts hitting my chest over and over are stronger than anything I've ever felt before, and my fingertips are frozen.

"I'm ... I'm dying," I gasp. Through dips and twists in my vision, I vaguely register that Sherwin isn't moving. Isn't reacting. Calling for help. Saving me.

He stays where he is.

He doesn't move his hand.

"You're killing me ..." I murmur.

I push to my feet to grab my phone, but the second I stand, everything rushes around me, and my ass hits the couch again. I can't process any of his words, but how can I when he's watching me die?

"You need to ... sitting ... breathing under control ... hurt yourself."

I have no fucking clue what he's saying. I'm tired. So tired. My lungs are burning with every failed breath. The deeper I try to breathe, the worse it gets, and the darkness passing over me solidifies to numb resignation. This is it. It's over.

⊏⊐

"XANDER ..."

I take what feels like the first real breath I've ever taken. My head burns around it, and my eyes are heavy, but I follow it up with another one.

"That's it. You've got it."

I recognize the voice. It's vague and far away.

"There we go ..."

Slowly, I open my eyes. I'm sweaty, my hands are shaking, and I'm still in Sherwin's office. What could have been seconds or minutes or hours feels like I've woken up weighing an extra fifty pounds, and I'm more exhausted than ever.

"Was there a trigger?" he asks kindly.

I can't answer him. That was way too strong and fast, and I'm disappointed I'm still alive.

Because if I'm alive, it means my brain won. Again.

It wasn't a heart attack. I'm just fucked-up.

I'm never going to be better.

Never.

Seven's already making improvements with his therapist, and I so badly wanted to make him proud. I wanted to keep Molly around and prove to Derek that I'm worth it.

That might be my biggest lie yet.

"Did something set you off?" Sherwin repeats.

My lips barely move as I say, "A smell."

"Something specific?"

That's the hard part. It doesn't smell like anything I recognize. It doesn't smell like *anything*, and it's hard to know if it's a

smell at all or if my brain is getting its wires crossed. But whatever it is feels so familiar, like a memory, and it always throws
me back to when I was invisible, worthless, weak. Like a hit of
nostalgia that makes me panic instead of feel good.

I haven't changed at all.

"Do you want me to bring Seven in?" he asks.

It takes all of my energy to smile. "No. I'm okay." It feels
like someone else is speaking. Smiling. Thanking him for the
session.

"Before you go," Sherwin says, "I think we should talk
about seeing a psychiatrist. For medication."

# Chapter Twenty-Eight

Derek

"Sorry to drop by like this, but he hasn't been answering his phone." It's been twenty-four hours, and considering I hear from Xander all day every day, I couldn't go home after work until I'd checked in.

Maybe he's ignoring me on purpose, I don't know, but I'm also not the type to play games and sit around questioning.

Fuck. I really am an old person.

"Ah, yeah," Christian steps aside. "He's in Seven's room."

"Am I okay to go up?"

"Sure." He glances overhead, wavering on saying more. "I don't think he's in a great space, like, I dunno. Go easy."

And that gets me moving. What the hell happened?

I take the stairs two at a time and head along the hall. I've only been upstairs once, so I'm not completely confident which room is Seven's, but after knocking on two closed doors with no answer, I finally hit the right one.

"Come in."

I puff out an exhale before pushing the door open.

"Hey," Seven says, glancing up from where he's scrolling on his phone, like me being in his bedroom is a totally normal thing. Xander's tucked up under his arm, and Molly's hugging Xander from behind, watching a movie on his laptop.

"Hey, sorry to stop by. I hadn't heard from Xander in a bit, and I was worried."

It's clear Xander knows I'm here because his back goes tense under his T-shirt, and he burrows down into the pillow.

Seven and Molly exchange a look before Molly pauses his movie.

"How was work?" he asks, like Xander isn't ignoring me.

"Fine …"

He reaches down to pat the vacant spot by Seven's legs. "Wanna watch the movie with me? Seven thinks musicals are boring."

"Hey," he grumbles. "I'm sitting here, aren't I?"

"Not watching."

"My ear holes are open." Seven looks over at me. "Boyfriends are bossy."

My eyes drift to the back of Xander's head. "I can't wait to find out."

Molly gently shakes Xander's shoulder. "You're being rude."

"Tell him to go away," comes his muffled voice.

The three of us share a look. My first instinct is to be hurt, then offended, then want to say fuck it and leave. Did he really say that? Like I'm not in the room?

Before either of them can answer him, I get in first. "Did I do something wrong?"

His voice is a lot quieter this time. "No."

In that case, I'm not going anywhere. "Then say it to my face. Tell me you want me to leave."

Molly looks like he's trying not to laugh.

"I … can't."

"Why?"

"Molly," Xander whines.

"Don't drag him into this," Seven says, unwrapping his arm from Xander's head. "Use your words."

"I hate you both."

Molly pats his back lightly. "No, you don't. Same as you don't want Derek to actually leave."

"What's going on?" I ask.

"I don't want you to see me like this."

"Like what?"

There's a long moment while the three of us wait for him to decide how to answer. In the end, Xander slowly sits up, and when he looks over, he's the most un-made up I've ever seen him.

Messy hair, reddened eyes missing their contacts, and face so pale the bags under his eyes stick out.

I'm so used to seeing Xander look nothing short of perfect that this … it both breaks my heart and puts it back together again.

"I'm a mess," he says.

"What have I said about you talking shit about yourself?"

He wrinkles his nose, where his freckles are even more prominent than usual, and I decide then and there that it's definitely a calculated move. A distraction.

"Don't try to be cute with me," I say softly. "Be honest. What's going on?"

"I'm never going to be good enough for you."

"Pretty sure that's for me to decide."

His laugh is humorless. "And you will. Soon enough."

"Is it the time thing? That I'm scared of losing my job? What?"

"My psychologist thinks I'm self-sabotaging by wanting someone unavailable."

Well, that plain pisses me off. Funny, isn't it? That I'm the one who advocated hard for him to talk to someone, and that same someone is telling Xander I'm not the right guy.

And maybe I'm not.

Maybe his psychologist is right.

But I'm not going to work off maybes.

Someone else's doubt doesn't get to be my doubt, and if Xander wants me, I'm his. I wasn't lying about that.

"Look at me."

If anything, he looks down further. "Haven't got my contacts."

"Good. Then maybe you'll see me clearly this time."

Slowly, his suspicious eyes meet mine, and I shift closer for good measure.

"Yeah, I am unavailable, Xander. Because I'm already yours."

"W-what?"

"I thought that was fucking obvious, but I guess I have to say it. No, we're not having sex or officially in a relationship, and I hate it too. But we need this time to get to know each other outside of a medical context, and I'm so glad that we're doing that. I've learned so much I didn't know about you, and the more I learn, the more I fall for you. I'm not playing games. There's no one else for me, and I'm happy to wait out all the time we need to for us to be able to start this thing right. If you are."

"But I'm a mess," he whispers, and from the corner of my eye, I see Seven's jaw clench.

"That's a lie, and you're the only one who believes it. For months now, we've spent most of our free time together, and there hasn't been a single time I've thought that."

He scoffs. "That's because I hide it from you. My panic

attacks are getting worse. I had the most fucked-up one in my shrink's office, and that's right after having one the night before. I'm not getting better."

Maybe that's his problem. Maybe he's too busy looking at himself like he's something to fix instead of looking at himself as a perfectly normal person who these things happen to. It's not on me to adjust his whole perception of himself, and I'm glad he's seeing someone who can help, but the fact remains that Xander might never change. He might not want to. Maybe hating himself is his comfort blanket, and it's on me to decide if I can spend my life with him exactly as he is.

"Your panic attacks aren't you," I finally say. And it's that, more than anything, that makes me grateful we're taking our time. I'd cared about him for so long, but I only cared about the side I saw. The side that swung between his not-give-a-fuck attitude and that deep vulnerability he didn't always have the strength to fight.

Xander is so much more than that person.

I'm not going to be gentle with him anymore.

"Here's the thing. I've made my choice. I can't offer you anything official, but that doesn't mean I'm not solely committed to seeing where this goes. I've seen you during your most vulnerable moments. I refuse to be your carer *and* your boyfriend, but I know what I'm signing up for. I know every-thing about you. Your past, your fears, how you can't always control the things your mind does. I also know about how fucking talented you are. How good. How you still want to see the best in people, even if you need them to prove it to you before you'll let yourself trust it. We're both coming into this relationship with baggage, and if mine is too much for you, then that's fair. It's a call you have to make. Not now, but soon. Because I'm also willing to wait for my person."

Xander's lips part, and I hate that he's still eyeing me like he's not sure whether to believe me or not.

So instead of pushing further, I lean in, press a hard kiss to his lips, and before I leave, I meet his gaze and say, "And for what it's worth, you have the most beautiful fucking eyes I've ever seen."

I'm out of Seven's room before any of them can say anything because while it sort of kills me that Xander didn't immediately jump into my arms and tell me another year of all this is worth it, I also know it has nothing to do with me. He needs to figure out where his head is at, and that's fine.

It's okay.

I'm just going to be nervous as fuck while I wait for him to figure out what he wants.

I linger in the hall for a moment, wondering if he'll follow, but when the door to the bedroom opens again, it isn't Xander coming after me. It's Seven.

Hey, maybe this time, he *will* punch me in the face.

His footsteps slow when he sees me, and when he's only a few feet away, he collapses against the wall.

His tattooed hands cover his face, and seeing a big man like Seven fold into himself is something I've never witnessed before.

"I love Xander. So, so much."

After everything Xander's told me, I don't doubt it. "I know."

"Basically, since we met. I don't know if he's told you this, but we were in the same foster home. I'd hear him crying every night, and it used to kill me. But I ... I have a lot of issues. Don't trust people. Can't talk to people. I kept an eye on him, but it was a few weeks before I ever said a word."

"What did you say?"

"I told him sometimes I can't sleep too." Seven drags his hands back, and his eyes are all shiny. "He started sneaking into my room every night, sitting right at my door, and he'd fall asleep on the floor. He didn't leave my side during the day.

Didn't say much, and neither did I. I don't really remember what changed, but one night, he was crying, and I got the urge to hug him, so I did. It was the first time I'd touched someone in years. I think we both needed that hug."

"You probably did."

Seven swallows loudly and looks over at me. "But it's been really fucking hard loving him alone."

It suddenly occurs to me that I've never heard Seven swear before. I've also never thought to ask him if he's okay. I've always seen him as this strong, capable force.

Tears spill onto his cheeks, and it makes me realize that I *really* should have asked. "I'd do anything for Xander, and I'd defend that man to death, but it's … it's a lot. He won't help himself, so I've been doing it solo for so long. Then I found Molly. That guy's the strongest man I know. He takes so much of mine and Xander's crap on, and it all bounces right off him. I think he saved me. Like Xander did once. And now …" He scrubs at his face. "I don't know what's going to happen between you both, but I know you get it. I know that you know exactly what you're signing up for, and damn, I hope he lets you because, well, I think *I* need him to."

I'm the one to pull Seven into a hug this time, and I second-guess whether I should for a moment before his arms fold around me. "Everything he's told me, I … he might have saved you, but I know you saved him too. I'll never be able to thank you enough."

He pulls away, and he slumps back against the wall like his energy has deserted him and left him limp.

"I'll never not be there for him," Seven says. "But since you've been hanging out, I think it's the first time in my life that I've slept okay."

"You've done so much for him." I want to make sure Seven knows that I see it. "It's my turn now."

His short laugh is watery and full of relief. "I'd tell you good luck, but I get the feeling you won't need it."

"Not even a little bit." Xander is fresh air in my life. I look at him and see a future. I see fun and talent and curiosity. My life was stale, a set of must-dos, just a bare expanse of only having getting old to look forward to.

Xander changed all that.

That's the man I'm falling for.

"If he decides he doesn't want to wait around for me, I'm still only a phone call away. Anything you need. The respect I have for you … like, fuck."

He manages a half smile. "Thanks. Sometimes I feel like dirt offloading it all onto Molly."

"Then don't. Just call me."

"I think I will." He looks up suddenly. "Oh, hey. I think this is the moment I'm supposed to tell you that if you mess with him, I'll kill you."

"Okay, get it out of your system."

"If you mess with him—nah, I can't do it. We both know he'll be the one to kill you. But I can promise to help him hide your body."

"Noted."

My potential death aside, I'm still reeling from this conversation. Getting to see this other side of Seven isn't something I ever expected. I didn't think it was possible to like him more than I did when Xander told me what Seven did for him.

Turns out I was wrong.

Xander was right though.

Seven and Molly are my people, too, now.

And I'll do everything I can to do right by all of them.

# Chapter Twenty-Nine

Xander

When I knock on Derek's door, I'm armed with an easel, a huge pad of paper, and the type of determination I haven't felt since I vowed to make sure that Seven and Molly got together.

If I could fight for them, why the hell can't I fight for myself?

*Because you don't deserve Derek.*

The thought hurts because, deep down, there's something in me that believes it's true. I refuse to play into that feeling, though, because I don't want to be this way anymore.

He opens the door, and seeing his face is a blast of happiness. His smile is cautious, and I get it, but hopefully, I can learn how to stop it from looking like that again.

"Good morning," I say, and he quickly steps aside to let me in.

I'm still feeling raw from the other day, and my mind has

never been more exhausted in my life, but for the first time ever, there's something new there too. Something that feels good.

I've thought a lot about what he said. I've thought a lot about what Sherwin, Seven, and Molly have all said. My other roommates too. All the people who care about me have been trying to tell me for so long, and I never listened.

I want to help myself … for me.

Not Derek, not Seven or Molly. I'm unhappy. So fucking deeply unhappy. For years, I had myself convinced that things were fine, that I was functioning the way I was supposed to, but it was all a lie. My angry spirals, my medical episodes, that deep need for attention that goes beyond a want and turns into a toxic rage … it's not fun anymore.

The problem is that the attention I get from those things gives me so much dopamine it's become an addiction.

I don't want to live like that.

So on the way here, I picked up the medication that I swore I'd never take again. It's a different brand from when I was younger, so I have to trust that things will be different this time.

Still, I surge ahead until I'm in the middle of Derek's living room, then set the easel down and rest the pad on top of it.

His front door clicks closed, and it's like a vacuum pulls tight around us. "I've missed you."

My resolve immediately crumbles. "I missed you too."

Derek takes two steps closer, and I hold up both hands. "I'm gonna need to stop you right there. If you touch me, I might maul you because I'm still feeling extra sensitive, and the thought of having sex with you is so goddamn tempting right now."

"Oh. Okay."

"Yes. Sit, please."

Derek redirects to the couch.

"That's better." I suck down a deep breath and pull the lid off one of the markers I've brought with me. Then, across the top of the page, I label three columns. One with "rules" and the other with yes and no.

"What's this?"

"Yeah, I'm going to need you not to talk either. Your voice is way too sexy and should be illegal."

He laughs.

"Laughing is also off the table."

"Wha—Xander!"

I grin at him over my shoulder, and thank fuck he looks amused. "What?" I ask innocently. "Out of the two of us, you're the one who's sex on legs."

His gaze immediately drops to take me in. "Yeah, that is definitely not true." And with the stuff my wet dreams are made of, he presses down on his dick.

"Enough of that, you slutty muppet."

Derek laughs louder this time, and somehow, it's even worse. I need to get through this list before it kills me.

"I'm here today for us to draw up ground rules for our rela-tionship," I tell him. In the first column, I write the word "boyfriend," and then before he can chime in, I tick yes. "Now, I know this can't be public or official or anything like that, but I have my reasons for this."

He stretches his arms out across the back of his couch, and fuck me. Is that the hottest move a man can make? It might just be.

"Arms down, please. I need my blood up here." I tap my temple, and Derek immediately tucks his hands behind his back. But then that only makes his shoulders rounder. I'm screwed. "You know what, I'm going to talk to the paper."

"If that's what you need to do."

"Yes. So. Boyfriends. Now, the reason I want to use this word is because Seven and Molly basically heard you confess your undying love for me anyway, and second, I hardly leave the house and don't have friends beyond them, so I literally have no one to tell. No risk. And for you, obviously you won't say anything at work, but my friends know, and Manny one hundred percent guessed it, so he'll be cool too."

"Uh-huh."

"We're basically that anyway, minus the sex." The longer he doesn't say anything, the faster my doubts creep in.

"And calling me your boyfriend is important to you?" he asks.

Damn, I love his voice so much. So smooth and deep, it was always the thing that helped anchor me through my hardest moments. "Yes. I've never had a boyfriend before. Apparently, I have the trust issues of a wet paper bag, so I really want to know what it's like. With you."

"Deal. Boyfriends."

I barely hold back a fucking squeal. Be cool, Xander. We've got this.

I clear my throat. "Next order of business. Affection. I've got this broken down into four main categories. At home, at—"

Derek's hands snake around my waist. I'm too busy freaking out over the fact he's touching me that it takes a second to compute as he kisses behind my ear. "Can I admit something?" he asks by my ear.

"Yeah …" My voice does that weird, shaky thing that happens when I'm excited.

"Not hearing from you for two days has been the hardest fucking thing. And I think, just for tonight, I want to forget about the rules and spend some real time with my boyfriend."

My knees aren't working right. "Like … like what?"

"Like, maybe …" His lips run along my neck. "Something we've both been so patient for."

Sex. He wants to have sex. I'm too excited to even stop and

worry about whether I've manscaped recently. I turn in his arms. "Will you fuck me in your bed?"

He chokes over his words. "Yeah. If that's what you want."

"I want."

The thought of Derek's body hovering over mine as he thrusts uncontrollably is something that's teased me for a long time. He takes my hand and leads me into the short hall before stopping. "I need to make it clear that this is only for today. You get that, right?"

"Of course. But …"

"Yeah?"

Other than right now, I respect that Derek needs to keep sex off the table, but there's something I need as well. "I want affection."

"What?"

"Like, constantly. I know when we're in public, that's out, but I really need to be touched. Always. Even something little makes me feel so …"

He tugs me toward him. "Yes." Then Derek dips his head and presses his lips to mine.

I melt against the feeling. I'm hungry for his taste, his kiss, the way his tongue is commanding against mine.

Derek lifts me from the ground, and I wrap my legs around his waist as he carries me into his bedroom. It smells like him in here, feels like him, and I wonder how many nights he's lain in his bed and thought of me. I wonder if it even comes close to how many nights I've thought of him.

He lays me down, hands on either side of my shoulders as he holds his weight up. "I'm happy for this to go either way," he says in that low, smooth voice. "I know you haven't done this before, so if it's easier for you to fuck me, we can do it that way."

Not going to lie, that thought is hot. I don't think I can imagine how it would feel for him to be wrapped around my cock like that, but at the same time, in all of my fantasies, he's been inside me. He's held me so tight I couldn't breathe and filled me inside and out.

I want to know what it's like.

There'll be time for all the other sex in the world later.

"I need you inside me," I say. "I need you to need me like that."

Derek's exhale is shaky. "Trust me, I really fucking do."

He breaks away from me to go to his bedside table and grab a bottle of lube and a condom. He tosses them both on the bed, then stands over me.

"I don't know how you're real, Xander. You are so fucking sexy."

I almost tell him he's got those lust goggles on again, but I bite my tongue. "Aren't you going to undress me?" I rasp.

The groan he lets out is almost feral, but when he touches me again, it's sweet. It would be so easy to mistake this for love as he slowly pushes up my shirt, kissing every strip of skin as he reveals it. He doesn't rush, just takes his time to hold me, kiss me, almost like he can't get enough.

He slides down my body to kneel beside the bed and then reaches for my fly. My dick is straining against it, and it's sweet agony as he slowly works my shorts open. Derek kisses his way up my inner thigh, and when he gets to the bottom of my shorts, he grips my waistband and tugs my shorts and under-wear down as one.

Those gorgeous eyes of his flare with lust, and it makes my cock throb.

Then Derek does something I'm completely unprepared for. He leans forward, and my cock sinks into his mouth.

"Oh, fuck," I cry, fisting the sheets. I refuse to come before he's inside me, but this is making it really goddamn hard. I've never had a mouth on my cock before, but I refuse to believe that anyone has ever given a blowjob like this. He licks his way down my shaft before pulling torturously off again.

My balls are already tight.

"If you do that again, you're going to be drinking my cum."

Derek chuckles. "That sounds delicious."

"I really need you to fuck me though. Whether I come or not, I need you inside me."

He presses a kiss to my balls, then just behind them.

"W-what are you doing?"

Derek's eyes darken. "I'm hungry." Then he ducks his head and buries his face in my ass.

Derek's tongue flicks over my opening as he sucks my sensitive skin. It's sensory overload. His stubble scraping against me, his tongue making my nerves buzz, the scent of him in his sheets, the way he moans as he works me over, and then, looking down. Seeing his head between my legs.

He presses against the backs of my thighs, bending my knees right back against the bed. He licks me one last time before pulling back, watching me as he rubs my hole. He's panting slightly.

"You ready for a finger?"

"Yes." I've done it before on myself, but there's no denying Derek's fingers are much wider than mine, and his cock … that's going to be a tight fit.

I'm leaking onto my stomach as he picks up the lube.

"Why don't you get naked too?" I ask.

Derek shakes his head. "Can't. If my dick's out, I won't be able to stop from touching it. And it doesn't get relief until it's inside you."

My thighs twitch, and he grins up at me as he clicks open the lube.

It's cold as it hits my skin, but Derek's warm fingers follow it, and when I'm ready, he presses one inside. A long, smooth breach that I can't believe is happening.

"You took that so well," he says.

"I need more."

"I know. Just let me handle it."

I groan as his rough voice goes right to my balls. "We're back on the no-talking rule."

Derek laughs, and for a second, that sweet, happy man flickers behind how turned on he is. "Is it turning you on when I talk to you?"

"Too much."

"What about it is working you up? My voice? Me telling you that you've got the prettiest hole I've ever seen? Or …" He presses a second finger inside. "How greedy your body is for me? How ready you are to be fucked by me?"

I'm ready to sob. "All of it."

The bastard fucking smirks. "Good to know."

He uses one hand to loosely stroke my dick as he stretches me open. It's taking all my willpower to hold off, but fuck me. I've had his hands on me one whole other time, and Derek didn't touch me like this back then. That was sex to get off. This is sex to drive me out of my fucking mind.

"I'm ready," I beg. "I'm ready for more."

He's taking sick pleasure in stroking his fingers slowly in and out. I can feel every movement. I'm so acutely turned on to every single thing he's doing that I forget to worry about literally anything, and when Derek stuffs a third finger inside me, it's heaven.

I'm so overwhelmingly full, and I can't imagine what it's going to be like once it's his cock. I need this. Need to feel owned and consumed. To know he needs my ass as much as I need his cock.

"You're going to be so fucking tight," he rasps. He's working me open with his fingers, and while it's weird and uncomfortable, it doesn't hurt. Mentally, it's the greatest thing I've ever experienced, but at least the stretch has taken a tiny bit of the desperate edge off.

Derek lets go of my cock and leans down to kiss me. I could survive with just this for the rest of our lives, I think, because it's that fucking good. But now that I'm getting a taste of sex, that I know what it's supposed to be like, how it's supposed to feel, I'll take every opportunity to indulge that he gives me.

We're kissing for so long that when he pulls back, his lips are puffy. "That's as ready as I can get you," he says.

"Then it's time to fuck me, isn't it?"

Concern crosses his forehead. "It might hurt. It might—"

"I don't care. This is what I want."

There's a second where I think he's going to argue with me, and then he relents. "Okay. Lay on your side so I can get behind you."

I'm fucking nervous. I didn't expect to be, and they're good nerves, but they're there anyway. I watch over my shoulder as Derek strips off, then rolls his condom on and covers himself with lube.

"Still good?"

My poor ass feels empty. "I need you so bad."

Derek lies down behind me, pressing against my back, and when he kisses along my shoulder, it melts me. "I'm going to put myself in, then it's up to you how fast or slow you take me. Okay?"

I nod quickly, desperate to feel it, and when the fat head of his cock presses to my hole, I'm so eager I try to thrust back onto him.

Derek grabs my hip. "We need to be kind to your little virgin hole," he warns, right by my ear. "I've got a fat cock, and this isn't going to be easy."

My eyes almost roll back at how Derek can be his same considerate self while talking like *that*.

"Please." I'll do or say anything to get him to push inside already.

"You have no idea what your begging does to me, bug."

The pet name makes me whimper, and he finally, *finally* pushes forward.

The stretch is more than I was prepared for. I'd thought his fingers made me feel full; his cock is making me feel ripped open. It doesn't hurt too badly, but there is a slight burn, and for one wild moment, I doubt that I can do this. Derek pauses to add more lube.

"What if you're too big?" I ask.

"Then we'll stop."

"I don't want to stop." I try to shove down again, but Derek's hand stays steady on my hip. Lucky he does, too, because the small movement was too much too quick, and it legitimately hurts for the first time.

A hiss escapes my teeth.

"I need you to be patient, or I'm taking it away."

"You can't."

"I can. I want this too, but I'm not going to let you hurt yourself."

I take a long breath to try and help calm down. At least the sharp pain that's thankfully fading helped reduce my desperation. "Okay. I'll be careful."

"Good. Just move slowly, and stop whenever you need to."

Unfortunately, whenever I need to is way too much for my liking. He wasn't lying about being big or that this wouldn't be easy. But I'm fucking determined.

"That's it," he mutters, adding even more lube. We have to have gone through half the bottle by this point. "You're doing so good. Just a bit more. Keep going."

"How far am I?"

He chuckles, husky and deep. "I'm not going to answer that."

"Fuck."

"It's okay. Watching you try is so hot. It feels so fucking good."

That's exactly what I need to hear. His praise helps me keep going. To keep trying. I wish he'd told me how far I have to go, but his lack of answer means it's probably still a lot. I'd only been half-serious when I'd asked if he was too big, but I'm starting to get worried that he might be.

"I don't think I can do it." Even though I'm trying to hold it back, the panic hits my voice. I want to do it. I need to.

"Shh …" His grip tightens on my hip, holding me still, as his lips return to kissing me. All along my shoulder, my neck, my jaw. "We're not in a hurry. If you need to stop, we'll stop, but I know you can do it."

"What if I can't?"

"You can. You're doing so good I know you can take the whole thing."

"Can … can you do it?"

"You want me to take over?"

I refuse to stop, but I need some help here. "Please."

"Okay."

Derek wraps his arms around me and draws me into a kiss. He begins slowly. A gentle rocking of his hips, fucking me with whatever I managed to get inside.

It feels better than I thought it could. I'm spread open and vulnerable, but with every tiny thrust, Derek works himself deeper. He clearly knows what he's doing, and I swear to fucking god he must have the patience of a saint because it takes forever.

But it doesn't hurt.

And when he presses his hips tightly to my ass, he's panting hard.

Locked together like this, feeling fuller than I ever could have imagined … it's the greatest moment of my life. I clench down around him, overwhelmed with how much I love that.

"I knew you could take me," he says.

"I need you to fuck me now."

Derek rolls his hips, lighting up a fucking mind-blowing spot inside me. His cock passes over it, again and again, and I swear I'm already on the edge.

All those times I'd tried for a one-night stand, I'm so fucking grateful none of them ever worked out. When Derek fucks me, I can feel genuine care coming from him. The same deep want I have. That's what I need. It's not something I would have gotten from a random in a bar.

Derek groans out some mixed-up curses before moving faster. "Watching you take my cock is turning me on so much."

I glance down to where his hips are pounding against mine, my needy, neglected dick jutting out in front of me.

"Touch yourself, baby. I need you to come."

I'll give Derek anything he asks for. I wrap my hand around my shaft, and the relief is immediate. Derek's going to get his wish sooner than later because as I jerk off with him moving inside me, I lose track of reality.

This is too good to be true.

This feels way too big to be happening.

The way my heart has a happy ache as he holds me tight and works to get us to the end. My back is sweaty against his chest, his breath is hot in my ear, and I'm floating out of my head, waiting for my orgasm to hit. It's so fucking close now.

"Look at me," he orders.

I turn my head, meeting his greeny-browny-golden eyes.

"So. Fucking. Beautiful."

That's it for me. My balls throb, and then I'm coming in my fist, orgasm wrapping tight around me and curling my toes over painfully.

Behind me, Derek cries out, gives two powerful thrusts, then stills, pressed tightly against me as his cock jerks inside my ass.

His rapid breathing is so loud, and when he collapses against me, arm circling my front, I realize he's sweaty too.

It takes way too long for my heart rate to return to normal.

"What did I tell you?" he whispers, nose by my ear as he struggles to catch his breath. "Fucking incredible."

And for the first time ever, I almost believe him.

# Chapter Thirty

Derek

I'm not convinced that having sex with Xander has helped. At all. Actually, no, I know it hasn't helped. Fucking him has made everything so much worse.

Whenever we're together and he laughs, the hairs on my arms prickle. When he brushes against me, my gut swoops. When he's giving me that cheeky, challenging stare, my blood heats to unreasonable levels.

And whenever he's unreasonably tired and irritable, this ache starts behind my sternum, and it's impossible not to hold him and never let go.

Yeah, my dumb ass has gone and fallen for him.

There are days when I question what the point of all this waiting is. We've already had sex, I've already crossed all kinds of ethical lines, and fuck—it's been a year. Clearly, nothing predatory is going on between us.

Yet there's this deep sense of responsibility urging me to take my time. I don't want to look at Xander as fragile, especially when I know what he's been through and what he's capable of, but I get the feeling the wait is good for him too. He's naturally impulsive, has fuck all emotional regulation, and this, making us both wait, it's giving me the confidence that we're in this for the right reasons.

Those reasons get murky sometimes, though, especially when he has his ass hanging out of his shorts or he's curled up at my side.

For a grown-ass man, I've been jerking off worse than a teenager.

Xander lets out a long yawn from where he's tucked under my arm. We're watching some mockumentary he found, and while I don't have a huge interest in professional dancers, I sit through it for him.

"I could never be that athletic," he says sleepily. "Not like certain football players."

"Yeah, I don't classify as athletic either. Playing ball is more about fun for me."

"You always win though."

I didn't think he'd noticed. "Lucky streak," I say, playing it off while feeling way too good about myself.

He blinks up at me innocently, and it's one of those days where he isn't wearing his contacts. Even though he knows I love his natural color, he's also explained that sometimes, the purple contacts are like armor. On days where he isn't feeling great, or loveable, or like he's worryingly close to the edge, he'll wear them.

Today isn't one of those days.

"If I was super, super tired and accidentally fell asleep, would that violate our rules?"

"Yes."

"But—"

"If you think you're going to fall asleep at four in the afternoon, you should probably head home now."

He groans, pouting prettily up at me. "But I'm so warm and comfy. You wouldn't really kick me out, would you?"

"Sure would."

Xander huffs. "Fine. Be mean. Whatever, I don't care."

"Uh-huh." I grin as he pulls away from me and sits forward on the couch with his arms crossed. This is one of those moments where I want to wrap my arms around him from behind and smother him in kisses. I know it's what he needs as well, which I think is why I want to do it so badly.

But kisses went in the no column, along with platonic sleepovers.

Cuddles and physical affection went in the yes.

I'm regretting absolutely all of it because clear rules mean that we can't fudge things or "accidentally" be less than platonic.

Xander made sure of that, proving he's more of a grown-up than I am.

"What if I leave, catch a cold, and then end up with pneumonia and die?" he asks, and I take back my grown-up assessment.

"When it's hot as hell out, I think we can take our chances."

"Gambling with my life. Wow. Thanks."

I can't help but laugh when he throws a grin back at me. My fingers card through Xander's hair, and he immediately leans into my touch. Like a cat or a puppy. Definitely not like he's being shitty with me over soliciting his impending death.

"You're the one who made the rules," I remind him.

"Actually, they're your rules. I just wrote them down."

My thumb skims the shell of his ear. "Are you not happy? Do we need to reassess?"

"I …" He sighs. "No, sorry. I'm fine. Mostly. Will be glad

when we can be an actual couple and I can straddle your waist and suck face whenever I get the urge."

My lips twitch. "How often do you get the urge?"

He runs an assessing glance over me. "At least four times a day."

"All the great things I have to look forward to."

"It would be nice to know you were struggling as well. Just a bit."

Is he freaking kidding me? I ignore the still-playing TV show as I rest my forehead on his shoulder. Xander has to know this is fucking killing me too. The fact he's here and actively advertising that he's available and wants me makes everything so damn hard.

I remember what he feels like, and tastes like, and how eager he was for my cock. Those things are going to ruin me, but I keep looking forward. Keep focused on what we could have ahead versus what a shitshow things would be if we gave in now and I wound up in front of the nurses' board.

Will waiting the full two years suddenly make our relationship okay? Fuck no. But we'll have a much better chance of proving it's real and not some type of Nightingale syndrome.

I want that reassurance as well.

From my end, I know that my feelings are real. I know that when I look at Xander, I see a man who makes me happier than I've ever been. That I'm attracted to him, yes, but I'm also growing really strong feelings for him. Feelings a lot like love.

On his end, I want to believe he feels the same way. I know that Xander doesn't think I've done anything wrong when it comes to us, but I also don't know how he feels about me, specifically. And if it came out that his feelings only existed because I was some kind of safety for him, that would be uncomfortable.

"You know for a fact that this isn't easy for me," I remind him. "No need to be a brat about it."

An email notification dings on my phone, and I reach over to grab it. Expecting junk, I'm about to swipe it off the screen when I pause.

Nursing International.

My free hand leaves Xander's hair and presses to my mouth. Either this is an email telling me the interest I put in when I got back from Ghana is a no-go, or … or I'm going to have a very hard choice ahead of me. I almost don't want to open and read it.

Almost.

I'm way too fucking curious not to though.

And when I scan over what's there, I'm torn between happy or depressed.

They want me to go to Cambodia.

The screen goes out of focus, as my heart slowly rips apart.

I have to say no … right?

All the amazing feelings from Ghana hit me again. That sense of purpose, of knowing I was making a difference. It was hard at points, and I hated being away from here, but it also had this deep sense of rightness that I've never experienced before.

But if it was hard to leave Xander then when he was only my patient and a guy I cared about, it's going to be nearly impossible now.

Especially when I know how vulnerable he is about people leaving him.

The problem is, it's also getting increasingly harder for me to be around him. I'm no saint, but I like to think I'm a decent guy who genuinely wants to do the right thing, and this relationship has become a mess. My feelings for Xander go way too deeply for us to keep up this casual, flirty friendship …

boyfriendship ... which means before long, we'll end up sleeping together again.

And again.

And again.

There's no way for me to argue my case that I was trying to keep boundaries when I'm fucking him every way from Sunday.

This would give us a forced break. Time apart where we can't be tempted, and once I'm back, well ... we deal with that when I'm back.

But how do I do what's best for me if it isn't best for Xander?

I'm not sure what gives me away, but Xander suddenly turns toward me. He studies my face for a moment, and I pretend not to notice.

"What is it?"

What the fuck do I say?

Obviously, I have to lie because there's no way I can take this. It doesn't matter how many reasons I find for why I should go, there's one more important reason for why I shouldn't. Being away from Xander would kill me.

And that's part of *why* I should be going. Should accept and fuck off and try to block out my feelings for a little bit longer.

Xander steps in before I get the chance to lie to him.

He plucks my phone from my hand and scans the email himself.

Then he looks up, and the expression on his face wrecks me. "You're going to Cambodia?"

## Chapter Thirty-One

Xander

I've never felt my stomach hollow out quite like this. Like I haven't eaten for days, and now all that's left sitting there is this dirty mass that's trying to bring on my anxiety. I can feel it pulling at me. That darkness.

But the weird smell doesn't hit, and for now, I'm able to hold it off.

The meds don't always work. They haven't fixed me. But I do feel like they're this extra barrier of defense.

"No," Derek immediately answers. Then he whispers, "Maybe."

"Maybe," I echo the word, but the meaning behind it is gone. "Maybe."

"Xander …" His phone disappears from my grip, and his hands replace it. Large, warm, strong. I can't lose them. "Look at me."

Yeah, I can't do that. Not right now. I'm shutting down and

trying to hide, and the first thing I hide is my eyes. Why the fuck didn't I wear my contacts over here? What if I cry and my eyeballs end up all red and ugly, and he looks at me and decides Cambodia is a much better idea than the stupid, bratty piece of shit he left behind?

"Xander. I said look at me, and I mean it. Now."

My gaze snaps up to clash with his, and somehow, it's even worse. I can't lose him, I can't lose him, I can't lose him.

"I applied for this after Ghana. I told you about that, remember?"

Slowly, I nod my head. I think he's mentioned it a few times, but I've been happy to ignore the very vague thing that was only maybe happening in the future.

His hands tighten over mine. "I'm going to talk, and you're going to let me finish before you try to cut in. Understand?"

A small part of me wants to tell him to fuck off to Cambodia and find a new boyfriend and be happy and forget all about me. It's instinct. Something that easily would have fallen from me before without pausing to think about it as a way to protect myself. Thankfully, my rational side is still some-what in control, and it's so strange to be able to stop those thoughts in their tracks, even as I feel like I'm unraveling.

"Okay," I whisper.

Then Derek does that thing he's only done a few times before. Where he presses a hard, fast kiss to my lips. Like a reassurance. A reminder. "The thing I love to do most is help people. That's why I became a nurse. Knowing that I'm actively making someone's life better fulfills me in a way I can't describe, and the two things at the top of my hypothetical dream board have always been Nurses International and keeping bees."

"Bees?"

He gently places his thumb over my lips. "Ghana was fucking hard, and it forced me to face a lot about my privilege, but it also showed me all the ways I was lacking. The sense of family between the people I cared for there was strong and real, and it made me realize how I didn't have that. How much I wanted it. Since I came back, since I found you ... I've added one more thing to the top of my dream board."

I wait for him to go on. Is having a family part of his dream board? If so, that's going to fuck some things up for us because I hate kids taking for granted their perfect families and their safe upbringings and—

"It's you, Xander."

"Me?"

Derek slumps back into the couch, arms across the back of it as he stares at the ceiling. His shirt is pulled up, showing off that stomach I want to lick, and he looks tired for the first time since I've met him.

"Come on, Xander." His voice is rough. "Do you really think I'd be fucking around as boyfriends and waiting until we can be together properly if I didn't think you were the real thing? If I didn't look ahead and see my future with you in it?"

These shivery sort of nerves hit me. "The real thing?"

His eyes look as wet as mine feel. "I'm trying to do right by my license, but what I feel for you ... it's too big. And I'm tired. I don't think I can keep fighting it."

"I want you," I tell him. "I don't care how, I just want *you*. I'll wait forever. I don't care. Just please, please don't leave me."

His eyes squeeze closed. "Don't."

"I can't ..."

"Please, just ... let me think."

Thinking is bad. Thinking will convince him to go. It's what convinces everyone to go. They love me for a while, and then they stop and think and realize I'm way too much effort and way too hard to love, and then I'm alone again.

"Don't cry," he whispers.

"Sorry." I blink wildly, trying to force myself to stop. I don't want to cry. I don't want to disappoint him. But not dating Derek has been the greatest time of my entire life, and I don't know how I'll survive without it. I don't know how to look at the future and not see us there. Because I can't stop myself, because I can't keep it inside, and I'm desperate to make sure he doesn't leave, I choke out, "What about your dream board?"

"I think … I think that's why I need to do this."

I can't stop the tears anymore. It hurts too much to think about him being gone, him moving on. I'm spiraling, and I know I'm spiraling, but it takes me a moment. Just a moment to realize something.

This is a regular spiral.

One that a lot of people experience.

My chest isn't closing up. I'm not smelling things that aren't there. I don't feel like the literal world is literally ending. Just my tiny slice of it.

It still hurts. It's still horrible and depressing, and I'm not sure that I'll survive it.

But I'm not dying. At least not yet.

So I do the hardest thing I've ever done. I swallow deeply, force the negative thoughts back, and when Derek reaches forward to cup my face in the way I love so much, the way that makes me feel so small and fragile compared to him, I meet his eyes.

"I'm sorry," I say. "I'm not handling this very well."

"No, I'm sorry. I'm so fucking sorry." His cheeks are wet with tears, and it's such a weird thing to see someone as relaxed and put together as Derek cry. "I want to make the right choices, and I don't know what that is."

"Staying with me."

I see it right then. The way his eyes dim.

"You don't want to."

"It's not that." He strokes my cheek, and I'm so glad he's

touching me. "I want to be with you more than anything, and at the rate we're going, it'll mean risking my license. Walking away from nursing and helping people. Every single day with you is a struggle because I want to be able to treat you the way you deserve to be treated. I want to give you everything, Xander. Everything. But I can't right now, and it's fucking killing me."

"You're not happy?"

"Not because of you. With you, I'm the happiest I can ever be. I wasn't lying about us having a future, but if our relationship gets out, if I'm reported by someone—"

"Who'd report you?"

Susan from the pharmacy immediately comes to mind. "If any other medical professional got wind of this, they'd *have* to report it. Like it or not. And if we keep going the way we're going, someone at work *will* find out. I'm not a very good liar."

"So ... so what does this mean?"

His hands find mine again. "The trip is a four-month placement. It's ... well, full honesty, it'll be fucked to be away from you for that long, but at least if I'm physically in another country, then it's buying us some time. It'll be a year and a half by the time I get back, and ..."

And we'll only have to hide for another six months. Roughly. I'm trying really fucking hard not to freak out. "What if you decide that I'm not worth it?"

"If I decide that, I'll decide that, whether I'm here or not. That's your anxiety asking that question, not you. Can you honestly tell me that I've done anything in the last six months to make you think that I'm fucking around? Do you really think I'd be risking my job for something that didn't mean so much?"

Knowing Derek, I know he wouldn't. "Four months is a really long time."

"Don't I know it?" He plays with my index finger. "I'm so

torn. If I stay and we're found out, that's going to be a lot of stress added to our relationship. If I leave ... I need to know you'll be okay. I can't go if it's going to mess with you. If you're going to doubt how I feel at all."

And that's the thing, isn't it? If we're together, Derek is always going to consider how I feel. What I need. Maybe, this once, maybe I need to do the same for him. Even if it means hiding how much it hurts, even if my brain is going to tell me for four whole months that he's never coming back, even if I wake up in a cold sweat every night, convinced he's dead, I can't stop him from going.

Because he'd never stop me.

"I don't think I'm capable of not doubting it. Or of being okay. But ..." I'm worried for a second that the words won't happen. "I want you to go."

"Xander ..."

"I'm not selfless very often, so you need to take it."

He still doesn't look convinced, and I think it's that indecision more than anything that makes me certain.

"You're going," I say, expecting it to kill me. It doesn't. "I'm going to text you every day until you're back. I'm going to be thinking about you always. And when you're back, we'll be that much closer to being together." My voice shakes. "I don't know if you know this, but I sort of have abandonment issues. Just a tiny bit." I swallow roughly. "I'm always so convinced that people are going to leave me. Maybe it's time I trusted someone to come back."

When Derek's mouth comes down on mine, it's sweet fucking torture. It feels like we kiss forever, but we both need the connection. The promise.

When I can't take it anymore, I pull back, forehead rested against his. "I have one request though," I say, breathless.

"Anything."

"Can ... when you get back ... can we have sex? It's going

to be hard to deal with you leaving me, but that might help me get through."

"I'll be counting the days," he promises. "I'm coming back to you, bug. Always. Don't forget that."

I swear to fucking Bertha, I will try.

# PART THREE

# AUGUST

XANDER:

Is it home time yet?

DEREK:

I've only just boarded the plane.

XANDER:

So ...?

DEREK:

Four months. We can do it.

XANDER:

You're really overestimating my impulse control.

DEREK:

I miss you too, bug. I really miss you too.

# SEPTEMBER

DEREK:

A cute cat adopted me today.

XANDER:

Tell that fucker I said to back off.

DEREK:

Too late. She's claimed me. Though, I won't be surprised if she's taste-testing me before gathering her rabble army to maul me.

XANDER:

Tell her I'm the only one allowed to do any mauling.

DEREK:

Are you ... jealous of a cat?

XANDER:

Of course I am. She gets to spend time with you and I don't. Bring her home and I'll cut off her tail.

DEREK:

I hear being violent toward animals is the markings of a sociopath.

XANDER:

Not animals. Just her. You're my Derek.

DEREK:

I am. It hasn't gotten any easier, you know.

XANDER:

Fucking duh. I'm going through it too.

DEREK:

Did Seven give you that hug for me?

XANDER:

Yeah. I didn't let go for about ten minutes.

DEREK:

So once we finish texting, that's how long I need to imagine hugging you for. Got it.

XANDER:

Do you and Seven message a lot?

DEREK:

Probably every other day.

XANDER:

Maybe I need to cut off his tail too.

Now, about this cat. Is it cuter than me?

DEREK:

Impossible. But you might need to send me a picture to be sure. In those shorts I like. You know the pair ...

# OCTOBER

DEREK:

Happy halfway mark!

XANDER:

Don't talk to me.

DEREK:

I'll go then …

XANDER:

How the fuck—THE FUCK—are we only halfway? You mean I still need to get through all that AGAIN?! FUCK, DEREK.

DEREK:

You've done so good.

XANDER:

Fuck good. I hate good. I wish I'd told you that you weren't allowed to leave.

DEREK:

Keep going, you're making me feel really good about my decision to be over seven thousand miles away.

XANDER:

Seven THOUSAND. What if I die before you get back?

DEREK:

I'll leave early to cry at your funeral.

XANDER:

You're such an asshole.

DEREK:

Just matching tone here, bug. This really how you want to spend this conversation?

XANDER:

Fiiiiine. Happy halfway. It's been three weeks since my last panic attack.

DEREK:

Fuck. Wow. I'm so proud of you.

XANDER:

Thanks. I think ... I'm maybe a little proud of me, too.

---

# NOVEMBER

---

XANDER:

How do you hit fast forward on this thing?

DEREK:

What thing?

XANDER:

Time. Life. Everything. I'm getting impatient.

DEREK:

You? Impatient?

XANDER:

How is this month somehow slower than all the other months combined?

DEREK:

Only eighteen days left!

XANDER:

Only, he says. ONLY.

DEREK:

Concentrate on that big commission of yours
and it will fly.

XANDER:

The asshole's being really picky.

DEREK:

He's paying you a lot of money, he's allowed
to be.

XANDER:

Do me a favor?

DEREK:

Anything.

XANDER:

Leave your sense of logic in Cambodia.

DEREK:

No can do.

I got you a present today.

XANDER:

Is it that you're coming home early?

DEREK:

Haha, no. But now my present feels like a
letdown.

XANDER:

It won't. I promise. Eighteen days. Fuck, Derek.
I get to see you in eighteen days.

DEREK:

It almost doesn't feel real.

XANDER:

Don't think I've forgotten about your welcome home. We had an agreement.

DEREK:

Bug, it's all I can fucking think about.

# Chapter Thirty-Two

Xander

Seven's holding me from behind, a little for support and a little to stop me from running through the front doors of the airport like a wild person. Derek should have landed almost an hour ago. Does it really take this long to get through customs? I have zero desire to leave the country, so I'll never know, but it's feeling really, really long.

Did the plane even land? What if it went down somewhere and it's plastered all over the news and we're standing here like fucking muppets waiting for a man who's never coming?

What if—

I grip Seven's hand and take a long breath, remembering to ground myself before I let the thoughts go any further.

The automatic doors slide open again, and a group of people walk out. They head in all different directions, but one slows. Cranes his neck above the people around him. Looks around until he spots us.

It's fucking him.

I break free from Seven and bolt. I'm running faster than my cardio-deprived body really should be running, and maybe I'll die from oxygen depletion, but I don't even care right now. I need to get to Derek.

I slam into him so hard an *ooompf* leaves his chest, and he stumbles backward a step. But he drops his bag from his shoulder to wrap both arms tightly around me.

"Fucking finally." His deep groan fills my ear as his face buries into my neck.

I can't let him go. I'm going to be glued to him for the rest of our lives because that four months was brutal. There is no fucking way in the history of ever that I'm going to be able to do that again.

"I was starting to think your plane crashed and you were stuck in the mountains and were going to have to eat one of the other passengers to survive …"

He chuckles and presses a kiss to my throat. "You do know that I flew across an ocean, right?"

"You do know my catastrophizing isn't logical, right?"

Derek squeezes me harder. "I missed you so fucking much."

I pull back, needing to see his face. Just like last time, he's scruffier, his hair is longer, and he's way more tanned than he was when he left.

And he's still the most handsome man I've ever seen.

"I didn't think you'd ever get home."

He brushes my hair back with his big hand. "Nothing would stop me. And …" His eyes search both of mine, drinking me in, all the longing and need and love I feel reflected back at me. "Fuck it."

Derek's mouth crushes down on mine. I squeak into the unexpected kiss, opening for his tongue, toes curling in my shoes, and I swear my head goes so light I might float away. My hands wrap fists into the front of his T-shirt, and when Derek finally pulls away, my whole face feels flushed.

"I needed that," he sighs.

"*You* needed that? I was a second away from begging for it."

His smile is broad and free as he kisses me one more time, takes my hand, and then grabs his bag again. He leads us over to Molly and Seven, who both swamp him in a hug.

"It feels fucking good to be back."

"Thank crickets," Seven says, taking Derek's suitcase from him. "Now Z can stop his wallowing. I swear I haven't had sex in a month."

Molly scoffs. "I blew you in the bathroom yesterday."

"Fine. I haven't had sex in my bed in a month. You need to come over and remind Xander where his own darn bedroom is."

I'm way too happy to give a shit about the teasing. My hand is securely in Derek's, and I can't stop staring at him. At his green, brown, yellow messy eyes. At his hair that needs a serious wash. At what's almost a full beard. At the kind lines by his eyes and the way the veins in his hand stand out when he squeezes mine.

We slide into the back of Seven's car, and I don't stop until I'm pressed up against him. Derek wraps his arm around me and kisses my head, but it's not enough. I need more.

I need to wriggle into his skin and live there.

"You want to head to your place?" Seven asks, glancing in the rearview mirror.

"Yeah. I need to shower this plane off me."

My gut sinks. I'd been hoping Derek would come over and that I'd be able to convince him to stay, even if it meant me having to take the couch. If he's heading home, I'm going to have to say goodbye. Again. Seven's already given up half of his day to pick Derek up; I can't ask him to drive back out to Derek's house to grab me later.

Even *I* know there are limits.

But I'm not ready to say goodbye already. I don't think I can. If Derek goes home and then I go home, how do I trust that he's really back?

It's been a few days since my last attack, but before that, it was almost a month. I'm working hard to go longer and longer, but this is exactly the type of thing that will send me spiraling again.

And I remind myself that's not on Derek. I'm in control.

"Hey." He squeezes my side, and I look up. "You going to come with me?"

Fuck, I want to more than I can say. "I don't think Seven will come back and get me, and the thought of getting an Uber …" Trusting a stranger to drive? No way in hell.

Derek shakes his head. "First, I would drive you home before I let you do that, and second … I don't want you to go home."

I perk up. "What?"

"Stay the night."

"At … your place?"

"Yup."

"But … the rules …"

Derek's teeth scrape his bottom lip. "You know what, Xander? Fuck the rules."

I can only blink at him. "Oh … I've heard about this."

"About what?"

"Those bugs that lay eggs in your ears that burrow into your brain until you slowly go insane."

Molly giggles.

Derek uses all his energy not to react. Probably. "I'm ninety percent sure that isn't a thing, but I'm one hundred percent sure I don't have an infected brain. But Cambodia was really fucking good for me, and now that I'm back, I'm doing some reevaluating. Starting with you."

"If you break up with me—"

"Don't finish that sentence." He tugs my hair playfully. "I'm not breaking up with you. The opposite, actually."

"Which … is?"

His eyes soften. "Will you be my boyfriend? Officially?"

I'm too stunned to speak. Because that's exactly what he went away to avoid. "I'm confused … I thought … there's, like, six months, and then—"

"Fuck it. Fuck them all. Maybe they find out and I lose my license and do something else. Maybe I quit. Maybe I … I don't know. All I know is that not being with you doesn't make sense. If I'm fined or stripped of my license … I'll figure it out. I love you, Xander. And the fact I had to be away from you for so fucking long doesn't *make sense*. I want to make you happy. That's it. That's top of my dream board."

"Shiiiirt sleeves," Seven groans. "You better say yes, Z, or I will."

"Not if I get there first," Molly adds.

But even with their threats, I can't make the words form. I fall against Derek, face in his neck, cursing the stupid damn stupid seat belts for making it impossible to crawl into his lap.

"What do you say, bug? Can we make this work?"

"We always could." I grit my teeth so I don't do something annoying like cry. Again. I'm so sick of crying. "I love you too. I love you so much it might kill me."

He chuckles, hand a steady anchor on my back. "Let's call that plan B. For now, tell me you'll be mine, and we're good."

"I'm yours. I've always been yours. I can't believe you finally caught up."

I'd been prepared to stick it out another six months. Another year. Another ten. It didn't matter to me. Public or not public. I'll take whatever I can get. Sherwin can tell me that's unhealthy all he likes; he doesn't know Derek.

"Thank you for waiting for me," he whispers. "I'm going to spend forever proving I was worth it."

Derek doesn't need to though. "Dare-bear, I've always known."

# Chapter Thirty-Three

Derek

Xander barely gives me time to take a quick shower before he's dragging me toward my bedroom door. There are no complaints coming from me because I've missed Xander more than I would have thought I could. When I went to Ghana, the distance was acute, and I felt it every day as much as I tried to turn off from the emotion. This was a thousand times worse.

Having Xander missing me as much as I missed him, remembering his smiles and how he fits in my arms, it was a lot.

Four months was a lot.

One month into the trip already had me regretting it. I would have canceled and come home early then if the work I was doing wasn't so damn important. Every day, I had to focus on the people I was helping and not how much my heart ached, otherwise, there was a very real possibility I would have been on a flight home. The time apart was worth it though. It made it very fucking clear that Xander is worth whatever cost I have to pay to be with him.

Including my license.

Waiting the full two years is no guarantee our relationship will be deemed ethical anyway, and I'm too tired to fight something that's this right.

Xander kicks open my bedroom door behind him and tugs me into the room. Manny dropped off some basic groceries for me earlier, and it looks like that smart-ass made my bed too. I owe him one for that.

It doesn't take long for Xander to strip off my towel and shed his clothes. My gaze doesn't leave his incredible body, and he's drinking me in just as greedily. The second his underwear is kicked off, he grabs both my hands and tugs me forward as he drops back onto the bed.

I land on top of him, all warm skin against mine, and the contact is so sudden after months without that I hold him against me for a moment while it sinks in.

"Kiss me," he begs, voice already raspy.

I lean down and touch my lips to his. We both moan into the kiss, and electricity flows from it right to my toes. My cock hardens, trapped between our bodies, thickening the second Xander opens his mouth and swipes his tongue against mine.

It's a blast of heat and something sweet on his tongue. As we kiss, I sink my fingers into his soft hair, missing the way it feels and how he responds to my touch. I'm lying between his thighs, his legs bracketing my hips, and the tiny thrust he gives as he drags his hard length over my skin is intoxicating.

"Missed you," he whispers. "Missed you so much."

I hum, brushing kisses all the way along his jawline before sucking on the silky skin at his throat. His head falls back on a soft sigh, hands carding through my hair and holding me in place.

As much as my dick is buzzing to hurry things up, there's something weighty and indulgent about taking my time to be with him like this. To savor the kisses and the intimacy. To give Xander the connection he constantly craves.

I spend time with my hands exploring his body while he does the same. From his hair to his back, along his arms, over his chest, where I tease his nipples into hard peaks. I grip his ass and explore his hips, his waist, his cock. We kiss with me on top, then him on top. I'm in control before he takes over, and then once he's done, he hands control back. My skin is sticky with his precum, and I'm sure he feels the same, but we keep kissing and touching and then kissing some more.

My tongue learns every ridge and groove of his body before Xander does the same. Looking down, with him nestled between my legs, tongue dragging over my balls, and shrewd eyes watching my every reaction, has my body overheating.

"I need to come," slips past my lips.

He answers by leaning up and sliding my cock into his mouth. Xander's tongue massages the underside as his mouth fills with saliva. It's clear it's the first time he's ever done this, but skill means nothing when it's his mouth sucking me down. He hums around me, eyes fluttering, firm grip circling the base. His other hand is rubbing my thigh, dangerously close to the crease of my groin, and it's an overload on my senses.

I have to pull Xander off.

"We'll be doing that again tonight, but I think right now, I really want you to fuck me."

"Really?"

"Only if you want to."

Heat flares in his gorgeous gray eyes. "Show me how."

It's the kind of thing that's self-explanatory for the most part, but I know Xander isn't necessarily asking for an instruction manual. He views sex as more than how I usually see it, and if he's asking me to show him, it means he wants to know what I need. What I like. Thankfully, we have plenty of time to work that out together.

I coach Xander through how to stretch me. It's been a long, long time since I've done this, but it doesn't take long for me to remember how to relax into the intrusion. He's hesitant at first, clearly worried about hurting me, but when he slips two fingers into my hole and I rock back onto them, his confidence increases.

"This is amazing," he says, breathless.

"We haven't even gotten to the good part yet."

"Every part with you is the good part."

A smile warms my face. "I can't wait to feel you inside me. I want to watch you come."

He exhales through his nose, loud and full of want. "How—"

I wait for him to go on, but he doesn't. Reaching down to still his hand, I watch Xander until he looks at me. "What is it?"

"How do we … be close while we do this?"

"Close?"

Determination sets his expression, and he nods. "I want to feel you all around me. Smothering me. The only thing I want to taste, feel, smell, see while I'm inside you is you."

My balls ache at the thought of that. I pull his fingers out, unfold a third, and then guide them back to my hole. Xander presses them inside, doesn't stop until he's nice and deep, and his eyes don't leave mine the whole time.

"Feel good?" he whispers.

"So good. Stretch me out, then sit back against the head-board. I'm going to give you everything you need."

His impatience comes through in the way he hurries to get me ready. We'll talk later about how important proper prep is, but I'm experienced enough that I know even with him rush-ing, I'll be able to take him.

"How do I know when you're done?" he asks, forehead creased with concentration.

"When I'm relaxed enough that your fingers move easily."

"So … you're ready?"

I grin at his excitement. "I'm ready."

Xander pulls out and hurries to sit back against the head-board, where he watches me expectantly. I grab a condom and the lube he was using before joining him. His eyes are on me as I rip open the tiny foil packet, pull out the condom, and then take my time rolling it down his length. It's a turn-on to cover him, to get him ready for me, and the lust sitting deep in my gut is filling me with impatience.

I squeeze lube out onto his shiny red tip and then stroke in over the condom. His hands curl tight fists into the pillows beside his hips, and seeing him already so close makes me laugh.

"Don't come too soon," I warn him, brushing my lips against his as I straddle his lap. "I want to ride you until I come."

"Kiss me."

His begging tone can get me to do anything. I bring our lips together as I position my ass over the blunt head of his cock and slowly push down onto it. Xander's hands snap to my hips as he lets out a strangled cry, tilting his hips up to fill me faster.

"God, you're sexy." I look down at how every hard line stands out on his slim body. His pecs rise and fall rapidly, drawing my attention to his reddened nipples.

"How is anyone supposed to have a preference?" he asks, eyes glazed. "Inside you, you inside me." His lips brush mine. "It's all so amazing."

"Because we work together," I tell him. I've had preferences in the past. Some of those have changed based on who I was with, the stage of life I was going through, or how I felt at the specific time. With Xander, it's all about how we connected with each other, and I can do that either way. He can too. "Once we're done," I say, rocking slowly on his cock, "we're going to eat. Relax. Talk about the last few months. Then I'm going to fuck you next. Maybe eat your hole. Suck your cock."

"Fuck." His fingers dig in as his head drops back. "You're going to make me lose it."

"Then lose it. I want to feel you let go."

Xander grunts, canting his hips again, almost like he's testing me. The faster he builds confidence, the easier it is for us to get into a rhythm, and it doesn't take long for him to be thrusting up into me as I ride him. I bring our mouths together again, one hand in his hair while the other teases his sensitive nipple, and Xander's nails bite through my skin.

He's straining to last—I can tell in the way he's panting, how his limbs are shaking with the effort. I'm trying to get to the edge quickly, but I need more.

I reach for one of his hands and wrap it around my cock. "Touch me, baby. Get me off."

His eyes flicker up to meet mine as he works me over. His grip is blissfully tight, my thighs are aching with tension as I take his length, and a line of sweat rolls down my back, right as Xander gets that devilish spark in his eye.

"Come on me," he says. "Mark me as yours."

"Shit," I grunt, meeting his thrusts harder. My balls are so fucking full and ready, and with his hand on me, it doesn't take long. The pressure builds up to an uncontrollable level and then releases.

I groan through my orgasm, Xander milking my cum onto his chest as he presses his hips to my ass and stills. His eyes roll back as he comes, and it's the single hottest thing I've ever seen in my life.

He's still struggling to catch his breath when my limbs go weak, and all I can do is press my mouth softly to his.

"That was …" he mutters against my mouth. "Amazing. So amazing."

"Catch your breath, bug. Because that was just the start of it."

# Chapter Thirty-Four

Xander

I stretch out like a cat, feeling warm and happy and like if I open my eyes, it might all fall away.

So I keep them closed and try to latch onto the moment where Derek said he loved me and that he wants to make us official.

Lips meet my shoulder as a hand runs over my back. "Good morning, beautiful."

Okay, so it's not going away yet then. I blink my eyes open to find my very shaggy boyfriend smiling down at me. "Don't they have barbers in Cambodia?" I ask.

Derek's chuckle is deep in his chest. "They do. It's a beautiful country. But I only shave and keep tidy because the pharmacy requires it, so while I was there ..." He looks a little sheepish. "I let myself relax a bit."

"Do you like this look?"

His eyebrows lift a touch. "You don't?"

"Actually, it's kind of hot."

"Good." He presses a lingering kiss to my lips.

"I'm *very* pro beard, so you know."

He drops back against the pillow, eyes closed, happy smile drifting over his face. "That was a great welcome home. I don't think I'm going to be able to have sex for a month."

I'm sore but very, very satisfied. Three orgasms in one night was like a shock to my system, and if that's any indication of what Derek's capable of, I have no idea how he went so long without it.

"So …" I'm scared to bring up real talk and break this cute little bubble, but I need to know. "We're official?"

"Yup."

"And that means …"

"Whatever we want it to mean. Mostly that I'm not holding back, that we don't need to hide … I probably won't be posting our relationship all over social media just yet, because I'm not an idiot, but if we go places, I want to hold your hand. I want sleepovers and sex and for you to know that you're loved. Completely."

I sigh—half swoon and half uh-oh. "I hope you know that I'm not capable of being as sweet as you. If you're going to be saying things like that, you're going to be well above my level."

His smile doesn't dim. "I know who you are, Xander. You're not going to scare me away."

"What if I get really clingy and needy? What if I have five panic attacks every day? What if I lash out at you and be an asshole because I'm overwhelmed and don't know how else to handle it?"

"Then I'll feel grateful that I'm your safe space and be clear about setting any boundaries I need to." He strokes my hair. "But you need to be okay with me saying I don't like something without assuming it means I want to leave you. Does that make sense?"

"I don't know if my brain works that way."

"I know it will be hard to believe initially, but I need to know that you'll try. I need to feel safe in voicing my concerns without you taking it as a personal attack, otherwise, this won't work."

Even him hinting there's something that could end us makes my throat want to close up. But this is what he means. Trusting he'd come back to me after Cambodia was the hardest thing I'd ever had to face, but this might be worse. Because this is real now, and we're going to have to face each other every day. I'm not going to be able to hide all my sharp edges from him.

"If I promise to try and be mature about this, can you promise to not assume that I know what I'm doing or how to be the perfect boyfriend? I'm going to fuck up, and I'll probably push you away. It's not because I want to, but it's the only thing I've ever known."

"The fact you're having this conversation at all shows me how much you're trying. My hard limits are abuse and cheating. I'm here to work through everything else."

I snuggle closer. "Then so am I."

---

I WAKE UP TO VOICES, and it takes me a moment to realize I must have fallen back asleep. Derek's bed has the faint scent of fabric detergent but now mostly just smells like the sex we had last night.

It was good fucking sex.

His hands and mouth on me is my favorite thing in the world.

*Enjoy it while it lasts.*

I shake Seven's voice out of my head. I hate that my inner demon sounds like him—like it's more convincing coming from the voice of the person I trust most—but I'm determined to fight it. I won't always win, but trying is more than I've ever done before.

Instead of letting my thoughts go dark, I climb out of bed and look around for clothes. Given the unfamiliar voice coming from the living area, it's not like I can walk out there naked.

I find my shorts and then pull on the football T-shirt Derek wore the day I went to watch him with his friends. It reaches my thighs, so I figure that's covered up enough.

"Look who's awake," Derek says cheerfully when I leave his room.

Manny is sitting at the table with a coffee, and I'm assuming by the lack of surprise on his face that Derek already told him I'm here.

We really are boyfriends.

"Hi," I say nervously as I join Derek in the kitchen.

He presses a kiss to my head and turns the coffee machine back on.

Manny holds up his hands as I eye him. "Sorry to burst your little boyfriend bubble, but it's been four months. I had to visit my boy."

"Good thing you didn't come last night." I join him at the table.

"Yeah, I'm not dumb. There's no way I was walking in on that."

I tilt my head. "You knew we were together yesterday?"

"Yeah …" He glances over at Derek like he's asking permission for how much to say.

Derek takes over. "I told him last week that as soon as I got back, I was going to make things official with you."

"Cocky." I narrow my eyes at him. "What if I'd said no?"

Derek sets down my coffee in front of me, then takes my

chin and steers my face up. He leans in close, close enough to kiss me. "You really think you could have?"

"No." I groan. He's got me. There was no way I was ever saying no to him.

"Now we've got that cleared up, yes, I told Manny, and yes, I told him that I was planning to be occupied with you all night but that he could come over today."

"I'm like a cockroach," Manny says. "Can't keep me away."

"Lucky Derek likes bugs."

Manny laughs. "I can't believe that wasn't a turnoff."

"Ehh, he has enough good qualities to balance it out."

"Anyway," Manny says, glancing back over at Derek. "There is a reason I'm here. Other than to see your pretty face."

"Shoot."

"The subdivision is approved, and we're ready to sell. I know you said no, but come on ..." He waves a hand over the house. "You really want to pay someone else's mortgage for the rest of your life? You're getting *old*."

"He's not old."

Manny smirks. "He's *old*, old."

"You're the one with a kid," Derek throws back. He sounds distracted though, and when I glance over, he's looking around the room. "I don't think it's the best time."

"I love you, but we can't sit on this thing forever."

"Then sell it."

"Derek."

He shrugs. "It is what it is. I'm not ready to leave yet."

"By the time you build something, you will be."

"That's the other thing." Derek shifts his mug to his free hand and back again. "Getting the money for something like that won't be easy, especially after I've taken time off work and spent a chunk of my savings to go overseas twice."

"They didn't pay you?" I ask.

His expression shifts to indulgence as he looks over at me. "I was volunteering. They covered a little, but mostly, I was on my own."

I think he'd mentioned it at some point, but I guess it didn't hit me that he was gone for four months ... for free. No income. He had to have saved a bit to be able to do that.

"You're selling land?" I ask Manny.

"I'm trying to."

"For how much?"

His attention redirects to me. "Not sure yet. We have a number in mind, but we still need to get a sales agent out to look at it. That said, if Derek's offer came in around what we're happy with, it'd be his."

"Can I see it?"

They swap a look between them.

"Hey," I say to Manny. "Don't look at him. I'm talking to you."

"Well ... I don't see why not."

Thanks to people liking shitty art and my overheads at Bertha being low as fuck, I've saved a lot of money over the last few years. It's not enough to buy land and build a place, but it is enough to do half of that.

"How long does a house take to build?"

"Xander, what are you doing?" Derek asks.

Manny answers me. "I think it all depends. I haven't done it myself, but you'd need to get all the supplies connected to the block, then find a builder, sign contracts ... a year? Probably two?"

"Two years." I turn to face Derek. "What if we did it together?"

"Uh—"

I wave away what I know he's going to say next. "Yes, it's super soon. Like we've-been-together-for-a-whole-day soon. I know. I get it. But I'm not going anywhere, and neither are you, plus we can draw up contracts for a fifty-fifty split, then if, two years down the line"—my throat does that thing where it's trying to close over, but I push on—"things aren't, well, great and we're not ready to live together, *then* we sell."

I'm trying to ignore all the things I said and focus on what could be.

"I'm …" There's still something holding him back.

"You're what?"

"Well, maybe I like living here."

"Do you?"

"I … don't hate it. It's a good size, convenient location, close to work …"

Work.

Very, very close to work. "You're holding on to this place because of me, aren't you?"

"No, I—"

"You what?"

The way his eyes dim tells me everything I need to know. Instead of feeling dejected, or like he thinks I can't do this, or frustrated that he feels the need for a backup plan in case I derail, I steamroll all those emotions. "If you think you'll still need this place in two years, we're going to have a lot bigger issues than building a house together. Sure, I'm never going to be fixed, I'll always need help, but we've both established that the help won't be coming from you. I trusted you to come back; now you have to trust me to handle my shit. So if you're holding on to this place because of me, well, well, you just … stop it."

His lips twitch. "Stop it?"

"Yes, stop it. It's insulting."

"Okay. Fair point."

"Aww, am I witnessing your first lover's tiff?" Manny asks.

"Quiet, you," Derek says, then drags a chair over to sit next

262

to me. "You know what you're saying? That you want to buy a place, with me, and that once it's built … moving in with me would mean moving out of Bertha. You understand that, don't you?"

Well, I fucking didn't until he said that. My natural reflex is a big, fat no. No, I won't go. I won't leave my brothers and the safety of the house. I won't let any of them leave either. But realistically, I know that Derek would never live there with the rest of us.

So one day, if this is forever, I'll have to move out. I'll have to say goodbye.

"I … Seven …"

"I know. That's what I mean. You need to be sure about this."

"Can't I close my eyes, sign on the dotted line, and then ignore we even had this conversation?"

"Nope."

Well, fuck.

"Why don't you come see the land?" Manny suggests. "Have a look, then you can think about the details and let me know."

"One step at a time?" Derek suggests.

I nod. One step is something I can do.

# Chapter Thirty-Five

Derek

I'm still not sold about Xander and Manny's plan. We're going up there next week to check the place out, but I think this is one of those times where Xander is being impulsive. As much as it would be a dream to build a house there and to move into that house with Xander, I'm also not going to get too excited about the idea.

It's soon. I know that. For me, these feelings aren't new though; Xander's been it for me for at least a year now.

Even though I'm confident that he's in a similar place to me, I can't ignore the way the light left his eyes when I reminded him that moving in with me would mean moving away from his brothers. It should have been a given, but I knew he wasn't thinking that far ahead.

Buying a place with someone is also a huge commitment, and no matter how set I am on being with Xander, I need to be careful there too. I haven't asked him about his finances, but I'm starting to get the feeling that his getting "lucky" with his art is maybe more than he's let on. Taking advantage of him and his money isn't something I'm okay with, so the last thing I want is for him to make this offer for me only to wind up regretting it and then be stuck with his money tied up in a house he never wanted.

Who knew that relationships were so fucking complicated?

"She's going to kill me," Xander says as we walk up the path toward his place.

"Who?"

"Aggy." He sighs. "You're being ambushed. Seven gave me the heads-up a few minutes ago, but they're all waiting inside to meet you. Well, officially. You've already met them all except Aggy, and considering I promised her that I'd leave you alone and then did the complete opposite, as I said, she's going to kill me."

"You don't seem like the type to be scared of an old lady," I tease.

Xander throws me a look, all wide eyes and serious. "You haven't met her yet."

And now, I'm insanely curious. I remember catching a glimpse of her at the nursing home over a year ago, but since then, every time she's been there, Xander has done his best to make sure that we avoid her. I've played along because we weren't dating then, but now that I'm back, I made it clear that wouldn't be happening anymore.

He didn't believe me.

I guess Aggy felt the same.

We walk into the familiar, homey space, and when we walk down the hall and into the front living room … Xander was right. I think almost everyone is here.

Most of the guys I recognize either from the times I've

visited or from them bringing Xander into the pharmacy. Madden and his boyfriend. Gabe, who used to live with them and I haven't seen in a long time. Seven and Molly. Christian, Émile, and a woman who looks like the female version of Émile.

And Aggy.

Sitting on a lone armchair, cane resting between her feet with her hands planted on top.

"So you're the nurse."

Well, fuck.

I point at Xander. "Shouldn't you be questioning him?"

"My angel boy? *Never*."

And when Xander smiles sweetly over at her and Aggy smiles indulgently back, it's impossible to worry about being yelled at by an old lady.

Everything makes sense. Xander and his brothers. The safety of a home. Then, the one overindulgent adoptive parent figure who lives next door.

Xander has believed he's not lovable for most of his life.

Yet all these people loved him anyway.

"Before you get started interrogating me, I just want to say that I'll answer whatever questions you have because"—I gesture to all the guys in the room—"this is your family. You've watched over them when no one else would, and that's fucking incredible to me."

I'm not sure what she was expecting, but I've thrown her. Aggy looks around at the others, then turns her nose up. "Well, it's not like they gave me much choice."

"Aww, do you love us, Aggy?" Gabe teases.

"I'm with her," Female Émile says in a light British accent. "You're a bunch of idiots, but you're impossible not to love."

"Except for me," Madden says. "I'm lovable, but I'm not an idiot."

Penn laughs and pats his shoulder. "Sure, Madeline. And it didn't take us basically our whole lives to get our shit together."

"At least I get to see all of my boys happy before I die," Aggy says, rapidly bringing down the mood.

Or that's what I'm assuming will happen, but I should have given Xander more credit.

"I told you," he says. "You're not allowed to die first."

"You also told me you weren't going to go after that nurse of yours, and here he is. So I think I'll be forgiven if I keel over."

"Gabe knows first aid," Xander says. "He'll just revive you."

"If he does, he's out of the will."

Gabe snorts. "I can do resuscitation, not magic. Doesn't mean I wouldn't try though."

"Why can't you all let me die in peace?"

"Because you're not even eighty," Seven adds. "I've still got a good twenty years of annoying you yet."

"Suddenly, a hole in the ground is sounding a whole lot more appealing."

"Sorry," I cut in. "Are you all joking about someone's actual death?"

"Technically, it's Aggy joking," Molly points out. "We're all joking about her not being allowed to die."

"Speak for yourself," Xander huffs. "I wasn't joking at all."

They break out into bickering, and I do my best to fade into the background. I've seen Xander with his family, but I've never seen him like this. There's a lightness to him that he hasn't had before, and I really want to hope that I'm at least part of the reason why it's there.

"This never stops," a feminine voice says. I turn to the girl with the short blond hair. "I'm Elle. Basically their sister and easily the coolest person in their lives."

"Derek."

"Oh, I know." Her tone makes it clear I've been talked about. A lot. "The handsome nurse. Much swooning over you has been had."

"Xander's a dramatic one."

"Not just Xander, silly. Everyone. Handsome and a softie for our Z?" She presses both hands to her heart. "Perfection. Though I'm happy to have one other vaguely sane person in the house. Between Molly and I, we couldn't carry it all."

"Sane, huh?"

"What makes it worse is that my girlfriend's side is no better. Her brother is a wild one. Perry is staying with me for a while but won't say why, because he wants me to have plausible deniability, and I don't think that came out the reassuring way he intended. Love him to death, absolute sweetheart, but a class A disaster." She nods at the room. "Just like these muppets." Her voice is full of pride when she says that.

"I'm ready for it all."

"You say that, and then next minute, you're on a roof, pants around your ankles, with no clue how you got there. Christian sure has kept my life interesting."

"You were … what?"

Elle pats my shoulder gently, like what she said is perfectly normal. "Garden parties are the worst, darling. Never let me invite you to one."

"Noted."

She hums lightly. "It's sort of strange to think this is it."

"What is?"

"Well … Chris and my brother. Seven and Mols. Rush and the Hunter. Gabe moved out before I really knew him. Madden's just moved in with Penn. Things are changing, and I get the feeling nothing will be quite like this again."

She's echoing the thoughts I had about Xander moving out.

"Not all change is bad," I point out.

"Of course not. Change is growth, which I think is beautiful. But life tends to be segmented up into a whole list of befores and afters. Before you can remember, before you were a teenager, after you became an adult. High school and college. Before you had your license. Before you lost someone you loved. Right now, it feels like one of those dividing moments. Like we had before Bertha, and now after. Soon, there'll only be Kismet left. Ready to hiss at whoever comes next."

"You think the others will leave?"

"I think it's only a matter of time, love. Chris and my brother are hanging in there."

"Do … you think Xander, Seven, and Molly will move?"

She's quiet for a moment as she watches them. "Yes. But it hurts my heart to think about it."

"Why?"

"Because they're not supposed to be apart."

I know exactly what she means. I'm hoping things are easier for Seven now that he knows I've got Xander's back too. Now that Seven doesn't have to support him alone.

But how do you separate two people who have been through so much together?

I know what Xander went through the one time they tried, and while it will be different now, I never want him to have to choose. Xander's doing so well, and the last thing I want is for him to struggle more than he needs to.

How do I let him leave?

How do I let him walk away from the only family he's ever had?

A year, two years, ten. It will always be too soon for him.

A headache builds behind one eye as I realize I'm going to have to be the one making the hard choices here.

The squashed-face orange tabby trots into the room and plonks himself right on my feet.

"Hey, boy," I say, reaching down to scratch him behind the ears.

The whole room goes silent.

"You're … touching him," Seven says.

I glance up and find everyone watching me. "Am I not supposed to?"

Kismet lets out a *rawr* sound and wraps himself through my legs in a figure eight.

Elle reaches down. "Come here, you little demon kitty."

Kismet's back fur stands on end, and he hisses, darting behind my legs.

Elle grins at me. "I guess you're not as sane as I thought you were."

"What do you mean?"

"Kismet only reluctantly lets Christian touch him when Christian's in full worrywart mode. He just … showed you affection." Elle shudders. "Creepy cat."

"Creepy or misunderstood?" He rubs his head up against my calves.

"Oh, he's understood all right," Xander says, crossing his arms. "And he's about to get his tail chopped off."

I step away from Kismet before Xander gets stabby. "You're turning into a little sociopath again."

"You said you like when I'm jealous."

"It's cute, I guess."

Émile and Elle disappear to make everyone coffee, and I finally face up to Aggy's interrogation. Gladly.

"These things are so odd," Elle says, walking in, carrying a tray. "There are little eyes on everything. I think your house is possessed."

"Not possessed," Xander says. "I did it. They're my friends."

"Your … friends?"

He laughs as he takes a mug. It stares at him. And he stares back. Then he plucks one of the eyes off and flicks it at Elle. "It was a game. I'm over it now."

"I had no idea it was you," Seven says, not able to keep the worry out of his voice.

"I know. But like I said, I don't need them anymore."

I don't know why he ever did, but the way he says it makes me glad he's moved on.

With this, at least. I'm scared to change too much.

## Chapter Thirty-Six

Xander

"This is huge," I say, looking around at it all. Derek's swinging our hands between us, whistling like a fucking grandpa, and the way I love it is borderline vomit-inducing.

I'm not used to being … happy.

Not like this.

I've been happy for a while now, but that's part of the problem. Happiness always comes before everyone leaves, so I've never let myself stop and feel it. With Derek, I'm getting better at that. The meds help too, I guess.

Standing in a giant fucking field is not where I would have guessed that realization would take place, but this is it. Even with my constant doubt and the way I think I'm going to ruin everything, if I can ignore all that, for a moment, this feels like home.

"Our place is over there," Manny says, pointing to the house on the other side of the property.

272

It's two stories and cute as hell.

I like the thought of Manny and his family being close by, but it does make me ache for what I'll be leaving behind. When I move out, where will Seven and Molly go? Will they stay close to me? What if they—it's hard to breathe for a second—move to Massachusetts to be near Molly's dad? Even with Derek and how much I love him, I wouldn't survive that.

Like he can sense my panic, he gives my hand a firm squeeze. "What do you think?"

"I think … it's amazing. Big. Probably too far from Seattle if you stay at the pharmacy, but think about how many bugs you'll find up here." I'm teasing at first when an idea hits me. "Hey! Bees. There's more than enough space here for you to get your bees. That was on your dream board."

His eyes are creased sweetly. "It was. I thought the same thing when I first saw this place."

"You can make your own honey, and Molly will design a logo for you. That would be so cute."

"It would. I thought the hives could be set up further down by those trees."

I'm relieved, because while I love that he gets to do something he's passionate about, I'm still not on board with being a bug lover. The further the bees are from me, the better. I'll help them out by eating their honey.

"We'll need a decent-sized house," he continues. "We've got to make sure you have a large art room. Maybe with windows the whole way around, unlike the one you have now."

"The more light there is, the more I can see my flaws," I point out to him. "Why do you think I work in the dark?"

"Maybe you wouldn't think your work was so shitty if you could see it properly?"

He's got me there. I can see it, obviously, but I just … prefer not to. Then I don't feel bad about charging people my prices and sending something horrible. Sherwin mentally slaps me for that one. Apparently, self-hatred isn't a thing most people do, and he wants me to work on it. Go figure.

As much as I love the picture of bees and a house and a big open paint room, it doesn't feel complete.

"Maybe a pool," Derek continues, raising our joined hands to point. "And then there's plenty of room for the second house to go there."

I nod along with his vision, and it takes me a moment to process it. "Second … house?"

"Yeah. Or we make the main house big enough for all of us—I'm easy either way. I know Molly wants lots of kids, and you're not a big child person, so the two houses might be …" He trails off. "Are you okay?"

*Am* I? My mouth is hanging open, and there's a deep pressure settling over my chest. My heart is beating faster, and I feel all weird and light-headed.

But it's not a panic attack.

"Molly?" I ask, voice sounding wet.

"And Seven."

"A second *house?*"

Derek pulls a face. "I know, I'm being ambitious. It'll cost a lot, so we'll have to see what we can work out. Maybe save the pool for further down the track and—"

"You know the cost isn't what I'm freaking out about!"

He drops the act and steps forward, tucking my hair behind both ears. "They're yours," he whispers. "So they're mine. Did you really think I'd be okay with you moving all the way out here without them?"

"You … you want them here?"

"Of course." He almost sounds surprised I asked. "It wouldn't be the same without them. I thought this would make you happy … you look like you're about to cry."

I sniff. "Of course I'm about to cry. I was so scared to leave

274

them. Do you mean it?" Then, a horrible thought hits me. "What if they say no?"

Derek ducks his head, and when he glances up, there's an apology all over his face. "I brought Seven here yesterday. I knew they'd be on board, but I wanted to make sure of it before I mentioned it to you."

"And he said yes?"

His lips hitch. "Got as choked up as you have."

I throw myself into his arms, not sure what the fuck I did to deserve him. It doesn't feel real. It's too hard to wrap my head around. Getting to call this place home is one thing. It actually *being* home because I have the people I love most here with me is another.

Derek's giving me all that.

Derek's doing exactly what he said he would and is trying to make me happy.

*You don't deserve him.*

That fucking voice. I grit my teeth and push it back, refusing to let it in. I know it will win sometimes, but if Derek is keeping his end of the promise, then I'm sure as hell going to do the same.

I can't even imagine Molly and Seven with kids. Sure, I hate kids in general because I never got that chance to be one, but *their* children? Little Molly and Sevens? Getting to be Uncle Xander?

Wow. Okay. This is a lot.

I slowly pull back so I can see him. "You think I'm incredible."

"Yeah."

I shake my head. "No, I mean ... you think that, when you're the one out here doing all this. I know I'm not great with telling you how I feel all the time, but I want you to know ... how much ... that this means ..."

He gives me his *shut up* kiss. "I know, bug. We might have had a slow start, but it wasn't slow for me. My feelings were always there, and I used all our time together to learn everything I could about you. I know how you squint at your work when you're getting frustrated. And I know how you lean into me when I touch you. I know that loud music makes you happy, and being alone for too long sends you into a spiral. I know that you try to be tough and strong because it's all you've ever learned to be, but I also know how much you hate it. It exhausts you to have to pretend all the time. This is going to be your home, where you can be soft and stop fighting. We'll get you a puppy for while I'm at work during the day, and maybe one day, you'll come and volunteer with me. Teach art to kids in other countries, like you taught it at the nursing home."

That actually doesn't sound completely horrible. "Only with less swearing."

"True."

"And wherever we go, it needs to have a great health care system."

"Of course." Derek almost laughs. "And the other thing I know about you? You're not Xander without Seven."

I shift, not able to meet his eyes. "Does that … it doesn't bother you, does it?"

"Nope. Maybe if I'd never met you two like I did, it might have. Maybe if I'd never seen everything you two have been through. I don't know. But Molly and I have been talking a lot. Me and Seven too. The way you all support each other is beyond words, and I'm so looking forward to being part of that."

I reach up to stroke his beard. He's tidied it up and gotten a haircut, but it's still a lot longer than I'm used to. Who knows? I might have a sexy mountain man on my hands. At the end of the day, I don't give a fuck how Derek looks, as long as I can always see the kind eyes I fell in love with. "Looking forward to it? Derry, you already are."

There's a reason Seven and Molly are always texting him. There's a reason why I can't get enough. He's the stability we need in our lives, and he's everything else I need as well.

It's a relief to know that I don't have to be strong anymore.

But I'll choose to be because Derek deserves to be loved the way he loves me.

I'm going to spend my life doing exactly that.

---

## Epilogue

---

Xander

Bertha really was something special. The place I called home, where I built myself a family, where I finally felt safe for the first time in my life.

It's gone forever now.

I'm trying not to panic. Surprisingly, that's a lot easier to do when I look around at the property, at all our friends and family here for our housewarming, at the two small houses nestled side by side with a door between them for internal access between the two.

My forever home.

With my forever man. The one I'll propose to tonight when everyone leaves. The one who I know will say yes.

The past two years have been amazing. Derek and I have figured out how to be together without my anxiety getting in the way and without me relying on him for every episode. He's learned the difference between being a supportive partner and a carer. I'm still a work in progress, and he is too, and I think that's part of what makes us work so well together. We talk. We assess. We communicate what we need. It hurts sometimes, when he voices things I've done that make him upset, and it would be so easy for me to go back to that place where I beat myself up over everything. I'm getting better. The medication is going strong. And Sherwin actually made me laugh the other day.

The last volunteer trip Derek went on, I made it the entire six weeks without a single panic attack, and there wasn't a single moment where I didn't think he was coming back.

Arms wrap around me from behind, making me jump as Molly's soft laugh tickles my ear.

"Can you believe the houses are finally done?"

"No. It took forever."

"It was so worth it." He squeezes me tighter, chin rested on my shoulder. "Can I tell you a secret?"

"Of course."

"Seven took Dad out to dinner last night."

I try not to give myself away. "Oh, really?"

"Without me. Alone. Just those two."

"Right."

"I snooped and found a ring," he says quickly.

"Molly!"

"I couldn't *not* look. And technically, Will found it first, not me, so blame him."

"Hopefully, he proposes soon, then," I say, knowing full well he's planning to do it tonight too. We went shopping together for the rings and everything. "You're shit at keeping secrets from him."

"I'll keep this one."

We stand there on the front porch, watching as Kismet

creeps along the banister. Molly holds out his hand and makes the *pst pst pst* noise, but the dumb cat turns around and faces his butt at us.

"I'll win him over one day," Molly says.

"At least you don't have to share Seven with the monster. He keeps trying to steal my side of the bed."

"He really loves Derek."

Everyone really loves Derek. He and Gabe have NHL season tickets to watch Gabe's boyfriend play. Rush lost his damn mind when he saw Derek's formicarium, and they text nonstop about antish … *things*. Rush also bought a beekeeping suit thingie to help Derek when he gets his hives. Christian, Émile, and Elle take him out for dinner once a month, and Madden and Penn have invaded Derek's football games.

All these people I have to share him with.

And I couldn't be happier because he shares his people with me. Manny and his daughter, Delilah, invite me to their tea parties, his mom calls me for a chat every other week, and Constantine and I go mini golfing.

I still can't get over how much my life has changed, but through everything, my brothers are still here.

There are even days where I really believe they always will be.

"Hey," comes Seven's deep voice. I glance over at where he's hanging out of his front door. "Both of you get in here a second."

Molly pulls away, and we exchange a quick look before following. Our homes are still sparse since we only moved in a few days ago, but scattered between the boxes and mismatched furniture are my family.

Madden and Gabe are both sitting on the floor. Aggy has taken the only armchair. Christian is standing by the kitchen like he's too scared to touch anything, and Rush is wandering around, taking it all in.

"What's all this?" Molly asks as Seven slings his arms around him.

"Dunno. Ask Aggy."

I glance over at her self-satisfied smile.

"So, you've all officially gone and left me, huh?"

"I *said* we'd build you a house too," I remind her before she can set the guilt trip in.

Aggy waves me off. "I have enough houses, thanks."

"Enough ..." Rush cocks his head. "As in, more than one?"

"As in several."

My eyebrows shoot up, and a confused sort of silence falls around the room.

"You have all been a pain in my side since I met you," she says. "Christian with the tittie-grab and Seven with his music. I've had to teach Molly to cook from scratch, basically adopt Rush, have seen more of Madden than my poor heart can take, babied dear Gabe, and Xander, my love, I have never met someone with such an attitude in my entire life."

"You can talk."

She laughs. "And I love and adore every single one of you." She holds out a piece of paper. "I wanted to show you this."

When no one moves, I take charge and cross over to grab it. At first, I don't know what I'm looking at.

"It's ... is this *your will*?"

"Yes."

I scan over it. "We're on here."

"You are." She shrugs. "I never had children of my own, my siblings are all dead now, and when it comes to family, well, you lot might only have me, but ... I also only have you. I'm officially in my eighties, and I see my friends at the nursing home and how lonely they are. How little some of them are visited. You have all made what could have been incredibly sad years full of life, and I owe *all* of you *so much*."

A tear slides over my cheek that I angrily scrub away. "Stop talking like you're going to die tomorrow. We still have plenty of years left to annoy you."

"Oh, I'm planning on it. But whether I die tomorrow or twenty years from now, I wanted to make sure I had a chance to say thank you. I've had a very long life, and the years with you, well, they might be my absolute favorites."

The will is long forgotten as I tackle Aggy in a hug. My brothers are quick to join us, and between the sniffles and the wet patch on my shoulder, I know I'm not the only one struggling with emotion. I have no clue how many houses or what Aggy is worth; all I know is what she's worth *to me*. That value goes beyond money and property. It doesn't have a number. Just the huge expanse of my heart that will always be hers.

"Okay, okay," she says, brushing us away. "Shoo, and enjoy your party."

We shoo. And we enjoy. I spend the day surrounded by love, knowing that this is the start of the rest of my life. A life with Derek. A life with Seven and Molly. One day with their kids.

"Where have you been?" Derek asks, catching me as I go to walk past.

"Enjoying myself."

"I love that."

I snake my arms around his waist. "Apparently, Aggy's left me a whole buttload of money in her will," I say.

"Ah ..." Derek blinks. "Sorry, *where* have you been?"

I bury my face in his chest. "Is it weird that I don't care about *what* she left me, it's the fact that I'm in it? That I'm in *someone's* will. It's, like, not something I ever considered because of the whole, you know, no-family thing. She could have left me a stinky, old sock, and I'd still be amazed. Every time I remember it, I start crying again."

Derek's warm, reassuring kiss finds my forehead. My eyes drift closed, and I lean into the feeling, grounded in this one single moment where everything almost feels too much, but he's got me.

He's here.

He always will be.

"I think it's finally sinking in how loved you are."

"Yeah …" It's a confusing feeling. "Maybe."

Derek tilts my face up toward his. "And your hair looks so fucking good brown."

I huff a laugh, awkward as I always am when he mentions it. It's still a trial, so we'll see, but I think I'm liking it too.

I'm liking a lot about myself these days.

Except my stupid art. That's still terrible.

I wouldn't want to go and change *too* much.

Unlike Derek, who quit the pharmacy, moved to a clinic closer to here, and has embraced his full mountain man persona.

"Everyone will be leaving soon," he says, dropping his voice. "We going to have a quiet night in?"

"Sure will be."

If all goes to plan, I'll be making love to my fiancé in a few hours.

Or should I say *when* all goes to plan?

Because I trust Derek when he says he loves me, when he says he wants to love me forever. And I'm going to do the same for him.

I never have to worry about being alone again.

━━━

THANK YOU FOR READING THE ACCIDENTAL LOVE SERIES! IT FEELS LIKE ONLY LAST MONTH THAT THE HUSBAND HOAX RELEASED AND LOOK AT THE FOUND FAMILY THAT HAS GROWN FROM THAT.

IF YOU WANT TO READ ABOUT OUR LOVELY ELLE
FALLING IN LOVE AND MEET MY NEXT LEADING
MAN BEFORE ANYONE ELSE, PICK UP:
FRIEND FOR HIRE


I HOPE EVERYONE IS READY FOR PERRY!

# Acknowledgements

As with any book, this one took a hell of a lot of people to make happen.

The cover was created by the talented Rebecca at Story Styling Cover Designs with a gorgeous image by Michelle Lancaster, and edits were done by Sandra Dee at One Love Editing, with Lori Parks proofreading the bejeebus out of it.

Thanks to @capt.christine and @lis_photoart on IG for creating amazing artworks for my website editions.

Charity VanHuss you're the most amazing PA I could have ever dreamed up. Without you I'd be even more of a chaotic disaster and there isn't enough space to list the many hats you wear for me. Paige and Lara Janz, you round out my team in the most incredible way and I'm always excited to see what fun ideas you both have next.

Eden Finley, thank you for being there for all the doubt spirals and hand-holding. Whether you wanted to be or not.

My incredible author friends who beta read this book: you've made this so much better than I could have on my own.

To my team of sensitivity readers, I appreciate your expertise more than you know! Sam F, Michaela, Lexi Jesen, Steph Kay, Lindsey Chapman, and Lindsey C all gave amazing notes and insight into Xander and Derek's relationship, and Adam Gyllenhaal was a gem with his hilarious and thoughtful comments for both of the guys.

And of course, thanks to my fam bam. To my husband who constantly frees up time for me to write, and to my kids whose neediness reminds me the real word exists.

## My Freebies

Do you love friends to lovers?
Second chances or fake relationships?
I have two bonus freebies available!

**Friends with Benefits**
**Total Fabrication**
**Making Him Mine**

This short story is only available to my reader list so follow the
below and join the gang!

https://www.subscribepage.com/saxonjames

## Other Books By Saxon James

**ACCIDENTAL LOVE SERIES:**

The Husband Hoax

Not Dating Material

The Revenge Agenda

Just Romantically Invested

Not Catching Love

**FRAT WARS SERIES:**

Frat Wars: King of Thieves

Frat Wars: Master of Mayhem

Frat Wars: Presidential Chaos

Royal Scoundrel

**DIVORCED MEN'S CLUB SERIES:**

Roommate Arrangement

Platonic Rulebook

Budding Attraction

Employing Patience

System Overload

Forgotten Romance

**NEVER JUST FRIENDS SERIES:**

Just Friends

Fake Friends

Getting Friendly

Friendly Fire

Bonus Short: Friends with Benefits

**RECKLESS LOVE SERIES:**

Denial

Risky

Tempting

**CU HOCKEY SERIES WITH EDEN FINLEY:**

Power Plays & Straight A's

Face Offs & Cheap Shots

Goal Lines & First Times

Line Mates & Study Dates

Puck Drills & Quick Thrills

**PUCKBOYS SERIES WITH EDEN FINLEY:**

Egotistical Puckboy

Irresponsible Puckboy

Shameless Puckboy

Foolish Puckboy

Clueless Puckboy

Bromantic Puckboy

Forbidden Puckboy

Possessive Puckboy

**STAND ALONES WITH EDEN FINLEY:**

Up in Flames

The Bastard and The Heir

**FRANKLIN U SERIES (VARIOUS AUTHORS):**

The Dating Disaster

A Stealthy Situation

And if you're after something a little sweeter, don't forget my YA pen name

S. M. James.

These books are chock full of adorable, flawed characters with big hearts.

https://geni.us/smjames

# Want More From Me?

Follow Saxon James on any of the platforms below.
www.saxonjamesauthor.com
www.facebook.com/thesaxonjames/
www.amazon.com/Saxon-James/e/B082TP7BR7
www.bookbub.com/profile/saxon-james
www.instagram.com/saxonjameswrites/